A Match Made on Madison

Also by Dee Davis

A Match Made on Madison

Dee Davis

St. Martin's Griffin 🌿 New York

www.stmartins.com

Grateful acknowledgment is made for permission to reprint from the following:

Quote on page 151: © New York Daily News, L.P. Reprinted with permission.

Quote on page 267: AOL CityGuide content © 2006 America Online, Inc. Used with permission.

Design by Phil Mazzone

Library of Congress Cataloging-in-Publication Data

Davis, Dee, 1959–
    A match made on Madison / Dee Davis—1st ed.
        p. cm.
    ISBN-13: 978-0-312-35784-9
    ISBN-10: 0-312-35784-2
    1. Dating services—Fiction. 2. Manhattan (New York, N.Y.)—Fiction.
3. Chick lit.

PS3604.A9568 M37 2007
813'.6—dc22   2006048878

First Edition: April 2007

10 9 8 7 6 5 4 3 2 1

To Manhattan,
the most amazing place
on the planet

Acknowledgments

Although writers tend to spend most of their time in imaginary worlds, there's no way a book can be created in a vacuum. And to that end, I'd like to thank the folks who helped me with *Match*—particularly those who so generously allowed me to quote from their Web sites.

My sincere thanks goes to: Sharon Thompson and the Carlyle Hotel; Michael Coy, Jeff Apfel, and citysearch.com; Stephanie Wong and stylemaven.com; Jennifer Appel and the Buttercup Bake Shop; Sly Tang and hipguide.com; Melissa A. Tyson, Greg Barton, and menupages.com; Jason Maxwell and Chef & Co.; Dena Meyer and Cooperative Communities; Chrissy Persico, Edward Fay, and the *Daily News*; Wayne Lorentz and glasssteelandstone.com; Heather Cross and gonyc.about.com; Mark Kornblau and Zagat; Kimberly Oser and Barneys; Mary Billingsly, historichotels.org, and the Waldorf=Astoria; Ted Magen and Park Avenue Floratique; Renee Kibbler and cityguide.aol.com; imdb.com; and Alain Gayot and gayot.com. I'd also like to thank Charlie Suisman and manhattanusersguide.com; and Melanie Thernstrom and *The New York Times* for the article that inspired it all.

In addition I'd like to thank Lexie Oberwetter, Julie Kenner, and Kathleen O'Reilly—I sincerely couldn't have done this without you. And last but certainly not least—Jennifer Weis, Stefanie Lindskog, Hilary Rubin, and the fabulous Kimberly Whalen!

At the end of the day, marriage is a merger. An agreement by two parties to enter into a binding contract that will yield dividends for both. It's a zero-sum game with the underlying goal of propagating the species, and the overwhelming desire for a controlled form of intimacy. It's been that way since the beginning of time. Unfortunately, somewhere along the way we got a little sidetracked. It's my job to get us back online.

—**Vanessa Carlson, President, HEA, Inc.**

A Match Made on Madison

Chapter 1

Bemelmans Bar. *The Carlyle Hotel, 35 East Seventy-sixth Street (corner of Madison Avenue), 212.744.1600.*

Best remembered as the creator of the classic Madeline books for children, Ludwig Bemelmans once joked he'd like his tombstone to read: "Tell Them It Was Wonderful." Well, wonderful it was, and still is, at Bemelmans Bar. Named in honor of the legendary artist, Bemelmans is a timeless New York watering hole that has drawn socialites, politicians, movie stars, and moguls for more than five decades.

—www.thecarlyle.com

Another round please." I signaled the tuxedo-clad waiter with an impervious twist of my hand, the gesture undoubtedly not nearly as regal as I supposed. But then dirty martinis will do that to you. Two is really the limit even for the most dedicated of drinkers. And we'd already had three.

But this was a celebration.

And I wasn't paying the bill. Which was just as well.

Bemelmans is my idea of heaven when it comes to a bar. Small and intimate, with killer drinks, fiery-hot toasted edamame, and folksy art that puts one in mind of a children's storybook, it's absolutely perfect. But you could mortgage a Park

Avenue apartment and still not have enough to pay the tab—especially on a martini bender. So better that it was Althea's headache.

I'd save mine for tomorrow.

Althea Sevalas was my friend, mentor, and sometime rival. In truth, I'd absorbed all she had to teach me with the voracity of the young and hungry and then proceeded to go out and apply what I'd learned on my own.

Actually, I'm making it sound easier than it was. I don't know that I'd ever have taken the leap, so to speak, if it hadn't been for Franklin Pierpont's tendency toward dramatic scenes. Franklin is a billionaire geek with absolutely no social skills.

Althea had taken him on in a fit of absolute pity. And when his first match ended in a somewhat less than desirable way, he'd wound up standing on a ledge outside my office window—nineteen floors up. Obviously this sort of behavior is not good for the matchmaking business, and Althea, who suffers from vertigo, tasked me with talking him down.

Suffice it to say, it was not one of my favorite assignments, but after showing half of Manhattan my Perele panties, and losing a Manolo to windowsill gymnastics, I managed to talk sense into the man.

Of course it didn't hurt matters when it turned out that the policewoman who'd come to our rescue was not only a looker but also the heir to a computer fortune. A definite sign from on high. So when Althea insisted on taking credit for handling the whole fiasco, I saw the writing on the wall, and with a little help from the Pierpont-policewoman merger, I started my own agency.

At first there'd been understandable friction between us. After all, I'd walked away with all Althea's tricks of the trade, so to speak. But with a little time she'd realized that Manhattan was big enough for both of us and, albeit warily, accepted me back into her circle of friends.

She wasn't above twisting the knife a bit now and then, though. And having been invited to the wedding of the century was a coup she'd no doubt lord over me for years to come. It was a first and something I had to admit I aspired to achieve. Not that it was likely.

This one was a fluke. Matchmakers simply aren't considered wedding guest material. Too much a reminder of things best forgotten.

Which explains the reason for celebrating. And though it wasn't really my triumph, I didn't have a problem swizzling Bemelmans martinis in Althea's honor. Of course, I'd brought reinforcements—my friend Cybil Baranski.

"So I heard that even though the gown cost half a million, the bride still looked like overfed farm stock." Cybil adjusted her Oliver Peoples frames and leaned forward, eyes sparkling in anticipation.

Cybil and I have been friends since Trinity, and believe me, her love of gossip was a well-developed art form even then. Just ask Roberta Marston, the first girl in our class to go all the way. And, of course, being Cybil, she'd found a way to capitalize on her talent for digging dirt, getting paid handsomely by the Murdochs to write a syndicated international column that's become a glitterati must-read.

The bride in question was Susannah Barker, a long-shot latecomer in the race to secure the hand of multimillionaire Robert Walski. Of course, she had Althea on her team, which meant the odds were upped considerably despite what the rumormongers (excluding Cybil, of course) would have had one believe.

"Honey," Althea leaned in as well, her nose almost colliding with Cybil's. Dirty martinis are hell on depth perception. "When you're wearing a size twelve at your wedding, there's just not a lot a designer can do." We all looked down at the newspaper Althea had brought. In this case the picture was beyond words.

Judged against the ordinary world, Susannah would be considered attractive, I suppose. But Manhattan is a sea of size twos. I've always believed that the reason restaurants open and close with such velocity here is due at least in part to the fact that while most women deign to visit restaurants out of social necessity, they very seldom actually eat anything.

Anyway, suffice it to say, Susannah holds up her end in the support of Manhattan restaurants. However, her size wasn't the issue here. Her father's upstate mills were. And when Walski realized the advantages of merging his assets with hers . . . well, the rest is history.

But that's what it's all about, isn't it? Finding someone whose social background and financial assets are equal to or enhance yours? All this nonsense about true love and opposites attracting is ridiculous at the social strata we're discussing. Marriage is a merger. It's as simple as that.

The waiter arrived with our drinks and a fresh assortment of nibbles.

The only really bad thing about overdoing martinis is that they're worse than cannabis when it comes to the munchies. At least I can delude myself into believing that wasabi-dipped edamame aren't going to break the calorie bank.

I stared down into the smoky depth of my gin, swirled it a few times for effect, then looked across the table at Althea, cutting to the chase. "Did they acknowledge your part in the nuptials?"

"No. But everyone knew anyway. I mean it's not a state secret what I do." She tilted her head in a practiced way, the light hitting her tightened and tucked face in just the right places. Althea couldn't be considered young by anyone's standards. But she was well preserved. Thanks in part to good genes. And mostly to her plastic surgeon on the corner of Park and Seventy-third.

I used to think plastic surgery was only for the aged or repulsive. I think most people in their twenties would agree with that. But I'm not in my twenties any longer. And suffice it to say, I am on good terms with Althea's doctor. So far only for a little Botox lift; I mean, I haven't hit forty. But the little wrinkles at the corners of my eyes aren't exactly getting smaller. You know?

"I think it says a lot that they invited you at all," Cybil said, picking up a peanut and then dropping it guiltily back in the silver bowl. "I mean, no one really wants to admit that they need help finding true love."

"Well, in point of fact," I said, waving my martini at her, "we're not really interested in love—true or otherwise. It's all about combining assets—two parts making a more productive whole."

"You make it sound like a corporate merger." Cybil wrinkled her nose in distaste.

"And you, my friend, are entirely too sentimental." I frowned at her over the rim of my glass. It was an old argument. Cybil, for all her sophistication, was a hopeless romantic. Which meant that when it came to men, she invariably chose losers. Case in point, her current lover, Stephen Hobbs. But I won't go there.

"I'm not sentimental. I just believe marriage should be about more than just bank accounts."

"Well, of course it's more than that." Althea reached over to pat Cybil's hand. "There's the sex."

I almost choked on an olive. Althea was overly proper by nature. You know, the type who never curses and uses words like "bedroom frivolity" to talk about doing it. Obviously, the martinis were loosening her inhibition.

"And how exactly do you think an arranged marriage guarantees good sex?" Cybil either hadn't noticed Althea's slipup or just wasn't interested. She'd leaned forward, eyes narrowed in concentration. Or maybe just so that there'd only be one Althea.

I mean, we *were* on martini number four.

"Because—like attracts like," Althea intoned, as if the words held the key to all wisdom.

"Um, I think you mean opposites," Cybil said, still squinting.

"No, I mean like. Two people of the same background, the same financial circumstances, and the same ideology will invariably be happier than two people who simply respond to chemical combustion."

"Maybe in a merger. But in the bedroom, I'll take combustion." Cybil sat back, sipping her martini.

"In the short run, possibly," I said, picking up on Althea's theme. I did say she was my mentor. "But when the combustion fizzles—and it will—you need the bedrock to maintain the marriage. And besides, pleasure isn't limited to the perfect partner."

"That's why there are affairs." Althea nodded in agreement.

"Actually, I was thinking of vibrators. But that'll work." I smiled at her through my gin-induced haze.

"You two are entirely too cynical to be in your line of work," Cybil said, her glasses shining in the candlelight. "I mean, Vanessa, you even call your business Happily Ever After. How in the world can one have that without love?"

"I think," I started to lean forward, propping my chin on my hand, "that the two terms are mutually excusive, actually. Love generally does not lead to happily ever after—happily short-term maybe—but not ever after. Unlucky in love is the norm, not the exception. And for the record, my business is called HEA."

"That's just semantics." Cybil waved her hand, and the waiter hustled over, quite possibly for fear that she'd topple over. She shook her head at him and he moved back discreetly. "You're a matchmaker, for God's sake. That means you arrange for people to find true love."

"Only in fairy-tale land, darling," Althea said, sipping her martini. "This is Manhattan."

"So you're saying that no one in Manhattan marries for love?" Not only is Cybil a practicing romantic, she's stubborn as all hell.

"Not once you've reached a certain social status." Althea shook her head. "It simply wouldn't last."

Cybil opened her mouth to argue, but I cut her off. "There are socially prominent married people who are in love, Cybil, but it's just a perk. An added bonus. Not a necessity. And certainly not the norm."

"So you're saying that in order to have a successful marriage, love doesn't have to be part of the equation?"

"Exactly." I nodded to emphasize the point. "In fact I'd go so far as to say that more often than not love is a detriment to the process, not an asset."

"And your clients *know* you think this?" Cybil asked, her expression mutinous.

"Know it? Darling, they demand it." This from Althea, who was almost two-thirds of the way into her martini. The woman might be repressed sexually, but she can drink like a fish.

"Well, maybe not demand it." I believed what I was saying wholeheartedly, but in all honesty most of my clients needed a little convincing. "But they usually come 'round to my way of thinking."

"It all seems a little bleak to me," Cybil shrugged, "but, apparently it works; business does seem to be booming."

"Yes. Although I still think we were better as a team." Althea shot a pointed look in my direction, and I busied myself looking for something in my purse.

"Vanessa's doing fine on her own," Cybil said, jumping to my defense. "And your business isn't hurting either." She pointed to the newspaper, the Walski wedding headlining the society page.

"I suppose you're right." Althea sighed. "But think how well we'd be doing if we'd stayed a team."

How well *she'd* be doing is more like it. I owe Althea a lot, don't get me wrong. But being her minion had definite drawbacks. Most of them financial. And since I have a weakness for Versace and Prada, money is essential. Hell, even if I didn't have a thing for Italian leather, money would be essential. This *is* Manhattan.

"Did you see who's over there?" I asked, pointing to a table in the corner, more for diversion than from actual interest. "It's Mark Grayson."

Well, actually I suppose there was some degree of interest. A person would have to be brain-dead not to know that Mark Grayson was a cut above the rest when it came to wheeling and dealing.

"I saw him when we came in." Cybil tipped her head so that she could see him better. "That's Tandy Montgomery he's with." Cybil was always in the know, but was so used to the fact she sometimes forgot that the rest of us aren't hardwired for the latest buzz.

"A new poptart?" Althea asked, apparently as out of the loop as I was.

"No, she's the latest winner of that modeling contest. You know, the one on cable." The last word explained why I hadn't heard of her. Keeping up with the boob tube's latest flashes of fame is more work than it is worth. The minute you catch up, their five minutes in the spotlight are over and you have to start all over again. I had better things to do.

"Well, she's certainly not the right woman for *him*," Althea said, her eyebrows disappearing into her perfectly sculpted hair.

Mark Grayson was new money, but he'd come by it the old-fashioned way. Hard work. And I wouldn't have pegged him for the flaunt-the-starlet type. Still, he was a man—and given half a chance the gender tended to gravitate to vacuous, breast-enhanced types. All the better for me, really. I mean, if the right people came together on their own, I'd be out of business.

"Well, *he* seems to think so," Cybil said. All three of us were now staring over at his table. Not the most polite thing to do. Especially in Bemelmans. But copious amounts of gin tend to blur the line a little when it comes to social behavior. And it was sort of interesting, watching him make his moves. Like a sort of sexual science experiment.

"So what else do you know?" Althea and I both leaned toward Cybil expectantly.

"About Tandy or Grayson?" Cybil asked.

"Both," we said almost in tandem.

"Well, I don't know much about her. And I'm pretty certain she's not a permanent fixture—if you know what I mean."

"Does he always pick the same type?" Althea asked.

"Redheads?" Cybil asked, frowning over at the would-be model. "I don't think so. I know I've seen him with blondes before." The martinis were clearly clouding her brain.

"No, I meant the empty-headed-girl-of-the-moment type."

"You were expecting him to step out with flat-chested fortysomethings?" I quipped, but they weren't listening to me, they were too busy watching Wonder Boy and his latest girl toy.

"No," Althea said, shaking her head. "Of course not. I was just . . ."

"Sizing him up?" Cybil grinned, just managing to swallow her laughter. "So what did you decide?"

"Truth?"

Cybil nodded

"He's not the marrying type." Althea studied the man, her look calculating. "Of course, with proper persuasion . . ."

"He certainly seems the ideal candidate for your concept of marriage. Merger is his middle name," Cybil agreed.

"Hey, I'm sitting here, too." I frowned at them both, waving my martini glass at them. Not a good idea as it turned out, since the liquid also went flying. Fortunately no one seemed to notice except our still hovering waiter, who immediately produced a fresh napkin. "And, anyway, I found him first."

"Darling, no one found him. He was here before we were. And besides, if anyone can land him, you know it will be me. I simply have more experience."

Of course she was right, but I'd had three-plus martinis and I hated to be bested at anything. "Experience isn't everything. There's technique involved. And you always did say I have amazing instincts."

"Instincts, yes. Technique, not so much. Besides, I'm the one who landed Walski as a client." She sat back, crossing her arms as if she'd trumped me. But I wasn't about to go down without a fight.

"Walski practically had 'marriageable' tattooed on his forehead. Anyone with half a brain could have hooked him up."

"Maybe," she acquiesced with a shrug, "but not with Susannah Barker."

"How about John Pollard? He'd been notoriously single for years. And I managed to snag him almost right out of the gate. And marry him off, happily, I might add, three months later."

"Pollard could be Pierce Brosnan's twin. There's not a woman alive who wouldn't marry him if given the opportunity," she countered, tossing back the rest of her martini.

"Yes, but *he* wasn't quite as easy to please. And yet," I paused for effect, "I did it. Which means that I am more than up to the task of convincing Mark Grayson that it's time for him to take the plunge. And if we're really rolling out the big guns," I paused again for effect, "there's always Franklin Pierpont." Despite my subsequent defection, Althea knew I'd saved her ass on that one.

"Maybe you both should give it a go." Cybil's seemingly offhanded remark had exactly the effect she'd intended, both our heads turning in unison in her direction.

"How do you propose we do that? We can hardly share a client," Althea said.

"I'm not saying that you should."

"But you said . . ." This was getting interesting.

"I said that you should both try. I frankly don't think either of you will succeed. But a little competition might be interesting. You've got to admit, Althea, that Vanessa has become quite successful. And, Vanessa, you're always complaining that Althea gets all the attention. So why not prove who's the best by seeing which of you can snare Mark Grayson. And once there's a winner, I'll announce it in my column. That way everyone will see it. The verdict will be final. And one of you will be crowned the ruler of matrimonial Manhattan."

The idea had definite appeal. I mean, Althea might be mentor and friend but, let's face it, she was big-time competition as well, and the idea of proving myself once and for all was almost irresistible. Not to mention the idea of having the fact touted before most of the free world. I wasn't exaggerating when I said that Cybil's column was an international must-read.

I glanced over at Althea, who was trying to appear uninterested, but I could see the calculation in her eyes.

"So the first one to sign him as a client wins?"

"No way." Cybil laughed, idly rubbing her finger around the rim of her glass. "That would be too easy. In order to win, you have to dance at the man's wedding. I mean, marrying him off is the whole point, isn't it? Signing him as a client is only half the challenge."

"I don't know." Althea shook her head, her eyes on Grayson, who had paid his check and was now ushering runway girl out of the bar. "Matchmaking isn't an exact science."

"Oh, please." Cybil sighed. "You just spent half an hour telling me how marriage is nothing more than a business deal. Are you saying now that you're not up to the task?"

I popped an olive into my mouth, all the better to keep it shut. This wasn't a task to enter into lightly. I mean, this public an endeavor could very well backfire, leaving my newly flourishing business deep in Chapter 11. A matchmaker who fails doesn't get a lot of repeat business.

But the olive apparently had not gotten the message. It slid blissfully down my throat and my mouth seemed to open of its own accord. "I'm in."

There was silence for a moment, but I knew it wasn't going to last. Althea wasn't the type to ignore a gauntlet, and I had just thrown one.

"Then so am I, darling." What can I say, I know the woman well.

Cybil raised her glass. "May the best woman win."

We clinked and drank, and something akin to sheer terror settled in my stomach. Or maybe it was the martinis. Either way the contest was on.

It was me or Althea.

Winner takes Manhattan.

Chapter 2

Michael Coy. *The Corcoran Group, 660 Madison Avenue (between Sixtieth and Sixty-first streets), 212.605.9389.*

A contented downtown resident, Michael Coy seeks to make your real estate experience just as fulfilling with his results-driven approach and focus on customer service. Add to that his great integrity, trustworthiness, and respect for clients' time, and you get the makings of the only broker you'll ever need for your real estate requirements.

—www.corcoran.com

You didn't think I was going to tell you where I lived, did you?

But, since I'm not going to share that little tidbit, I thought I'd give you then next best thing. My broker. I mean, in New York finding the right apartment ranks just behind making certain you're dressed in this year's fashions. It's all about location—and closet space. And fortunately, thanks to Michael, I had both.

However, just at the moment I wasn't certain I cared. Not only was I entertaining the mother of all hangovers (I really should have known better), I was playing the role of apologetic mother for Waldo.

Seems he'd been doing his Colin-love-'em-and-leave-'em-Farrel impression again. Let me clarify before you head off in the wrong direction. Waldo is my cat. Actually Waldo is nobody's anything. It's more like I'm his person. And just at the moment, that was not a particularly enviable position.

You see, Waldo has had the hots for Arabella for months now, and apparently his lust led to a Houdini-like breakout that landed him inside my next-door neighbor's apartment. (She said she's got hair strands to prove it.) And anyway, push come to shove—which is absurdly appropriate in this situation—Waldo did his manly thing, and Arabella—a purebred Burmese—is now pregnant.

And since Waldo's heritage is more uptown than Upper East Side, it's not a good thing.

At least from Edna Melderson's point of view. Arabella actually seemed fine with it. And Waldo was positively strutting. But Mrs. M. was threatening board action, and believe me, that's a hell of a lot worse than being hauled in front of the headmaster for freezing Debbie Robertson's bra. (How were we to know it would stick to her skin and cause permanent damage?)

So instead of meeting Cybil at Bergdorf's for their handbag sale, I was standing in my apartment with an angry blue hair, and my second best friend, Anderson Wright.

Anderson runs one of the largest investment firms on Wall Street—which he thinks is irony at its very best. Testosterone land ruled by a queen.

I'd called him as soon as I got the message about Arabella. I wasn't the type to face danger on my own, I needed someone on point, and since Anderson was my neighbor on the other side, he was perfect for the job.

The fact that he'd brought his partner, Richard, was all that much better. The two men were not easily cowed and therefore the kind you wanted in your corner. And in this case, I needed the backup. If you check in the dictionary under "intimidating," you'll find Edna's picture. Hailing from Massachusetts, she has blood so blue you can actually see it running through her veins.

She's probably somewhere in her sixties, but you wouldn't know it to look at her. Never married, she has that perpetually sour expression of a woman who really needs to get laid. Add to that an assortment of clinical procedures, and she's sort of stuck in a perpetual grimace, poppy red lipstick only accentuating the fact.

Her blue-tinted hair is always pulled back into a chignon. Although the word is probably too elegant for the actual effect. And I don't believe I've ever seen her in anything except a vintage Chanel suit (she probably sleeps in them). Only, of course, hers weren't vintage when she bought them.

I don't think we've ever said more than hello and good-bye to each other in the three years I've lived in the building, her usual greeting a slight inclination of her head. As if she's granting me a favor just to go that far.

Anderson and Richard haven't had much more luck, although Richard actually carried Chanel bags into her apartment once (she gave him a tip). According to him, the apartment is a shrine to the fifties, complete with mahogany console TV and the scent of Chanel N° 5 mixed with cat litter.

The latter I have to admit I've been guilty of myself, although I keep the litter box in a closet. (We've already established that Waldo can get into or out of anything, so a folding closet door is no problem at all.)

Anyway, the woman is formidable at best. Quite frightening at worst. And as an original co-op member, she wields a lot of power in the building. All in all not someone you want for an enemy. And thanks to my randy cat, that's precisely where I'd landed.

This is exactly what I meant when I said that it was best for like to marry like. Look at the mess Waldo's made, and he's just a cat. A loud one at that. I'd shut him up in the bedroom when Arabella and Mrs. M. arrived, but kitty senses are keen and he was more than aware his lady love was in the next room.

"What I want to know," Mrs. M. sniffed, "is what you intend to do about this?"

Since it was somewhat after the fact, it didn't seem to me that there was really a lot I *could* do. I shot a look at Anderson, pleading for an out.

"Well, I'm sure Vanessa will be happy to pay for any vet bills you incur during Arabella's, um," Anderson swallowed a smile, "confinement."

This wasn't a small offer, either, as Mrs. M. favored a veterinarian who made house calls and specialized in feline acupuncture and holistic medicine. (I'm serious, check out housecallsforyourpet.com.)

"I assumed she'd do that much, but what I'm looking for," she shot an Elmira Gulch–worthy frown in the direction of the extra room, "is some kind of guarantee that *that* animal won't do this again."

Waldo's yowl echoed through the room, and I swear Richard crossed his legs. We all knew what the woman was alluding to, but I just couldn't see taking Waldo's manhood. It seemed a cruel punishment just for fulfilling a basic need. And besides, it takes two to tango. I shot my best venomous look in Mrs. M.'s direction.

"Of course, I'd be more than happy to pay for Arabella to be spayed." Hit hard, when they're not expecting it. I'd learned

that from my father. Let her cat be the one to suffer the indignation of losing gonads.

"That's not exactly what I had in mind." She stroked Arabella with bony fingers, her eyes narrowing until there was
nothing but eyeliner visible. My thoughts switched from Elmira
Gulch to that woman in *Sunset Boulevard*.

"Well, I'm sure as hell not going to cas—" Anderson pinched
the underside of my arm, but it was too late. Mrs. M. had followed the gist.

"My Arabella is a grand champion. And as such she is more
valuable if she can be bred."

"Just because Waldo isn't a show cat . . . ," I managed before
Anderson pinched me again. I wriggled out of reach, certain
that I was going to have marks.

"Your *cat*," Mrs. M.'s mouth pursed as she practically spit out
the word, "is a mongrel. And as such, a menace. While there
may be nothing I can do about Arabella's present situation, I
will not tolerate it happening again. To that end, you will either
solve the problem, or that animal," she waved a bejeweled hand
in the direction of the spare room, "will be evicted. Am I making myself clear?"

I clenched my fists, my vision going red. I really hated being
ordered to do anything. Fortunately Richard was well aware of
this fact.

"So," he said, standing up with finality, "Vanessa will look
into options for preventing another liaison and report back to
you. Certainly there are all kinds of variables to be taken into
consideration, before anything rash occurs. And should it come
to that, we'd of course need to be certain that both parties were
as represented. Authentication would be crucial, wouldn't you
say?" Did I mention that Richard is an attorney?

Mrs. M. fingered the Judith Ripka brooch at her throat, her

expression now guarded. "I'm sure we can reach some kind of agreement." The about-face would have been comical, except that we were discussing the fate of my cat's testicles. I glanced over at Richard with a frown, but he only shook his head slightly, his benevolent gaze still on Mrs. M.

"We'll be in touch," Richard dismissed her. "And as Anderson suggested, feel free to have the vet's bills sent to Vanessa. It's the least she can do."

With a sigh worthy of high melodrama, Mrs. M. waltzed (and that's an accurate description, really) out the door, leaving the three of us standing in a cloud of Chanel N° 5.

"Well, at least she didn't stuff poor Waldo in a basket." Anderson had obviously seen the resemblance to the Wicked Witch as well.

"But I don't understand why she backed off," I said, still flummoxed. "I mean, not to knock you, Richard, but she's pretty formidable. I'd have taken her over you in a bet any day."

Richard smiled. "Ah, but you see I came with ammunition. When you called I did a little checking. It seems there was a suit filed by the CFA several years back after Arabella won Best-in-Show at the National Capital. Apparently there was some question as to the authenticity of her pedigree."

An imposter. Kind of raised my estimation of Waldo's paramour.

"Additionally, I talked with the Beckers in 11C, and apparently their cat, also an unneutered male, has been known to find refuge in Miss Arabella's paws." He flashed his ladies-and-gentlemen-of-the-jury smile. "So I suspect that the last thing that Edna Melderson wants is a microscope on her poor Arabella's sexual habits and lineage. My advice? Put up window screens and you should be good to go."

"Or not go, as the case may be," Anderson said with a laugh.

There was a thunk, a click, and the spare room door swung open, Waldo falling into the room with the dignity only a cat can pull off.

"On second thought, maybe you should just lock the windows." Richard tipped his head toward the cat. "He does seem to have a knack for escape."

Waldo ignored all of us, walking over to the window and leaping up to sit lapping at a paw, watching traffic below—or planning his next rendezvous with Arabella.

I would wind up with a lothario for a cat. Sort of apropos, I suppose, considering my occupation.

"So enough with the cat," Richard said settling back on my white sofa. "Tell me about *Page Six*."

Anderson sat down next to his partner, his eyes twinkling in anticipation. Nothing made Anderson happier than a little gossip. And *Page Six* was as good a place as any to try to keep up.

"I have absolutely no idea what you're talking about." I rubbed my temples, wondering if I should dose myself with bismuth or just have a Bloody Mary. Hair of the dog and all that. The thought actually made the Pepto sound positively fabulous.

"You haven't seen the paper." It was a statement, not a question, but Richard was smiling.

"I wouldn't even be awake if it weren't for Mrs. M. and her seductive siren of a cat. Besides, I haven't been up to anything that would rate *Page Six* exposure." Well, except agree to a practically impossible bet on the off chance that I'd score the match of a lifetime. But we'd been discreet. Sort of. I reached for the still folded *Post*, quickly turning to the gossip column, which in all actuality is usually found on page ten.

I scanned the newsprint, settling on my name highlighted in bold. At least they'd spelled it right. There's a singer named Vanessa Carlton. She won a Grammy a few years back.

Anyway, I'm forever having people want me to be Carlton instead of Carlson. Of course, her life is probably better so maybe I missed an opportunity.

But I digress.

The paragraph cut right to the chase:

Manhattan glitterati with a desire to find the perfect mate have a new champion in matchmaker **Vanessa Carlson.** With her fledgling business giving the competition a run for the money, Ms. Carlson, 35, is definitely hot, hot, hot. Spotted last night at Bemelmans Bar in a heated discussion with mentor/rival **Althea Sevalas,** 52, speculation is running rampant. Sources swear that the discussion centered on downtown playboy **Mark Grayson.** If either Ms. Carlson or Ms. Sevalas were to score Grayson as a client, there'd be no question as to who ruled Manhattan's matrimonial mergers. For what it's worth, this writer's money is on Ms. Carlson. . . .

"Shit." I leaned back in the wingchair pushing the paper away as if it were offensive, trying to remember who had been sitting around us. Someone with a big mouth, obviously.

"It's not that bad. At least it doesn't mention the martinis," Anderson said.

I'd had to admit last night's lapse of good judgment when they'd arrived, if only to assure them that I hadn't suddenly contracted a fatal illness. Although at the moment I was doing a damn good impression. "But it does mention Mark Grayson."

"So that part's true?" Richard's salt-and-pepper eyebrows shot up.

"Yeah. I told you it was a wild night."

"Apparently." I couldn't tell if Anderson was reprimanding

my behavior or just wishing he'd been there for the party. "So spill the rest of the story."

"You sound like Paul Harvey." (I know that makes me sound like an old geezer, but my mother used to always listen to him on the radio.)

"Vanessa . . . ," Richard said, using his best badgering-the-witness voice.

"All right. We were discussing Mark Grayson. Betting on him, actually. Or I guess, more accurately, betting that one of us could marry him off."

"This is the same Mark Grayson who is rarely seen with the same woman twice?"

"The very one. He was there, at Bemelmans, with Tandy someone or other," I said by way of explanation—although in actuality it explained nothing. "Look, there were copious amounts of martini involved. Dirty ones at that."

Richard shuddered. "I don't see how anyone drinks those things. Give me straight Scotch any day." Thirty-year-old, oak-cask, private-label Scotch at that.

"Trust me, after the first one, you can't taste a thing."

"So can we move off of the cocktail lesson and onto the impossible dream?" Anderson asked, crossing over to the table to pour a cup of coffee. I'd thought the caffeine would cut through the morning-after queasies, but instead the smell had only exacerbated the matter.

"It's not impossible. I'm good at what I do, remember?" I frowned at them both.

"No one is saying you aren't." Richard's tone was soothing now. "But you have to admit that Grayson isn't exactly the life-time commitment type."

"Everyone is the type if you find the right match."

"Spoken like a true professional," Anderson said, waving his spoon for emphasis. "But Richard's right. This one is going to be tough."

"I know." I let loose a sigh emanating from soul level.

"Have you ever even met the man?" Richard scolded.

"No," I shook my head, feeling like a three-year-old on time-out. "But I've read about him. And I know the type."

"Seems to me if you're going to win this bet, you'll need a little more than the gossip rags' bletherings to go on."

"Well, I've heard more than that, obviously. I mean I do know a few people in this town." The drummers in my head had upped the volume, making it hard to think.

"Of course you do. But that's not the same as knowing the man."

"Obviously, I'll have to meet him. It'd be hard to convince him to hire me if I don't." I blew out a breath and fought against a wave of total panic. I should never have agreed to Cybil's insane proposal. Blame it on gin and greed.

"So do you have a plan?" Richard sat back, sipping his coffee, his expression carefully neutral.

"Actually . . . ," I paused dramatically, scrambling for an answer, then sighed. "No. Not yet."

"Well, I'd bet my practice that Althea not only has a plan, she's already putting the wheels into motion."

Unfortunately, Richard was right. Althea probably sat up all night scheming. I already mentioned she had no problems with alcohol. Four martinis probably hadn't even left her with a headache.

"So what am I going to do?" I know I sound really incompetent here. And I'm not, I swear, but in the heat of the martini moment, I hadn't considered the fact that I'd never even met the man. I mean I've really only been out on my own a couple of years. And quite frankly, in addition to Franklin Pierpont, my first few clients had come from Althea, or rather from her roster. And the rest I'd gotten through referral and word of mouth. I'd never really done a lot of hunting, per se.

The men came to me—most of the time.

The business itself is really very straightforward. $15,000 to sign on and $1,000 a year for one date a month—if it took that long, which it hardly ever does. (I really am good at what I do.)

Fees include home consultations and wardrobe advice, as well as a background check and, more important, access to my extensive database of women. All of whom have been vetted carefully and then trained in the nuances of fashion, society, and wifely deportment—for lack of a better term—the idea being that they offer ideal qualities that when matched with the right man will lead to wedded bliss.

I don't offer guarantees, but my success rate is rather impressive.

In truth, I've been matchmaking in one way or the other since I turned twelve and realized that men belonged with women and vice versa. I was about sixteen when I realized that the rest of the world was too bogged down in the idea of true love and soul mates to actually see the simple beauty of the perfect match, but with a little nudging, I managed more often than not to get the right prep school buddies paired off.

It wasn't until I met Althea that I realized I could make money doing it. And believe me I jumped when she'd offered to hire me as an assistant for her new matchmaking venture. Despite Althea's impeccable contacts and our concerted efforts, business was slow at first. For several reasons. First, the old-fashioned idea of a matchmaker (think *Fiddler on the Roof*) was an anachronism, and second, dot-com dating services were all in their fledgling states, offering seductive and inexpensive ways for couples to meet.

But the ugly side of the Internet soon reared its head, and those who had signed on with hope, signed off in revulsion. Enter the modern-day matchmaker. A necessary evil in our mobile and disenfranchised society.

In ages past, families stayed together, three or four generations sometimes, and it was the elder clansmen who were responsible for finding the right spouse for younger members of the family. Of course, the idea had its drawbacks should said child have his or her own ideas (Romeo and Juliet as an example), but overall the system worked because it recognized one intrinsic fact.

Like attracts like.

As I said at Bemelmans, it's really that simple. To build a long-lasting marriage it's important that core values be similar. As well as environmental factors, like where someone grew up, what their financial situation was, where they went to school, etc., etc. . . .

Although there are exceptions, most successful marriages are based on constants. Things that contribute to our psyche that only someone else with like experiences can understand. It's not foolproof, of course, but I find that it's pretty much a sure thing.

Why most people seem to miss this little tidbit I have no idea, but I guess I should be grateful as their ignorance is the reason Althea and I now sport rather sizable bank accounts.

Anyway, eight years after hiring on with Althea, I was ready to step out on my own (armed, as I said, with a few of her most recent clients), and HEA was born. However, all the experience in the world wasn't enough to guarantee that Mark Grayson would even listen to my proposal, let alone agree to let me represent him.

"So what do you think?" Richard and Anderson were both looking at me expectantly, and I realized that I'd obviously missed something crucial.

"Sorry—was off in a haze. What do I think about what?"

"Anderson trying to wangle an introduction?"

"You know Mark Grayson?" Hope sprang back with a rebound worthy of Michael Jordan.

"Not personally, no." Anderson shook his head. "But he has accounts with the firm. Large accounts. And as such, it wouldn't be out of place for me to make certain he's given certain perks."

"Like?"

"I don't know, actually. I'm still formulating the plan. But something along the lines of an invitation or tickets or something that would place him in a particular place at a particular time where you would happen to be as well. I need to think on it a bit."

"Not too long. As you pointed out, Althea will have already formed her plan of attack."

"No worries, I'll come up with something." His smile was comforting, and even if he couldn't produce the miracle I needed, it was nice to have such good friends.

"Well, considering Richard has already saved my ass, or rather Waldo's privates, today, I'd say you're two for two. I owe you both."

"You can take us to dinner."

That might sound like nothing in light of what they'd both done and intended to do for me. But Richard has a thing about only eating at the *right* restaurants. King's Carriage House, Cipriani, or Brasserie 8½. Which meant this month's handbag allowance was probably history. Still, it was more than worth it.

And besides, Bergdorf's was having a sale.

Chapter 3

Bergdorf Goodman. *754 Fifth Avenue (between Fifty-seventh and Fifty-eighth streets), 212.753.7300.*

An old-school department store for the ladies who lunch and the husbands who support them. All the top luxury designers are here, each with their own little branded area. But what's more, Bergdorf has an incomparable fine jewelry selection, an antiques gallery, gourmet foods, personalized stationery, and a name that means you've made it.

—newyork.citysearch.com

I adore shopping in general and Bergdorf's in particular. Everything in life is about presentation, and Bergdorf's has it down to a science. The mansard-style building itself is fabulous. Simple and elegant with a Parisian flair, it is the perfect foil for the merchandise it carries.

Inside the store each nook and cranny is accentuated by the sophistication of the architecture, starting with the Swarovski crystal waterfall in the front foyer and continuing on through the vaulted spaces on each floor. Even more miraculous is the view of the Plaza and Central Park out the upper-floor windows.

I read somewhere that Andrew Goodman had actually kept

an apartment in the building. Now that's my idea of perfect real estate. Great building, great view, and designers like Rebecca Taylor and Yves Saint Laurent only an elevator ride away.

Now, of course, there are women who would swear that they'd never shop at any department store. Not even Bergdorf's. I mean, most of the designers' boutiques are practically next door. But me, I like comparison shopping, and at Bergdorf's it's all there like a fashionista smorgasbord—all you can eat, as long as you can afford it, and sampling is totally free.

Case in point.

Handbags.

The riot of color filling the beautiful display cases was enough to make a girl swoon. Add to that the fact that they were all on sale, and it was possible to induce permanent coma, except that would mean missing out on the entire event.

Cybil was standing in front of a case full of Judith Leiber bags. Not something I'd ever want to carry, mind you, but they're great fun to look at. I love the really kitschy ones like the frog or the Barbie bag.

"You're late. I've been waiting for almost an hour." Cybil's smile negated the rebuke. That and the shopping bag in her hand.

"It looks like you found something to do." I nodded toward the sack.

"Shoes. I found the most amazing shoes." She opened the bag with a flourish, producing a Manolo box, patently ignoring the saleswoman's glare as she set it on the counter and opened it. "Aren't they wonderful?"

I have to admit I don't get the same rush from shoes that I do from purses. But I've also never been accused of having bad taste. And these were truly great shoes. A pink thong with a kitten heel and tiny daisies decorating the straps, this shoe was the epitome of fun and flirty. A guaranteed come-on to any male within a five-block radius.

"They're great." I held one up to the light, turning it in admiration. The saleswoman's glare faded at the sight of the shoe and soon she, too, was oohing and ahhing.

The great uniter. Manolo shoes.

"I thought so, too." Cybil nodded in agreement. "I couldn't resist."

The truth was she didn't have to. A fact that should have made me envious. But Cybil wore her old money well, and it never actually bothered me. Maybe because I wasn't exactly destitute myself. Or maybe just because I'd known her forever and her wealth was as much a part of her as the fact that she secretly adored Lyle Lovett's music and had an almost spiritual connection with Junior's Cheesecake.

"I love them. But we're here for purses, remember?" At that the saleswoman positively beamed.

"Anything in particular?" she asked.

Actually, I had my eye on a Jimmy Choo bag. A cute fuchsia number in patent leather. It screamed me. And would look fabulous with my new trench. But I was a big believer in delayed gratification.

"I guess I'll start with Marc Jacobs. Maybe the Guinevere tote in red?" The secret to good service in places like Bergdorf's is to let them know you know the merchandise. If you can knowledgeably discuss the new collections, it immediately sets you apart from the throng of tourists who wouldn't know a Falchi from a Fiore.

We followed the woman to the Jacobs counter.

Red was actually last year's color, but the purse was still

fun—and what woman didn't feel better wearing red? It was a beautiful bag, a little larger than I usually carried maybe, but worth considering.

I put the purse over my arm and turned right and left, admiring it in the mirror. Cybil stood just behind me mouthing, "It's too big," but I ignored her, concentrating instead on the soft feel of the leather and the length of the strap.

"I thought maybe you'd be a no-show considering the number of martinis we had last night," Cybil said.

"You know me better than that. I'd never let a hangover keep me from a Bergdorf's sale. Besides, I had an early morning wake-up call. Mrs. M."

"Waldo?" Cybil asked, pulling a face.

"My cat the lothario." I held the bag next to my coat, admiring the combination, and filled Cybil in on the morning's encounter and Waldo's narrow escape from the scalpel. I love my cat, but I also love my apartment. And if snip snip had meant I got to have both, well . . .

Cybil nodded as if I'd voiced my thoughts, but then we'd been on the same wavelength so long, sometimes words really weren't necessary. Her glasses today were Corinne McCormack, a wonderful new designer who, like Cybil, believes that a woman's glasses are as important as her shoes, or more important, her handbag.

Definitely my kind of girl. Almost makes me wish my eyesight were less than 20/20.

"It was really Richard who secured the battle," I continued. "Or maybe more importantly Arabella, the little tramp." We giggled over cat sex as I took a last look at the red bag, then shook my head, returning it to the saleswoman. Next up was Dolce & Gabbana. A mustard yellow tote with a wonderful leopard-print lining. But it was slightly bigger than the Marc Jacobs, and didn't look right with my coat.

"You already know what you want, don't you?" Cybil asked, picking up a light pink Valentino with tiny embroidered flowers.

"Sort of, but I need something to compare with to be certain, you know?" I reached over to touch the little flowers. "That would be fabulous with your new shoes."

"I know," Cybil said, holding the purse up to her shoulder. "It really is kind of fun."

"I think you should get it." The only thing I love more than buying my own bag is watching someone else score a great one. At Cybil's nod, the saleslady took it, satisfied that at least one of us was going to provide a commission.

We moved on to Lambertson Truex. The Roxbury bag. Kelly green, definitely an "in" color, it had cleaner lines than the Marc Jacobs and was about half the price.

Cybil eyed the bag, then shrugged, indicating exactly nothing. She'd always preferred more feminine looks, flowing with flowers. Me, I was more the tailored little-black-dress type. But then pink *is* the new black. The saleswoman, finally convinced that I was eventually going to buy something, withdrew from earshot. Cybil's expression grew serious.

"I didn't mean to go overboard last night."

"You drank less than I did."

"No, I don't mean that. I mean with the bet. I shouldn't have goaded you into it. I woke up this morning feeling really awful about it. I was just caught up in the moment. If you want, I'll try to talk to Althea. Get her to back off."

"Althea never backs off of anything. Besides, if I can publicly best her, it'd be wonderful for business."

"Yeah, but Mark Grayson isn't the type to jump at the idea

of a matchmaker in the first place, and now after the speculation in *Page Six* . . ." She trailed off with a shrug.

"Well, first off, not everyone reads *Page Six*. Especially serious business types like Grayson."

"No, they just pay someone to do it for them. Trust me, he'll
know about it."

"Okay, so he'll have an idea of what might be coming. That
doesn't mean he'll turn tail and run, or ban me from his presence. It just means he'll have his guard up. But I've dealt with
that kind of thing before."

"Maybe. But word on the street has Mark Grayson eating
people for breakfast, lunch, and dinner. To put it mildly, he's a
barracuda."

"Most men are when first facing the idea of settling down.
It's like taming a wild animal. Everything is in the approach."

"Well, I hate to question the analogy, but you can't even control Waldo."

"I can control him, I just don't want to inhibit his libido."

"Talk to me about that when Mrs. M. dumps the kittens on
your doorstep."

My skin turned clammy, my stomach twisting at the conjured image. "She wouldn't do that."

"Of course she would. She lives to make people miserable.
Especially if they hurt her precious Arabella."

The green purse suddenly lost its appeal, the idea of me as
momma to a herd of kittens, or whatever you'd call it, a bit too
much to contemplate. I shook my head to clear my thoughts. It
was time for the main event.

Jimmy Choo.

The bag in question was low slung and, in my humble opinion, incredibly sexy, and from the way Cybil was fingering its sil-

ver cousin I could tell she thought so, too. In truth, it was somewhere between fuchsia and raspberry, with pavé crystal accents.
Have I mentioned I'm a sucker for sparkle? Anyway, just as I suspected, it looked amazing with my trench coat (turquoise,
Michael Kors).

"I'm not going to let this go," Cybil said, her eyes meeting
mine in the mirror.

"The kittens?" I asked, twirling to look at the bag from all
sides, knowing damn well that that wasn't what she was talking
about. Tenaciousness is one of Cybil's more annoying attributes.

"No. Althea and the bet. We were talking about ending the
ridiculous thing before it starts."

"I told you Althea will never back down. And I'm not about
to let her stage a coup d'etat. It wasn't just *Page Six*, you know. It
made the *Daily News* as well. If I quit now it'll be the same as if
she'd won."

"But you don't even know this man."

"Ah, but Anderson does." I started to leave it at that, but
Cybil deserved full disclosure. "Actually he's never met him. But
Grayson has a lot of money invested with Anderson's firm. And
since he's the managing partner, I figure he can work something
out. At least an opening. In fact, he's trying to arrange something even as we speak. I'm meeting him for a late lunch in
hopes that he'll have news."

Cybil sighed. "You are the most stubborn woman I've ever
known."

"Except maybe for you." I shot her a smile, knowing that she
understood my need to continue with the bet. It probably was
foolhardy, but I couldn't back down, not with Althea. There
was too much water under that bridge. And besides, there was
potential for a huge payout. I mean, all kidding aside, Althea

and I were basically working the same pool of people, and until I proved otherwise, no matter how many successes I had, I would be considered her protégé.

And therefore second-rate. A head-to-head contest was the only way to prove I was truly worth my salt.

And surely that was worth the risk of failure.

"Look, all I have to do to beat Althea is stay one step ahead. Starting with Anderson."

"If you're going to beat Althea, you're going to have to find a way to grab Mark Grayson's attention and keep it. And then you have to convince him that despite all rumors to the contrary, he really is a marrying man."

"Piece of cake," I said, with a smile worthy of an Oscar.

The saleslady cleared her throat, obviously nearing the end of her patience. I turned, my dazzling smile still in place. "I'll take it."

In truth, I'd known I would all along. For fortification. A girl needed the right accessories to go into battle, and far be it from me to deny myself the proper accoutrements. And so feeling supremely self-satisfied, I followed the woman to the register. She wrapped the bag in tissue and then after I charged enough for two dinners with Richard on my card (even on sale), the prize was mine.

I waited impatiently while Cybil purchased the Valentino, tempted to pull my purse out and carry it immediately. But I've already mentioned the importance of delayed gratification, and carrying the shopping bag, knowing what's inside waiting for me, is half the fun, really.

I guess you've figured out by now that I take purse shopping very seriously.

"Can you come to lunch? We're meeting at Town." We walked to the revolving door and then out onto Fifth Avenue.

"I can't. I'm meeting Stephen." Cybil's face closed. A certain sign that she didn't want any comment from me.

I think I already mentioned Stephen Hobbs and my opinion of him with regard to Cybil. She's the most amazing woman. Really. Beyond all words. Generous to a fault, she loves deeply and blindly, without any thought at all as to what the consequences might be, more often than not including a trampled heart—hers.

It's not that Stephen is evil or anything. He's just not Cybil's social equal. And before you throw stones, please consider the fact that he's dumped her not once but twice, on a whim, because he felt as if she was inhibiting his art.

Have I mentioned Stephen is an artist? The penniless, live-off-a-benefactor, no-particular-aspirations kind?

And while an artist can be a wonderful addition to a dinner party, or a very exciting Bar Harbor fling, everyone who's anyone knows that an artist, no matter how sexy, is simply not the kind of man one considers for a permanent liaison.

Everyone, that is, except Cybil.

I sighed, resisting the urge to comment further. It was an old argument, and I had to believe that in good time Stephen would show his spots—again. And hopefully Cybil would ditch him once and for all.

Until then, it was better that I bite my tongue. Although that wasn't exactly one of my strong suits.

"He's taking you out then?" I asked.

"Actually I'm taking him. A celebration. He sold a painting." One.

I tried for positive support. "I didn't realize he had an exhibition?" I prayed she wouldn't mention Central Park.

"He doesn't. Although I'm working on it." Her voice had taken on a Pollyannaish perkiness that reminded me of our grade school days. "This was actually one he'd decided to throw out. A friend of mine saw it and asked if it was for sale."

Probably matched the color of her sofa. (I sound really bitchy here, don't I? It's just that I really worry about this guy.)

"Anyway, she bought it. So we're celebrating."

On Cybil.

I struggled for something supportive to say. Came up with absolutely nothing and so instead gave my oldest friend a hug, and prayed that she'd somehow see the light. Until then, no matter what I thought, I'd have her back. Hell, she'd do the same for me.

I waved good-bye, and a scant fifteen minutes later I was seated in Town, sipping a Bloody Mary while waiting for Anderson and his news.

Town is the creation of Geoffrey Zakarian, one of New York's finest chefs. The food is modern French, minimalistic, artsy, and divine. The restaurant itself, nestled in the Chambers Hotel on Fifty-sixth, is beautifully appointed. Two stories with cascading crystal and twenty-four-foot ceilings, it's restful— almost serene. Which makes it the perfect escape for lunch.

I was just debating the wisdom of ordering another drink when Anderson walked in, clad as usual in Armani. Anderson wears a suit better than anyone I've ever known. He sort of just inhabits the thing, making it seem a part of his total aura, or something. I'm not describing it well at all. But it's more than just being good-looking. It's an intrinsic soul-deep sort of thing.

Definitely no more drinks. I was turning philosophical. Always a bad sign.

"Sorry I'm a bit late." Anderson rushed forward, sitting down in the chair adjacent mine.

"Not at all." I smiled as the waiter handed him a menu. "I was early, actually."

"So did you find a purse?" He eyed the bag with interest, and I produced the Jimmy Choo with a flourish.

"Isn't it fabulous?"

He took it, held it up to the light, turning it this way and that, then handed it back.

"So?" I asked, impatiently, knowing he was milking the moment. "You like?"

"The color is totally you. And the lines are marvelous."

I breathed a sigh of total contentment and put the bag back into its tissue.

"Where's Cybil? I thought you were bringing her along."

"She already had lunch plans," I rolled my eyes, "with Stephen."

"Vanessa," Anderson chided, "you mustn't be so judgmental. Just because Stephen isn't your cup of tea doesn't mean he isn't right for Cybil."

"If you were talking about a normal relationship, I'd have to agree with you. But we're talking about a man with limited talent and even less ambition. He lives off of Cybil, until he feels boxed in, and then abandons her, leaving her crushed, only to return three months later to repeat the process. That isn't a healthy relationship—for anyone."

Anderson reached over to cover my hand. "I know you're saying all of this because you're worried about Cybil, but you can't tell her how to feel. And you can't change the situation just because you don't approve."

"I know." I sighed, turning my hand to squeeze his. "It's just that I love her so much, and I don't want to see her hurt. And unfortunately I can see it coming."

"Well then maybe it's a lesson she has to learn."

Anderson could be very Zenlike at times. Especially when the atmosphere suited it. And Town was wonderfully tranquil.

The waiter came to take our order and then as we settled in to wait, I cut to the chase. "Any progress on the Grayson front?"

"A little anxious, are we?" Anderson laughed.

"No. Just figure we might as well get to the point. Business before pleasure. And I assure you the escargot risotto is definitely all about pleasure."

"Fine, then we'll talk before eating." He leaned forward, took a sip of his Evian, and then smiled. "I've got two options."

"Two is wonderful considering that up until now I've had none. Tell me." I leaned forward, too, lowering my voice as if he were about to impart the wisdom of the ages.

"Well, the first is a sure shot. A Cancer Society benefit at the Pierre. Grayson is going to be there. Apparently his mother had breast cancer."

"She died?" I don't know why it hit me the way it did. Maybe because my own mother was growing older (despite the work of her plastic surgeon) or maybe because mortality in general seemed a bit closer than, say, when I was in my twenties.

"Yes, but it was a while ago, I think."

I nodded, digesting the information. I wasn't sure that it had value, but then forearmed is forewarned—or is it the other way around?

"Anyway, the point is that I've managed to get you seated at the same table. It seems the perfect way to angle an introduction."

"Will you be there?"

"Yes, Richard and I both, although not at your table. Three seats together at Grayson's table was a bit more than I could manage. As it is, we've displaced someone. But c'est la vie." He shrugged.

"It's fabulous. So why the second option?" I frowned, waiting for the other shoe to drop.

"The benefit isn't until week after next. And knowing Althea, I figured you needed something a little more timely."

"Like yesterday," I said, nodding my agreement, then sat back as the waiter set our salads in front of us.

"Right. So on to number two." He stopped to take a bite, murmured appreciatively over the greens, and then continued. "I did a little sleuthing—actually bribery was involved, but we won't go there. Anyway, I found out that Grayson is going to be at Bungalow 8 tonight."

"You're not talking about the Cavalli party, are you? The one for the new line?" I slumped in my seat, disappointment robbing me of my appetite.

"Yes. That's it. But why the long face?"

"Because I wasn't invited. Oh, believe me, I tried. Pulled every single string I'd ever unraveled. Even had Cybil try to wangle an invitation. No go." Anderson opened his mouth to respond, but I was on a roll. "Wait. It gets worse. Althea is going. She told me last night. If I hadn't been looped, I'd have killed myself right then, but I was busy trying to think of a way to snag a meeting with Grayson. And all the while she'd already beat me to the punch." I buried my head in my hands, feeling thoroughly defeated.

"If you'll just let me get a word in edgewise?"

I looked up at Anderson with a sigh. "Unless you've got an invitation in your pocket, there's nothing you can do. Althea's won."

"Oh, come on. You're made of sterner stuff than that."

I was, but it had just been a roller-coaster day. First Waldo, then Jimmy Choo, then Stephen, then the benefit at the Pierre, and then Althea and Roberto Cavalli. "I'm sorry. You're right." I squared my shoulders. "We'll think of something."

"Like an invitation?" He laid the perfect white square complete with gold engraved letters by my plate, and my breath caught as if I were Cinder-fucking-ella.

"You're kidding." I knew my eyes were shining, and I looked around for the pumpkin carriage.

"Nope." Anderson's smile was so full of self-satisfaction they could have added it to the menu. "It's the real deal. And you don't even have to be home by midnight."

I picked up the invitation, grinning like a fool. I was back in the game almost before I was out of it. All I needed now was the right dress.

And honey, that's a problem I know just how to handle.

Chapter 4

Girlshop. *819 Washington Street (between Little West Twelfth and Gansevoort), 212.255.4985.*

Wrapped up in a swathe of 1970s pineapple wallpaper, the virtual online store Girlshop has crossed the chasm into the brick and mortar world—smack-dab in the middle of New York's Meatpacking District. . . . Known for its collection of trendsetting emerging designers, Girlshop is a must-see destination for New York women.

—www.stylemaven.com

Girlshop started out online—a fabulous way to score great clothes from new and up-and-coming designers. But Laura Eisman realized in a flash that what worked in cyberspace could only be better in brick and mortar. Enter a renovated art gallery in the Meatpacking District and a snazzy retro feel that makes a girl feel positively glamorous. Add to that the fact that, compared to Madison and Fifth avenues, it won't empty your checking account, and you've got shopper's nirvana.

Usually I keep a find like Girlshop to myself. I mean, the fewer people who know, the more merchandise for me, right? But sometimes in the name of multitasking you have to bend the rules a little. I needed a dress and I needed to have a morning-after-first-date meeting with Belinda Waxman. Which meant I had to allow for a little overlap. Time management at its best.

Fortunately she was running a little late and I'd already managed to reject a gold Cigana slip dress, a multicolored confection from Zola, a white Sean Combs ruched-waist halter dress that made me think of Marilyn Monroe, until I saw it on me. Believe me, in certain dresses ample wins the day, and that word has never been used to describe the upper half of my anatomy. Not even with Victoria's Secret doing the lifting and separating.

On the plus side, the black lace Wendy Hill I was currently wearing looked pretty damn good in my humble estimation. I lifted a finger to my chin and twirled first right and then left, eyeing myself from the front and then behind.

"Perfect," Belinda pronounced, appearing more or less out of thin air. Her low-slung voice always made me think of velvet and whiskey, the kind of woman who sang torch songs in a smoky jazz club in the forties. "So what's the occasion?"

"The Cavalli party."

"The one at Bungalow 8?" she gasped, envy flitting across her face. "You really do rank."

I shrugged, figuring it was better not to go into too much explanation. But Belinda was quick on the draw.

"Mark Grayson is going to be there."

I stopped twirling, the dress deflating right alongside my enthusiasm. "You read *Page Six*."

"And the *Daily News*." She shrugged, her expression all attorney. "Face it, you're the talk of the town." Apparently discretion and martinis do not good bedfellows make.

"Let me get out of this dress and we'll talk." I nodded toward a chair and headed back toward the dressing room, the mirrored curtains giving an endless view of me and the dress. My own personal Rockette line.

But I digress.

Belinda and I have been friends for a couple of years now. I met her at a New York City Bar function I attended with Richard, and we'd hit it off. At forty, she was still a looker, with heavy auburn hair and a penchant for designers like Lida Baday and Marc Jacobs. She also had an amazing sense of humor and a solid bank account.

Perfect for my roster and, unlike a lot of the ladies I culti-vated, already savvy enough to take on the best of the best. In this case, Stanley Barrow.

Not that it was going to be an easy sell.

One of the downsides to this business is that no matter how many times I explain the type of woman a particular man will mesh best with, he isn't always able to turn off the precon-ceived notions in his head. Mainly that the only women worth dating have their breasts insured by Lloyd's of London. It's a male fantasy that isn't easily broken.

And Stanley had two ex-wives as testament to his attach-ment to the idea.

I slipped out of the dressing room and headed for the cash register, Belinda following in my wake.

"I'm sorry for the change of plans. But I'm sure you can un-derstand the necessity of a new dress."

"Best to go into battle in full regalia," she nodded, holding a pair of gold filigree earrings up to one ear. "These are gorgeous."

The sales assistant nodded. "They're Kipepeo. Eighteen karat gold on brass."

The three-inch disks were intricately shaped like perfect snowflakes, delicate and bold all at the same time. "They're great. You should buy them."

Belinda flipped them over to examine the price, and then shook her head. "I really shouldn't. I've been trying to save for a condo and with prices the way they are, every little bit helps."

With prices the way they are now, I am just grateful I already own my apartment. Although if Mrs. M. has anything to do with it, I may soon be living there sans Waldo.

Belinda caressed the curve of the earring longingly. Boy, did I know that feeling. And then with a sigh, she hung them back on the rack and waited as I paid for the dress. Talk about self-restraint.

The salesclerk handed me the bag, and we headed over to a Starbucks on Ninth Avenue. After ordering a couple of venti nonfat caramel macchiatos and waiting for the barista to perform her coffee magic, we settled at a window table to talk.

Last night Belinda and Stanley had had their first date. Usually I'd have debriefed at dawn, but in light of last night's hijinks (and this morning's hangover), the whole thing had sort of been relegated to a back burner, thanks to my total and complete panic over the bet.

Now, however, with invitation, gown, and carriage (Paris Limousine Service, 800-225-7131) all arranged, it was time to get down to business with the clients I already had.

Particularly with first dates, I like talking to the woman before the man—they're always more open, and it gives me insight for dealing with the client.

"So tell me. How did it go?" I waited patiently while she sipped her coffee, fighting the desire to rush the conversation. Much better to let Belinda take the lead.

She is a great lady, really. Married once a long time ago, she divorced and then put herself through law school, winding up as a partner in one of the city's top firms. She is a no-nonsense barracuda when it comes to business, but when it comes to personal involvement the mistakes of her past have kept her hamstrung. Afraid to take a risk, she's sequestered herself in her work, ignoring her desire for marriage and family.

Enter me. And more important, Stanley.

"He took me to Chanterelle." Her voice took on a wistful quality that had no resemblance at all to the hard-ass lawyer she plays by day. Of course, I already knew about the restaurant. I selected it, after all. Setting the stage is almost as important as the actual date.

Chanterelle is fabulously French and wonderfully TriBeCa and, and more important, it's over-the-top romantic, which is exactly what Stanley and Belinda needed.

"It was amazing," she continued, "really it was. It's just that . . ."

"What?" I tried but couldn't quite keep the sharpness from my voice. So excuse me for taking rejection personally.

"Well, Stanley was so distracted. It was like he had his mind on a million other things. I mean, at first everything was going really well, and then all of a sudden it's as if he just disconnected, you know?" She sounded disappointed, which told me two things. First off, she was interested—which was, of course, half the battle. And second, she wasn't sure exactly what had gone wrong—which hopefully meant it was more to do with Stanley's reticence to change gears than his actual opinion of Belinda.

"Do you remember what you were talking about when he disconnected?"

She took the lid off her macchiato and stirred it absently with a straw. "Just my work. I was telling him about a case I was working on."

Well, I, for one, can't think of anything less stimulating than legalese, but not so with Stanley. His Mean Streets TV series was based on a district attorney's office and staff. I mean, the man made his money off of legal mumbo jumbo.

"What kind of case, Belinda?" There had to be something more here, the key was figuring it out and nipping it in the bud, so to speak.

"It's a court battle over an inheritance. Old man dies leaving adult children and a second wife. The prenup is ironclad, but she's claiming duress and arguing that the estate should pass to her. The children—"

"You hit a hot button. It's the prenup." I cut Belinda off with a wave of my hand. "Stanley didn't have one the first time out. And his ex took him to the cleaners. So second time he had one that he thought would provide protection, but she managed to find a loophole. Not a pretty picture."

"I didn't mean to upset him." She removed the straw, twirling it between her fingers like a tiny plastic baton.

"You wouldn't have known." I cursed myself for the slipup. I'd briefed Belinda on Stanley's background, ex-wives included, but I hadn't thought to discuss his residual bitterness. Big mistake.

Fortunately this was date number one (I require two for each match; it gives involved parties time to relax and show their true selves instead of a fractured version brought about by first-date jitters), which meant that there was still time for salvage.

"So what happens now?" She sounded so wistful I wanted to hug her.

"Let me talk to him. I'll explain that you didn't know, and I'm sure that will be that. Everything was going fine up until then, right?"

"It was great. He's really funny. And he made me feel like he actually saw *me*, you know, not just the package I come in." She'd folded the straw accordion-style and was absently pumping it up and down with her thumb. "And you'll never believe this, our parents both have summer homes in the Adirondacks on the AuSable. I've probably passed him on the river. We both fly-fish," she added by way of explanation.

Of course, I already knew all of that. It pays to do one's homework. As I said, commonalities are the things that make for permanent connection.

"Well, it sounds very promising. I'll talk to Stanley and then get back with you to let you know how he wants to proceed."

The two-date rule was more or less absolute, but occasionally I had to accept defeat and let it slide. Which put the ball squarely in Stanley's court.

"I see." Now she sounded dejected. This was the part of the job I really didn't like. I didn't go into this business to break hearts, quite the opposite really.

"Don't worry, it was only the first date. Everything will be fine. You just have to have to be a little patient. All right?"

"Patience has never been one of my strong suits." As if to underscore the feeling, she flipped the now-mutilated straw onto the tabletop. It wasn't a pretty picture. I reached over to cover her hand with mine.

"It'll work out. You just have to have a little faith."

Her laugh was hollow. " 'Faith' isn't exactly a catchword in my industry. We deal in tangible facts. Everything in the detail."

"So concentrate on the fact that you had fun. Despite his backing off, I'm betting Stanley felt the same way. You belong together," I said, channeling a Miss America smile. "I know what I'm doing, so relax and let me handle this."

She nodded, although she didn't look completely convinced. Not that I blamed her. I'm good, make no mistake, but matchmaking is a very inexact science. All of which begged the question as to what in the world I'd been thinking agreeing to take on Mark Grayson. The man was a born bachelor. (Did you know that the term "confirmed bachelor" was a euphemism for gay in the forties and fifties? I had no idea. Nor, I suspect, does my mother, who throws the term around with the abandon of the totally uninformed.)

Anyway, all terminology aside, the honest truth is that I'm in over my head—no question about it.

"I heard that Althea's wearing Ungaro," Belinda said, segueing nicely into my panic.

The idea of Althea seducing a man with her wardrobe was almost laughable. Almost. The point here was that she was arming with stronger weapons than mine. But, quite frankly, my bank account couldn't support anything that pricey. I'd just have to rely on a combo of Wendy Hill, Jimmy Choo, and the new Manolos I'd bought last week. The sum of which surely equaled Ungaro. Especially when adorning my considerably younger body.

"I've got Manolos." It was an "I'll see yours and up the ante" moment and Althea wasn't even in the room.

"You'll do fine." Belinda smiled. "Just remember Grayson doesn't like phonies."

Oh God, I was a born a phony, came from a long line of them. Bullshitting was like a family name. "Do you know Mark Grayson?"

"Casually," she nodded. "Our firm has handled some of his corporate maneuvering."

"So spill."

"Really, I don't have all that much to share. But during a conference, Grayson asked for some stats we clearly didn't have. And instead of admitting the fact, a junior associate tried to bluff. Grayson caught him in the lie, and threatened to walk."

"What happened?" I sipped my coffee feeling a lot like someone had slipped a noose around my neck.

"The associate was fired, and we did everything but throw

ourselves prostrate on the floor. The man was pissed. And de-servedly so. All I'm saying is whatever you do, stick to the truth. And don't mince words."

"What else?"

"I don't know." She frowned, pursing her lips as she consid-ered the question. "He's very self-contained. The kind who ex-pects you to follow his train of thought even when he hasn't vocalized it. He's tough in that silent, condemning kind of way. Frankly, he scares the shit out of me. Too intense. You know the type."

"Oh God, what was I thinking? I must have been out of my mind to have agreed to the bet." No more martinis—ever.

"No . . . ," she started, then shook her head and grinned. "Well, maybe a little. But that doesn't mean you can't succeed. You just have to play to his weaknesses."

"Except that I have no idea what they are." There'd been ab-solutely no time for anything but the most cursory research. "I Googled him, of course. But even with that, it's hard to put to-gether a realistic picture. He's a deal maker. A whiz with prop-erty development. If you believe the press he's single-handedly revitalized something like seven major cities."

"Twelve, actually," Belinda interjected. "Three of them in Europe."

"Right, so the man's a demigod when it comes to urban real estate. But all work and no play . . ." I left the phrase unfinished.

"But Mark Grayson is anything but dull," Belinda countered. "I'm betting at least half of your Google hits stemmed from mention in the society columns."

"True enough. But most of it was strictly speculation."

"Fits with the strong and silent image." Belinda had started on my straw, the plastic already showing white lines of strain where she'd twisted it.

"But it doesn't help me." I'd fallen into quicksand and was sinking fast.

"I think the key is to capture his attention. Intrigue him. Men like him can't resist a challenge. They thrive on it. Throw down the gauntlet and I'm betting he'll pick it up."

"And throw it in my face." I was being flippant, but the idea actually had some merit. Some men needed to be led to the altar. Some just needed guidance on who to take along for the ride. Some of them had to be tricked into the trip. But with men like Mark Grayson, it was all about seducing them into the game.

And letting them think they could win.

I drew in a breath, girding my proverbial loins. "Good advice. Thanks. Maybe you should be the matchmaker."

"No way." She waved the dilapidated straw. "I can't even keep a boyfriend."

"Well, we're about to change all that." I smiled, firmly back on solid ground again. "And in the meantime, I appreciate the insight into Grayson."

"I read people for a living. Part and parcel of being a trial lawyer." Belinda shrugged. "But Mark Grayson isn't going to be an easy mark, and I figure you'll need all the help you can get. And between you and me," she leaned in close, glancing around her as if she were sharing state secrets, "I think it's going to take more than Manolos."

I opened my mouth to argue. Manolos were the crème de la crème of FMPs. One pair of four-inch heels and men practically crawled behind you begging. I had personal experience with the phenomenon. But before I could formulate a pithy retort, my cell phone rang.

Cybil.

Now, I'm all for business before pleasure, but Cybil trumps everything. We've been through too much together for it to be any other way. "Hang on." I shot Belinda a smile and flipped open my phone.

"What's up?"

For a moment there was only silence, and then a sort of muf-fled snuffling that was Cybil's version of holding back tears.

"You okay?" My heart skidded into overdrive, my mind whipping out all kinds of possibilities. Belinda leaned forward, her eyes questioning.

I shook my head. "Cybil? Are you there?

More sniffing. And then after a moment's silence. "It's Stephen." Another pause. "He's left me."

Relief flooded through me. That's not very kind, I know. But I've already made it clear what my opinion of Stephen is. So his leaving can only be considered a miracle. Of course, Cybil wouldn't see it that way.

At least not without a little help.

Chapter 5

Buttercup Bake Shop. *973 Second Avenue (between Fifty-first and Fifty-second streets), 212.350.4144.*

Buttercup Bake Shop is a place to walk into and feel deliciously overwhelmed by display cases filled with cupcakes in every color of the rainbow. . . . With information moving at the speed of light, the bakery lets you slow down and while away an afternoon sipping your favorite beverage and enjoying some delectable, nostalgic treats that spell comfort and love.

—www.buttercupbakeshop.com

Comfort was exactly what I was looking for. And I knew the best way to ease a broken heart was with chocolate. Melt-in-your-mouth amazing buttercream chocolate. And no one in Manhattan does that better than Jennifer Appel with her fabulous cupcakes. Under the circumstances, it was tempting to just go straight for the chocolate layer cake, but I kept my head and bought a dozen cupcakes instead.

No comments. It was an emergency.

Cybil lives in Sutton Place. A fabulous apartment with a garden terrace and a doorman who is better connected than most socialites. The apartment had been her grandmother's and, when the old girl had moved to the family compound in Southampton, Cybil had taken over the residence. It was the kind of place that people kill for. Literally. Six rooms with twelve-foot ceilings, casement windows, a fireplace, and original molding. Add in the completely renovated bathrooms and cook's kitchen, and you have the stuff of metropolitan dreams.

Just at the moment, however, none of that meant anything. What mattered was the fact that my best friend was sitting cross-legged on her white Berber carpet, surrounded by tissues and cake crumbs.

"So tell me exactly what happened." We'd been through the story a couple of times, but Cybil's tears had interfered with coherent discussion and I was a little hazy on the details. And from the little I had been able to glean, it didn't make a whole lot of sense. Not even for Stephen.

And for the record, let me be perfectly clear here, I might not have been lamenting Stephen's departure, but I certainly wasn't happy about the pain it was causing my friend. In fact, if I could have gotten my hands on the man, well, suffice it to say, I'd be moving from *Page Six* to page one in less time than it takes to say "local artist murdered."

"I don't know. It all happened so fast." She blew loudly into a Kleenex and then sucked in a fortifying breath. Even blotchy and teary-eyed, she looked amazing. Joe's Jeans, a faded Trinity sweatshirt, and a wonderful pair of red square-framed glasses. "I was a little late." She shot a glance at the Bergdorf's bag sitting in the foyer, as if it was to blame for everything.

"I hardly think that's a reason for walking out. Even when it's Stephen doing the walking." She frowned at the last, and I quickly softened the remark with a smile. "I'm only saying he can be a little irrational sometimes in how he reacts to things."

There was a dinner party once long ago where he'd refused

to sit at his assigned place because the table wasn't angled in just the right way. Bad karma or something. Unfortunately, the hostess was not amused and Cybil had had to tap dance around the gossip-enhanced story for months afterward.

Not that she'd minded all that much. She's too sweet for that. But I'm not sweet and I minded for her—a lot.

"I'm just saying there has to be something more than that."

She nodded, pushing her glasses up onto her head, tears welling again. "He hates me."

"Did he say that?" Stephen may not be the best when it comes to interpersonal relations, but he's never struck me as the malicious sort.

"No. Not in so many words." She took a large bite of cupcake, defiantly ignoring the glob of frosting that landed on the carpet. Her housekeeper was not going to be amused.

"So what exactly did he say?" I folded my arms, ignoring the cupcake calling my name as I leaned back against the overstuffed sofa cushions.

"At first everything seemed fine. He ki . . . kissed me." There was a pause as she pulled herself back into control. I've always maintained that Stephen must be a hell of a lover. I mean for all the grief he'd caused Cybil, it was just easier to believe there was a payout of some kind.

"And then what?" I bit my lip, trying to hang on to my patience. Right now Cybil needed to hear it all out loud, to process it, and hopefully to realize that it was—in the infamous words of Martha Stewart—a good thing.

"We sat down and ordered champagne. It was a celebration," she reminded me.

"Right, the painting you sold."

"I didn't sell it. It sold itself." From the garbage heap. "Anyway, we didn't talk about the painting. We talked about you and the bet. And my part in it. He knew I was having regrets." She shot me an apologetic grimace, but I waved it away.

"I'm assuming Stephen didn't approve?"

She blew out a breath and shrugged. "What upset him was the manipulation involved. He just doesn't believe love can be coerced."

"Who said anything about love?" I'm usually not defensive about what I do. But somehow criticism from *Stephen* seemed a bit much.

"All right then, matchmaking. Whether you believe it or not, it's the same thing."

"No, it's not." I started to launch into exactly why it wasn't, and then realized that we weren't drowning in buttercream because of my career choice. "But that's not the point. We're trying to figure out what happened between you and Stephen. Why the preoccupation with the bet?"

"He'd seen the rough draft of the column I was writing." She waved at the computer console in the corner. Mind you, if you didn't know there was a computer inside, you'd never have guessed the fact. The armoire itself was eighteenth century. English. Solid cherry. Cybil's six-greats grandmother's. The transformation to computer console had been Cybil's idea. And even though it had been done with elegance of good craftsmanship, no one had had the nerve to break the news to her grandmother.

"You're not listening." There was a hint of rebuke in her voice, and I forced my thoughts front and center.

"I am. I swear." I smiled. "You were saying that Stephen read your article."

"Rough draft," she nodded, still eyeing me skeptically. "Anyway, I think it pissed him off that I was aiding and abetting your cause, so to speak. And he'd had the whole morning to work himself up about it."

"All because he thinks love should hold sway?"

"Pretty much."

"But I've been matchmaking as long as he's known me. And you and I have always lived in each other's back pockets, so surely that can't have anything to do with why he walked out." Despite the ridiculousness of the notion, guilt washed through me. I might have been secretly delighted with the breakup, but I'd never have done anything to precipitate it.

"Of course it wasn't because of you." Cybil's reassurance was immediate and heartfelt, but I had the feeling there was more to it.

"What aren't you telling me?"

"Nothing." She shook her head. "Honestly."

"Cybil . . ." I gave in to the urge and grabbed a cupcake from the box. Hell, wasn't sugar supposed to be good for a hangover?

She sighed. "Look, Stephen thought you were a bad influence on me. At least with regard to your views on relationships." I opened my mouth to retort, but she waved me quiet. "I think the real truth is that he knew you didn't approve of him. And so he worried that you were going to talk me out of our relationship."

"What relationship?" The words were out before I could stop them, and I stared down at the cupcake, feeling about an inch tall. "God, I didn't mean that the way it sounded."

"I know you didn't." Have I mentioned that Cybil is a saint?

"I just meant that he's the one who walked out on you, not the other way 'round. So it can't be my fault." I wasn't sure how we'd gotten to this—but I sure as hell wasn't going to take blame for Stephen Hobbs's inability to commit to a relationship.

"No, of course not. You just asked what we talked about, and that's where we started. He was mad at me for helping you manipulate Mark Grayson."

"I don't think Mark Grayson is the malleable type. But that's beside the point." I licked off a bit of frosting and let the chocolate confection melt on my tongue while I studied my best friend. "We're trying to figure out what happened with Stephen."

"I know. Believe me, I've been over it and over it. But none of it makes any sense."

"So, what? He just stood up and said, 'I can't believe you're enabling Vanessa's torrid manipulations, I'm out of here'?"

Cybil almost choked on a cake crumb. I slid to the floor, pounding her on the back, and then both of us dissolved into giggles. Chocolate and misery—it'll do it every time. After we'd snorted enough to give my mother apoplexy (she doesn't believe a lady should laugh out loud), we sobered and sat for a moment, staring at the remnants of the cupcakes.

"I don't think it had anything to do with the bet, Van. I think it was more about the differences between us. I think maybe in his own way Stephen was trying to tell me that you're right."

"Say again?" It was as if the pope had just declared a holiday for priests at Scores.

"I said that I think he realized the gulf between us was too big."

I glanced over at the Bergdorf sack in silent agreement.

Cybil laid her head against the coffee table for a moment, and then sat up, the tears spilling out onto her cheeks. "But you're both wrong." The words lacked conviction, and I suddenly felt like I'd shot my best friend.

"Look, maybe it wasn't that at all. Maybe he was just looking for an excuse."

"To dump me."

"Sorry. I'm not helping, am I?" This was shaky ground. And even though we'd been here before, it didn't make it easier.

Whatever their differences, Stephen had connected with Cybil in a way that was difficult to sever. And the fact that he kept coming back also meant that it was harder to accept his defection as fait accompli.

"What else did you talk about? Besides the bet. Did you talk about the painting?"

"Not really. I mean it was the point of the lunch. And we did order the champagne, but beyond that he didn't say much about it."

"Did you tell him how the sale came about?"

"Not exactly. I told him the woman had a friend in the building." Highly unlikely when one considered that Stephen's studio was far enough uptown that it was almost the Bronx. "She saw the painting in the hallway. Loved it. And asked around about the artist."

"So why didn't she come directly to Stephen?"

"He wasn't in." She dipped her finger in the cupcake frosting, twirling it around until it clung to her finger like cotton candy. "I told him she recognized the name and his connection to me. So gave me a call. From there it was a simple matter to arrange the sale."

An ugly idea occurred to me. "Did the woman actually see the painting?"

"Yes."

"Outside the studio?" I felt like Jack McCoy going for the jugular.

"No. Not exactly."

"You asked her to buy the painting."

She licked the icing off her finger and blew out a breath. "Yes."

"Did she even like it?"

"Of course she did." Cybil's answer was a little too glib.

"Is there any way that Stephen could have figured out the truth?" Talk about manipulation.

"No." She shook her head to underscore the words. "Absolutely not. Abby would never tell."

Abby was an old friend. One I'd certainly trust. "I agree with that. But there are other ways for information to leak. You of all people should know that."

"I know. But I don't think that's what this was about. If he'd known about Abby, he'd have confronted me with it. Wouldn't he?" She interrupted herself on a sob. "I really thought we were going to make it this time."

"Honey, it'll be okay, I swear it." I reached for her hand, feeling a lot like crying myself. Of course there was no way I could be certain it would be okay. Hearts could be fickle. Especially the really sensitive ones—like Cybil's. But overall, the organ was amazingly resilient.

"I don't see how," she sniffled, taking another bite of cupcake. "Everyone is going to think I'm such a fool."

Everyone was going to be doing handstands in their Cesare Paciottis, but that little fact was best kept under wraps.

"If anyone is the fool, it's Stephen." In more ways than I could possibly innumerate.

"But *he* dumped *me*." If she hadn't been my best friend, I swear I would have slapped her.

"My point exactly. The man's obviously not thinking clearly. You're the best thing that ever happened to him. So what exactly did he say when he ended it?"

"After he'd said his piece about you and manipulation, we made small talk about shopping and the celebration. And then everything just sort of trailed off into silence. You know, the uncomfortable kind that you can't seem to cut through." Been there, done that. And wouldn't wish it on anyone. It's like waiting for the other shoe to drop, and you just know that when it does it'll be covered in dog poop. "He just kept shaking his head, and staring at the fois gras." He probably didn't know what it was. But then again, far be it from me to pass judgment on anyone.

"And then what?"

"The wine steward arrived with the champagne. And before he could pop the cork, Stephen just stood up and said it wasn't going to work. I don't know who was more surprised, me or the sommelier." She absently picked up a couple of crumbs and popped them into her mouth. "And then he walked out." Her eyes welled with tears, as she tried valiantly to swallow a sob.

"Maybe this is for the best?" I knew it wasn't going to be a popular sentiment, but it had to be said.

"That's not a very nice thing to say." Cybil scowled at me, dropping the last bit of cupcake back into the box.

"I know. But it doesn't make it any less true." I waited a minute, trying to find the right words. "You said it earlier. You and Stephen aren't on the same page when it comes to life experiences."

"I didn't say that. I said that I thought Stephen might think that."

"Okay." I held up my hands in surrender. "Point taken. But what I'm trying to say is that maybe you were right. Maybe his reticence to stay in the relationship is based on the fact that the two of you are from different worlds. And despite the fact that you're willing to ignore the differences, it's a little harder from his side of things. Maybe he just couldn't deal with that anymore."

"Great. My pedigree ruined my relationship."

"No. It wasn't you at all. It wasn't even Stephen, really. It was the two of you together." I reached for another cupcake and forced myself to stop midway. I wasn't the one who'd lost a boyfriend. "I'm not saying this right. What I mean is that I truly believe that Stephen cared about you. But in the end, he just wasn't ready for a real relationship."

"With me," Cybil said, the words tinged with self-deprecation.

"With *anyone*," I quickly assured her. "Stephen's a free spirit. And I think sometimes people like that are better off on their own. I mean, the phrase 'happy artist' is probably listed in the dictionary under 'oxymoron.' The point, Cybil, is that this isn't your fault. It isn't even Stephen's. It's just the reality of your stations in life."

"You sound like Jane Austen."

We'd read her books in high school. Well, actually, Cybil read them. I sort of got the gist vicariously, if you know what I mean. I've never been a big reader.

"I sound like a realist. Look, I know you care about Stephen. And I know this hurts like hell. I'm just trying to say that maybe there's a silver lining out there somewhere."

"Well, I wish it would hurry up and get here."

I fished in my bag for the invitation. Who said fairy godmothers had to be old and have wings? "It may be closer than you think." I held it out with a flourish.

"My God, this is for the Cavalli party." Even through the tears I could see excitement sparkling in her eyes. "How in the world . . ."

"Let's just say I have friends in all the right places. Anyway, the point is that you can be my 'plus one.'"

She started to smile but the reflex died before it could fully blossom. "I don't have anything to wear."

Cybil had enough couture to fill a boutique at Bergdorf's, but

I didn't even hesitate as I held out my bag. "Of course you do. This will look amazing on you."

She took the sack and opened it, the Wendy Hill looking resplendent inside. "It's gorgeous." She paused as she contemplated the dress. "Mark Grayson is going to be there, isn't he?"

I nodded.

"This is your battle gear." She closed the bag and held it out to me. "I can't take it. You need it."

I pushed her hand back. "Not as much as you need to feel beautiful tonight. I've got lots of other dresses. Besides, I'm not trying to attract Mark Grayson. At least not in that way. What I look like is irrelevant." That, of course, was a blatant lie and we both knew it. But Cybil did need the dress more.

"I've got the perfect shoes." She hopped up, crumbs raining down on the carpet, already heading for her closet, her heartbreak not forgotten but at least numbed for the moment with the prospect of a new dress and a hot party.

Priorities and all that.

Chapter 6

Bungalow 8. *515 West Twenty-seventh Street (between Tenth and Eleventh avenues),* *212.629.3333.*

The name and decor are meant to invoke memories of the Beverly Hills Hotel and old Hollywood; thus the palm trees, concierge, and inevitable NO VACANCY sign glaring into the night at this far–West Chelsea spot. We would advise being utterly fabulous before attempting to cross the threshold or you'll be doing the walk of shame. Trust us.

—www.hipguide.com

Bungalow 8 has topped the Manhattan club scene for several years in a row now. And in a town famous for overnight failure, this is not a feat to be taken lightly. But then Amy Sacco, the brains behind LOT61 and Bette, knows her stuff. And the tightly guarded door only makes it more alluring. Maybe it's the NO VACANCY sign in the window.

Anyway, as we pulled up, I could see the usual assortment of cleavage-baring wannabes staggered amid Gap-clad gawkers and the occasional B-list celebrity. Even though tonight's soiree was strictly invitation only, hopes of crossing the velvet frontier still apparently ran high.

Fat chance.

Plastering on my best ice princess smile, I stepped out of the town car. Cybil followed suit, looking stunning in the Wendy Hill. Frankly, it looked better on her. I'd chosen an Alberta Ferretti. It was two seasons old, granted. But it was also formfitting and red. And did I mention backless?

If I had to call it, I'd say the two of us looked pretty damn good, especially when you considered the fact that we'd been gorging on cupcakes not three hours earlier. We paused on the sidewalk, playing for the paparazzi.

Cybil usually drew a decent amount of attention. Between her position with the Murdochs and her old family money, she warranted at least a photo or two. And me, well, I had buzz. The kind that can turn on you in an instant, granted, but at least for the moment I was hot.

After a couple of minutes of smiling at no one in particular, I grabbed Cybil's hand and we moved past the crowd, as the beefy guy at the door smiled in recognition and waved us inside. I could hear the whispers rise as the Victoria's Secret wannabes tried to figure out exactly who we were and why we were able to achieve what they had not—entrance into one of Manhattan's coveted hot spots.

It was all over in seconds, but I confess it gives me a thrill every time. That's probably not the chic thing to say, but it's true nevertheless. Limelight is a double-edged sword, there's no doubt about it, but it's a kick, too. It has to be, right? Otherwise no one would want it, and television shows like *Extra* would be out of business.

Inside the club you could actually feel the vibrations from the music. On a normal night Bungalow 8 holds about a hundred people, and the strict door policy keeps it to that, maintaining the intimate feel of the place. Tonight, however, the

place was overflowing, a short runway jutting out amid the potted palms, Cavalli-dressed mannequins emerging from behind
glittering curtains in an endless stream of amazing couture.

Trays of the club's infamous watermelon martinis wended
their way through the crowd, the excellent waitstaff making certain that no one was left without libation. I passed on the martini
with a shiver of memory and chose champagne instead.

"Quite a crowd," Cybil whispered, sipping a martini. Obviously her stomach was stronger than mine.

"And then some." I nodded to a hard-bodied man in Tommy
Hilfiger, shirt open to the waist. He flexed as he walked past us,
and I resisted the urge to pinch to see if it was real.

Three scantily clad twentysomethings passed in his wake,
their eyes locked on his now undulating derriere.

"*Bungahos*," Cybil said, with a catty smile almost reminiscent of pre-breakup.

Bungahos were women (and I suppose men) who hung out at
Bungalow 8 with startling regularity. Hangers-on who could get
in—*just*—and intended to make the most of the fact.

"I don't think so. The look isn't right." I nodded at blonde
number two. "Definitely off-the-rack. My guess is they've been
admitted as part of someone's entourage."

Cybil tilted her head, studying them as they walked away.
"You're right. My vote is Banana Republic."

Now, please understand that in normal life there is nothing
at all wrong with buying clothes from Banana Republic, but if
you're trying to capture the attention of someone of the opposite sex in a place like this, you have to dress for the challenge.

Unfortunately these girls hadn't gotten the memo. I smiled
kindly, thinking what I could do for them, and then pushed the
thought aside. I wasn't here for recruits.

"You see him?" Cybil asked, as usual reading my thoughts.

"No." I shook my head, trying to pitch my voice beneath the music. "But I can't see more than about a foot in front of me. There're too many people in here."

As if on command the Dolce & Gabbana crowd shifted and there beside a potted palm and a red velvet banquet I saw a flash of gold Ungaro and the perfect symmetry of an auburn pageboy.

Althea.

Fortunately, she was talking to an editor from *Woman's Day*. Martha something-or-other. If memory served, the woman was a chatterbox. Which at the moment suited my purposes perfectly since it bought me valuable time.

Assuming, of course, Althea hadn't already found our quarry.

The thought sent panic coursing through me, but a long sip of champagne stopped it cold. I traded in my empty glass for a full one, letting the frosty bubbles bolster my courage.

"If he's here, he'll be up there," Cybil said, gesturing to the glass-enclosed VIP lounge above our heads. If getting into Bungalow 8 took connections, getting up to the VIP lounge took credentials.

Thank God Anderson had them. Which meant that my gold-edged invitation trumped the bulk of the crowd holding simple white ones. Althea's, of course, would have gold as well. So the race was on.

"Help me get through the crowd." I was already moving, using a strategic smile, as well as a well-placed elbow, to work my way forward.

Cybil moved to my left, flanking me on that side. It was a dance choreographed through years of clubbing. We might have been on the wrong side of the age equation, but what we lacked in skin tone we more than made up for with experience.

In fact, we'd almost made it to the überbouncer when I felt a hand on my arm.

"Vanessa. I knew you'd be here." Speaking of young and perfect.

Devon Sinclair was a client. One I'd taken on in a fit of optimism that I had a feeling I was going to live to regret. In all truth, he was too young for this game. Too many wild oats to sow. A wunderkind on Wall Street, with a seven-figure income and the pubescent mind of a teenager.

If a male could in fact be a bungaho, Devon fit the bill to a T. Except that in addition to all the philandering, he supposedly yearned for 2.5 kids and acreage in Westchester. Hailing from somewhere southwestern, he had that rare combination of boyish charm and Mensa IQ. Common sense not coming into the equation at all.

So far I'd set him up with four women without success. His reticence was helping my income and ruining my average. But I had high hopes for my latest choice. Lindy Adams was as delicious as she was connected. A year younger than Devon's twenty-six, she was Barbie to his Ken. A perfect couple.

At least on paper.

Judging from the buxom brunette clutching his arm, things were playing out true to form.

"What are you doing?" I asked, sotto voce.

"Having a good time." His smile was meant to be disarming, but fortunately I was immune.

"With her?" I shot a pointed look in the brunette's direction. She responded by pouting, her eyes narrowing in a decidedly unflattering fashion. This one recognized a good package when she saw it.

"Oh, my God," Cybil said, cupping a hand over her eyes. "Is that Armando Diaz?" Diaz was one of Hollywood's hotshot producers, a fixture at Bungalow 8 and a sure draw for bimbos of all persuasions.

"Where?" Chesty asked, her eyes going wide.

"Over there." Cybil pointed toward a man holding court by the bar.

"Oh." The woman's voice would do Jayne Mansfield proud. And with an excited squeak she tottered off on five-inch heels, the crowd miraculously parting in the way that could only be accomplished by a double D.

"What was that all about?" Devon asked, frowning. "I just met her."

"You're supposed to be with Lindy. What happened?"

"She's here." Devon shrugged and reached for a cigarette, only to realize he wasn't allowed. "Damn Bloomberg." He slid the silver case back into his pocket and smiled sheepishly. "She's in the restroom."

"And you've already picked up another woman?" I tried but couldn't keep the dismay out of my voice. "Devon, you said you wanted to find a wife."

"I do. It's just hard to ignore the eye candy. You know what I mean?"

If he'd been ten years older he'd have sounded pathetic, but he wasn't. He was young, hot, and successful, and in Manhattan that made him a commodity.

"Look, Devon, I took you on against my better instincts. Don't prove me right."

He actually managed to look chastised. It was the same look that had sucked me into overriding my intuition. "I'm trying."

"Maybe a little less clubbing and a little more serious face time with your date?" It was just a suggestion but I delivered it with the authority of a five-star general. It wasn't what you said as much as how you said it. I learned that from my mother, the queen of innuendo.

"You're right. I know you're right." He sighed, his gaze traveling up and down the amazing length of one of the Cavalli models.

"Devon." I sighed. "Go find Lindy. Make me look good. Okay?"

He nodded, his attention switching from the model to me. The once-over was less enthusiastic, but there was admiration there. "I'm not sure you need my help. That dress is hot."

I was old enough to be, well, his sister, and I had no illusions about how I looked. But it was a good dress. "Thanks. But flattery isn't going to work. Go find Lindy."

"Fine." He grinned. "There are worse fates. Like maybe chasing after Mark Grayson?"

God, the whole freakin' world read *Page Six*.

"I'm not chasing him."

"But you are here to see him?"

I frowned, recognizing the look in his eyes. "Anderson has a big mouth."

I'd met Devon through Anderson. Devon worked for Anderson's firm. Different department, but Anderson had an eye on him anyway. To hear Anderson tell it, Devon's insight into the market was extraordinary.

I tended to picture him in a cowboy hat. Stupid, I know. Blame it on the accent or his penchant for using the word "ma'am" all the time.

"I think he's upstairs," Devon said, tipping his head toward the VIP lounge. "Can you get in?"

"Of course," I responded, fighting irritation. The real truth was that without Anderson's invitation I wouldn't have even been able to get into the party. But no one wants to feel inferior to a kid. Even a handsome, well-off one. I flashed the invitation for good measure and sent him off with instructions to find Lindy.

A glance in Althea's direction confirmed I'd been right about the *Woman's Day* editor. She was still talking.

"I'm going to run to the ladies'," I said to Cybil. "Keep an eye on Althea. I'll be right back." It was a risky move. I had the advantage and should have probably taken it, but I needed a moment to prepare.

I moved through the crowd, stopping a couple of times to air-kiss women I knew, or thought had potential for my list. By the time I reached the restroom, I'd handed out quite a few business cards. If nothing else, at least it would increase the buzz.

Once through the door, I exhaled and dropped the social smile. After all the hot bodies pressed together outside, the ladies' room felt like an oasis. I moved to the mirror, pleased to note that despite the crush I hadn't melted. My makeup was in place, and my dress really did look fabulous. I opened my lip gloss (Chanel Glossimer #65, I swear by it) and was just about to put it on when Lindy Adams walked out of a stall.

Usually Lindy Adams is one of those perfect blond princesses we all wish we'd grown up to be. The American ideal. Rich daddy, perfect figure, and hair that could inspire the "I'm worth it" people to copy the color. She's the kind who turns heads—male and female—wherever she goes. The whole package, as it were. It's enough to make a normal woman want to throw up.

Except that she's also one of the nicest women I've ever met. The kind who donates to charity because she really cares. And remembers your birthday with frightening regularity. We'd been friends for a couple of years. I'd met her at a Humane Society function—a cause, it turned out, we both shared a passion for. And since then, we'd often worked together in the effort to find safe, loving homes for abandoned animals.

Okay, enough with me as a do-gooder, the point here is that Lindy didn't look beautiful at the moment. In fact, she looked downright defeated. And it didn't suit her at all. There were smudges of mascara beneath both eyes, and the end of her nose was red.

She'd clearly been crying, and I had a pretty good idea why. Damn Devon.

"Lindy, honey, are you okay?" I asked, trying hard to find a motherly tone.

"Vanessa." Her perfectly sculpted eyebrows shot up in surprise. "I didn't know you were going to be here tonight."

If it had come from anyone else's mouth, it would have been an insult. But from Lindy it was just honest surprise.

"It was sort of a last-minute thing."

"Mark Grayson," she said with a nod.

I won't repeat any of the words that sprang to mind except the bit about busybodies in this town. "Right," I nodded. "Grayson. But he's the least of my worries at the moment. I ran into Devon a few minutes ago. He said you were here."

"He brought me," she said, swinging her Kevin Mancuso hair. "Not that he seems to remember the fact."

"The brunette." I didn't see the point of mincing words. I mean, the mascara was already smeared.

"You saw her?" Again the eyebrows rose, but this time in anger.

"Saw her and sent her running in Armando Diaz's direction."

There was a quiver of a smile, but her eyes still filled with tears. Today, apparently, was my day for dealing with wounded women. "He'll just find another one."

"No worries, there's more than one director here." My attempt at a joke fell flat. "Look, Lindy, the way I see it, you have two choices. You can either abandon the whole thing or you can fight fire with fire."

"I don't know what you mean." She sniffed. The downside of being such a lovely person is that she hadn't a clue how to play hardball when it came to a man. Which is, of course, exactly why she had me.

"All right. Let's cut to the chase. Do you like Devon?"

"I do." She nodded, dabbing at her tears. "Except for the roving eye."

"So you don't want to jump ship?" I waited while she thought about it.

"No. I really think it clicks between us. It's just hard to get him to settle down."

"But it's what he really wants." I said it to myself as much as to Lindy. The boy was a handful to be sure, but in his own way he was sincere. "All right, then, here's what you need to do." I took a deep breath and gave her my best "I'm queen of the world" smile. "You've got to give him some of his own medicine."

"I beg your pardon?"

"Play hard to get. I know it defeats years of feminist fighting, but the best way to hold the attention of a man like Devon is to stay just beyond his reach. You know most of the people here tonight, right?"

"Most of them," she echoed in agreement.

"All right, so find a couple of the really cute ones and dance your heart out. Flirt, smile, whatever it takes. Keep it just this side of entanglement. And make sure that Devon sees you."

"Are you sure that will work?" She looked skeptical. Which was to be expected. Lindy was the kind who played fair. Which was why she was in the Bungalow 8 bathroom in tears.

"Yeah, think *Grease*."

She gave me a blank stare. God, I was getting old.

"It's a movie. From a Broadway musical."

Still no reaction.

"Never mind. The point is, you're going to make yourself more attractive simply by seeming to be unaffected by his lack of attention. My guess is that Devon has had a long line of adoring girlfriends, and although that's appealing on paper, it's kind of cloying in real life. Meaning his roving eye is more of a defense mechanism than anything else."

"And you think that if I play hard to get, he'll lose the defenses."

"Hopefully." I could be wrong, of course, but I tend to read people pretty well, and Devon was nothing if not predictable. "Look, Lindy, you're everything he wants in a woman. And I think given the right jolt, he's a good fit for you as well. You just have to make him see it that way. Sometimes the best way to catch a fish is to lure him into the bait. That's why they're called fishing lures."

She nodded, although I wasn't entirely sure she followed the analogy.

The door opened behind me, Cybil following in its wake. "Althea is on the move."

I nodded, my blood pressure jumping up a couple of notches. "I've got to go. Are you going to be all right?"

Lindy smiled, pulling off her Stella McCartney sweater to reveal the shell pink camisole underneath. "Better?"

"Once you fix your mascara, you'll knock 'em dead."

"Devon is the only one I want to knock anywhere." Spunk is a good thing.

"Well, save that for after he capitulates. And looking like that," I eyed her from head to her Rene Caovilla–clad toes, "I think it's a sure thing."

"The movie." She said with a smile.

"You've seen *The Sure Thing?*" It wasn't as old as *Grease*, but I've have thought not as well-known.

"On DVD," she nodded. "I love John Cusack."

I felt tottering-on-my-cane old.

Cybil tilted her head toward the door. "Althea?"

I nodded, checked my dress and lipstick, and followed her out the door.

"What was that all about?" Cybil asked as we made our way toward the VIP bouncer.

"Trouble in match-made paradise. Devon's wandering eye didn't go unnoticed."

"So what's with *The Sure Thing?*"

"Actually it was *Grease*, but she missed the reference. I was telling her to fight fire with fire. You know the drill."

"Make herself desirable and scarce."

"Exactly."

"But surely in the long run she'll just have the same problem all over again."

"If it wasn't Devon I'd have to agree. But he wants to settle down, remember? And I'm certain that Lindy is exactly what he's looking for. So it's just a matter of him accepting the fact."

"And once he does, you'll have another notch on your belt."

I shot her what I hoped was a caustic look. "I prefer to think of it as another success story. A happy couple. That's what it's all about."

Cybil didn't look impressed, but I didn't have time to argue. We'd reached the überbouncer. Fortunately, the magic gold border did the trick. I flashed the invitation and we were accepted as VIPs.

The upstairs room was quieter and less crowded than downstairs, but still there was a hum of activity. I scanned the room for signs of Althea or Grayson, finding both easily. Grayson was ensconced in a corner talking earnestly with Walker Frazier, another real estate mogul.

Althea was only a few feet away, but she'd been stopped by Liz Smith, the Texas transplant and ruler of all things titillating. I subconsciously took a step back but Cybil's hand on my arm was blocking my retreat.

"You can do this."

"No, I can't." I don't know if I've mentioned it, but I'm a certified chicken when it comes to actually getting my fingernails dirty. Cindy Adams was moving my way though, and if Liz was the queen of gossip, Cindy was definitely a duchess. They were both lovely women, but anything was fair game with the press, and unless I wanted to spill my guts, it was best that I keep moving.

"Go on," Cybil said, giving me a shove in the other direction. I felt immediately guilty for not listing her among the stars of the columns. She's right up there, believe me. And even more important, she's the best friend a girl could possibly have.

Especially in sticky situations.

I made my way around the edge of the room, pausing for one moment to look down at the undulating crowd below me. I spotted Lindy, hair flying as she held her arms up and moved with the music. I didn't recognize the man dancing with her, but it was enough that he was dark, Latin, and to die for. About ten feet away, Devon stood with his eyes glued to Lindy, the redhead at his side trying in vain to gain his attention.

Score one for the matchmaker.

Chapter 7

Roberto Cavalli Showroom. *745 Fifth Avenue, thirty-first floor (between Fifty-seventh and Fifty-eighth streets), 212.308.5566.* **Cavalli Boutique.** *711 Madison Avenue (corner of Sixty-third Street), 212.753.7722.*

Italian designer Roberto Cavalli relies on his mature fashion experience to guide his eye in creating his collections of fashion couture. . . . Today, Cavalli's unique creations adorn the likes of Anthony Hopkins, Sting, Alicia Keys, and many other style-conscious celebrities and couture aficionados.

—www.lifeinitaly.com

There was an appreciative titter followed by all-out clapping as the man himself, Roberto Cavalli, approached the microphone on the runway at Bungalow 8. He had an air about him that made you feel like anything was possible, and despite my need for haste, I found myself staring down at him with something akin to awe.

In the business for something like thirty years, he'd passed from noted designer into legend. Brigitte Bardot wore his clothes. Along with scores of more modern glitterati. Even me. (Although it's only a scarf, and I'm not technically glitterati.) Noted for his love of animal prints, Cavalli just has a way of

feminizing clothes to make them sensual and seductive. Definitely my kind of designer.

And judging from the still-echoing applause, the party was a
success. Cavalli's wife, Eva, had joined him at the podium.
Theirs was the kind of coupling I strove to create. Beautiful,
successful, each perfectly accentuating the other.

All of which served as a reminder that I had far more important things to do than stand at the window staring down on
Cavalli and his adoring fans. I turned my attention to Mark
Grayson's table and sucked in a deep breath. It wasn't like I
hadn't done this kind of thing before; it was just that I'd never
done it with so many eyes watching.

Or at least it felt that way. In truth most everyone's attention
was attuned to the man on the runway below.

Perfect timing.

I hoped.

Grayson was alone now, tapping away on his BlackBerry, not
even Cavalli himself, it seemed, could pull the man away from
his messaging.

"Go," Cybil whispered, one sharp finger nudging my spine.
"Before Althea breaks free. I'll handle Cindy." A quick look as-
sured me that my nemesis was still deep in conversation with
Liz, probably planning my demise.

Squaring my shoulders, I waded between trays of martinis
and happy partygoers, a cool and hopefully gracious smile pasted
on my Chanel-coated lips. I've always believed in the adage that
if you visualize something you can make it happen; in fact, in
many ways I've come to depend on that inner sight to help me
achieve success.

All that remained was to convince Grayson that I was exactly what he needed. Tall order, but I was up to the challenge.

I mean, he had everything I look for in a man. Brains,

money, looks, and class. His background was a bit scruffy, but if the gossip rags were to be believed he more than compensated for any lack of upbringing with charm.

And besides, who wouldn't want a man with all that money? He was an irresistible combination. All he needed was the right woman.

I glanced back at Cybil, and she nodded in support. Swallowing to calm the butterflies that had suddenly blossomed in my stomach, I squared my shoulders and mentally prepared for battle. Althea had seen my approach and was heading for Grayson as well. But I was still in the lead, provided I kept moving.

My feet, fortunately, didn't share my brain's hesitation, and in three short steps I was standing by the banquette. It's funny the things you notice in times of stress. There was a bottle of Chivas on the table. About a quarter empty. Several glasses surrounded the bottle, but only one held whiskey. Apparently Grayson wasn't inclined to share.

His suit was impeccably cut, his French cuffs straight from the boardroom. Leisure and work were obviously one and the same with this man. I mentally ran through the tidbits I'd gleaned over the past twenty-four hours and realized with dismay that I basically knew nothing at all about the man.

Well, it wouldn't be the first time I'd had to wing it.

I shook myself from my reverie. Althea was closing in fast. It was now or never.

Grayson looked up with a frown. "Can I help you?" he asked, his eyes narrowing as he tried to place me.

"I think maybe you have it backward, Mr. Grayson. I'm here to help *you*." The words were out and there was no way to pull them back, but the minute they came out of my mouth I knew they were ridiculous.

"I beg your pardon?" His frown deepened as recognition set

in. "Wait a minute," he said, holding up a hand to ward me off. "You're one of the matchmakers." The last was clearly not meant as a compliment. So much for a rousing start.

It wasn't the first time my chosen occupation had been ridiculed, but unfortunately it was the first from a prospective client. But I wouldn't have lasted a minute if I succumbed that easily. So despite the lukewarm welcome, I stuck out my hand. "Vanessa Carlson."

"Mark Grayson," he said, taking my hand. To his credit it was a firm handshake, the kind some men reserved only for members of their own species. He might hate matchmakers but he was an equal opportunity handshaker, and since limp-noodle handshakes were a pet peeve of mine, I had to admit grudging admiration. "I don't suppose you're going to go away now?" He asked, his eyes telegraphing arctic blizzard.

"It would go better for me if I could at least have a couple of minutes of your time."

He waved at the seat opposite him with a not-so-flattering sigh, and I slid into the booth, my mind trying valiantly to come up with an angle that might appeal to the man. In my peripheral vision I saw Althea hovering a few yards away, her fingers digging into some poor woman's arm with a ferocity that was sure to leave a mark.

"Drink?" Grayson asked, pulling my attention back to the task at hand.

I nodded, grateful when he poured only half a glass. I'd already had more champagne than I needed. And wasn't there some rule about wine and whiskey? Or was it just simply whiskey is risky— period? Especially in dire business situations.

I took a sip. "Thank you." We both knew I was thanking him for a hell of a lot more than the drink. Principally for not embarrassing me in front of the elite crowd gathered in the VIP lounge.

"I wouldn't jump the gun, Ms. Carlson," Grayson said, draining his glass and pouring more. "The only thing keeping me from having you evicted from my booth is the fact that I have a couple of things I want to say."

"I'm assuming it's with regard to the bet."

"Yes." The monosyllabic word seemed to echo through the room. It was almost as if the crowd paused. But, of course, that was ridiculous. Grayson wasn't that powerful.

I waited, watching him over the rim of my glass, knowing full well he was waiting for me to apologize. But I wasn't going to do it. The truth was, I wasn't the slightest bit sorry. I might wish that it hadn't gone quite so public. But I stood by the idea that he, like all men, was in fact the marriageable type. He simply had to be presented with the right woman.

Silence stretched for what seemed like hours but was in fact only a few seconds. And then an amazing thing happened. Mark Grayson smiled. It was like he'd morphed into a completely different person, the laugh lines around his eyes immediately making him look younger and more carefree.

"I'm betting you're pretty good at poker."

"I'm not much of a gambler. I prefer sure shots." The minute the words were out of my mouth I realized my mistake, and so did Grayson.

"That would explain why you bet your friend you could get me married off." All hints of the smile were swallowed by a scowl.

"Actually, the bet was that one of us, both professionals, mind you, could find the right woman for you."

"And marry us off," he repeated stubbornly.

"Well, that's the usual conclusion when a man finds the right woman."

If possible, the frown deepened. "And what if the man doesn't want a woman?"

"You're gay?" I knew the answer to the question, of course, but it seemed the right tone for a comeback.

"Of course not."

One point for me.

"So ultimately, you're going to want to settle down. I mean, if nothing else, don't you want an heir?"

He paused mid-drink, his eyes narrowing as he considered the question. "I can't say I ever thought about it."

"Well, unless you want to raise a child from your wheelchair, it's time to start. Besides there's more to a marriage than just progeny."

"Right," he said, his tone impatient. "This is when you start talking about true love."

"No." I shook my head. "I'm talking about a merger of assets."

"Fancy words for the same thing."

"Not at all. Love can certainly play a part in it all. But it doesn't have to. I'm talking about an honest merger. Two people with assets that are better when combined than solo."

"So by assets you're talking about money." Almost despite himself curiosity replaced animosity.

"Certainly that's one part of the equation. I think that any large inequity in financial strength can cause serious problems in any merger. In fact, if it's too lopsided, it becomes a takeover. And in matrimony, takeovers rarely succeed."

"Surely, you're discounting arranged marriages where someone trades social station for capital."

"Quite the contrary," I said, surprised to find I was actually enjoying myself. "In the situation you're referencing, there is still an exchange of assets. They may not be the same, but the two have equal stature. And certainly the combination of assets makes both sides better off than they were before the merger."

"Point taken. But without love, how can such an arrangement survive?"

"I wouldn't have taken you for a romantic."

"I'm not." Maybe I just imagined it, but it seemed he emphasized the statement just a little too much. "I'm just making a point. Love isn't a myth."

"No, it's not. But its importance for marriage is highly overrated. I think that even in marriages where there was love as an instigator, you'll find that the longevity of the union is based on commonalities and equal or at least complementary assets."

"And if love isn't an instigator?"

"Then desire is."

"I beg your pardon?"

"Not that kind of desire," I said, swallowing the last of my whiskey. He promptly refilled it, and I took the action as a sign that I was making at least a little progress. "I'm talking about desire for a lasting relationship. The need for a combination that creates a better whole."

"That sounds more like a sound bite than reality." He leaned forward, his mind clearly trying to find ways to dismiss what I was saying.

"All right. Let me make it clearer. Two people, each at the top of their respective games. Each of them has strengths, and each of them has weaknesses. Because they're basically winners, their virtues outweigh their faults. However, they still have weak spots. But if either of them were to find a partner whose strengths covered their weaknesses—a person whose value system and upbringing created additional common ground—then the couple would be stronger than either of them were on their own."

"All right. Let's assume I buy that." Which, of course, clearly meant that he did not. "Why does a person like you need to become involved in what is, for all practical purposes, something anyone with a Dun and Bradstreet could accomplish on their own?"

"Because most people work from the misguided belief that they're searching for true love. And in most cases," I glanced over at Cybil, and immediately felt guilty, "they never find it. But the myth is so damn persistent they can't seem to get past it. In other words, they're looking in all the wrong places."

"And you steer them to the right ones?"

"Exactly." I smiled at him as if he were a prize pupil. Unfortunately, I don't think he appreciated the gesture. "Look, for whatever reason, I have the ability to recognize when two people are suited for each other. And my job is to facilitate their meeting."

"Sounds archaic."

"Which is precisely why it works. It's basic to our nature to want to procreate. From there comes the chemical combustion we mistakenly refer to as love. To base an entire relationship on that combustion is a huge mistake. Enter the matchmaker. A neutral entity who can see beyond pheromones to make sure that a marriage is based on commonalities rather than chemical attraction."

"What if the *pheromones* happen to be present in an otherwise sound merger. Are you saying you'd reject it?"

"Absolutely not. It's sort of like a bonus round."

"Love is icing on the cake?"

"Well, we're talking about lust, not love. And after a certain amount of time that's going to fade. Part and parcel of the animal, I'm afraid."

"And love?" he insisted, his gaze intent, and in some indefinable way unsettling.

"Well, in most cases, I believe that love—the kind that lasts—grows from mutual respect, from shared experience. It comes out of the seeds planted when two people share the same background, the same values."

"And sex?" He meant the question to throw me off, but I'd played this game before.

"Is a natural by-product of the merger but shouldn't be considered part of the equation."

"Even if I accepted your so-called rationale," he paused, picking up his glass, contemplating the contents, "I still don't see what it has to do with me. Other than that I'm obviously good fodder for the columns."

"Well, first off, we never intended for it to go this public."

"That's hard to believe, considering the venue you chose for announcing the bet."

"Bemelmans isn't exactly a public forum. And it was a private discussion."

"Held at the top of your very inebriated lungs. I was there. Remember?"

"You couldn't have heard us." I swallowed, trying to hide my mortification.

Grayson just sat there, his expression unreadable.

"Look, there were martinis involved," I offered as explanation. "Lots and lots of martinis. But the idea of helping you to find the right match was an honest one. The gin only fueled the fire."

"But you had absolutely no reason to believe I'd want your particular brand of help. It so happens that I'm perfectly comfortable being single. To be honest, I've never even considered marriage. I travel all the time. I live, eat, and breathe business. I'm difficult on a good day and impossible on a bad one. I'm simply not matrimonial material."

A gauntlet if ever there was one.

"All the more reason to let a neutral party find your match."

"I just said that there isn't one."

"No. You just gave me a laundry list of excuses you've used to avoid the idea of intimacy."

"With good reason."

"Mr. Grayson, I'm very good at what I do. And I wouldn't be pushing you if I didn't believe that somewhere behind that austere exterior you have a beating heart that would be better served if presented with the right woman."

"Bullshit." The expletive startled me. Obviously I'd hit a nerve. Two points for the matchmaker. "You're interested in me because if you can find me a match, you win not only a bet, but potentially the apparently coveted position of Manhattan's top matchmaker."

"I'm not saying that doesn't play into it. But it's not like I just picked you at random." Actually that's pretty much exactly what happened, but there was absolutely no sense in revealing that fact. "I honestly believe that the right marriage would improve your bottom line on more levels than you can possibly imagine."

"My bottom line is fine." This time he almost growled at me. I was definitely hitting a hot spot.

"That doesn't mean it couldn't be better." I waited for the idea to sink in, knowing that bigger and better was Mr. Grayson's middle name.

"And better is exactly what I can deliver." Althea's husky voice had never been less welcome. "I'm sure you're more than aware of the fact that Vanessa learned everything she knows from me."

"What I'm aware of, Ms. Sevalas, is that the two of you have managed to turn the media spotlight squarely on my personal life. And since I've spent years taking measures to avoid exactly that, I can only say that were I inclined toward marriage, which I am not, I most certainly would not allow either of you the opportunity to meddle in matters that are clearly none of your business."

With a glare he stood up, and without so much as a by-your-leave, walked away from the banquette, leaving me and Althea, and a half-empty bottle of Chivas.

Chapter 8

Madison Restaurant. *965 First Avenue (corner of Fifty-third Street), 212.421.0948.*

The lines go out the door on weekends because everything is good. Pancakes, French toast, omelettes, potatoes . . . all just what you'd expect from a great neighborhood diner. . . . Madison is a great place to go late at night with friends or on a lazy Sunday afternoon.

—www.menupages.com

In my case, it was late night, and thank God for friends. Grayson's dismissal at Bungalow 8 had thoroughly soured the evening. And to add insult to injury Althea had made it clear that I had not only ruined it for myself, I'd ruined it for her as well. And so feeling totally chastised I'd grabbed Cybil, retreated to higher ground, and called in the cavalry—Anderson and Richard. It wasn't so much that I thought they could do anything, more that misery loves company.

And pancakes.

If the Atkins diet ever became mandatory, I'd have to kill

myself. Carbs may be a dieter's worst nightmare, but they are my best friend. Particularly those very special carbs associated with breakfast. It's sad, I know, but eating stacks of pancakes, waffles, or biscuits and gravy makes me feel secure.

My mother wasn't the culinary type, and my father hated takeout, so we had a cook. Imelda. She was amazing. One of those ample-chested, happy people who always knew when a kid needed a hug and a cookie. Or two. Or three.

Now that I think of it, it's amazing I'm not a size 2X.

But the most wonderful memories I have of Imelda center around Saturday mornings. My parents slept late, and I didn't. So most Saturday mornings I could be found in the kitchen, warm and cozy, eating whatever Imelda had conjured from flour, eggs, butter, and usually lots of sugar. It was heaven.

And addictive.

I'm still a sucker for pancakes, and the Madison Restaurant serves up some of the best in Manhattan.

"I've never understood why you don't eat syrup," Anderson said, his own stack of pancakes swimming in the stuff.

"Because they're perfect as is," I replied around a mouthful of pancakes.

"You mean drowning in butter." Cybil nodded toward the little pile of empty butter cups beside my plate. Not that Cybil was behaving any better, mind you. She was already halfway through her French toast complete with butter *and* syrup.

"I like them this way, okay?" I defended my pancakes with a wave of my fork.

"I like them that way, too," Richard said, making me feel infinitely better for no particular reason at all. Richard had opted out of breakfast altogether, choosing coffee and pie instead.

I'd ordered hot tea in hopes of countering the risky whiskey I'd consumed at Bungalow 8 (not to mention the champagne).

"Based on your SOS, I'm assuming things didn't go well at the party?" Anderson shot a look at Cybil for confirmation and then reached across the table to pat my hand. "I'm sorry."

I sighed, grateful that no one had mentioned the "incident" until the food had arrived and I'd managed a forkful or two of comfort. "It didn't start out badly at all. In fact, I honestly thought he was responding to what I had to say. But then Althea showed up and in less time than it takes to download something to your iPod, we were dismissed."

And that was a kind word. Left sitting at the losers' table was more the ticket.

"So maybe it was Althea," Richard said, as always my knight.

"No. It's not fair to blame Althea. She hardly got a sentence out. I think the reality is that what I mistook for a spark of interest was actually more like a cat toying with a mouse, with me playing the part of the mouse."

"It can't have been as bad as all that. He asked you to have a drink," Cybil said, dipping a bite of French toast in syrup.

"Only because he wanted to tell me to fuck off."

"Did he say that?" Anderson's frown made me smile.

"No. Not using those exact words, anyway. He was actually very polite. Even let me run on about my theory of marriage."

"Like attracts like," Richard and Anderson said in unison.

"Right." I shrugged. They might not like the idea, but they'd seen firsthand that it worked. "Anyway, I think he was letting me go on to see if I'd hang myself."

"Which you didn't." Cybil nodded with satisfaction.

"Yes, but it still didn't do me any good. The man made it perfectly clear that hell would freeze over before he let either of us find him a match. No more martinis for me."

"Don't make promises you can't keep." Richard's lips twitched with laughter, but to his credit he held it in.

"Oh God, can you imagine how much fun the papers are going to have with this?"

"Not me," Cybil promised, crossing her heart. "In fact, I'm not really feeling up to writing anything at all."

"Poor darling," Anderson said. "Vanessa told us about Stephen."

"He'll come back." Richard nodded to underscore the thought. "He always does."

"I don't know." Cybil shook her head. "Something about this time felt final."

"Well, then you'll find someone new. Someone utterly fantastic." Anderson pushed back his plate of pancakes. I've always marveled at his ability to leave half of his food untouched. I simply can't ignore food if it's in front of me. Especially pancakes.

"In theory that sounds wonderful," Cybil said. "But it isn't so easy to meet men in this city."

"Tell me about it." Anderson shot a loving look at Richard, and I almost wished I had someone like that in my life. But one look at Cybil wallowing in breakup misery and I was reminded of why I didn't. Richard and Anderson were the exception, not the rule.

"Maybe I can find someone for you." I actually wasn't at all certain it was a good idea to mix business with friendship, and Cybil seemed to have no problem finding men. It was just keeping them that had proved difficult. Although that sounds harsher than I meant it.

What I'm trying to say is that Stephen wasn't the first guy Cybil had dated that wasn't, in my humble estimation, worthy of my friend.

"No thanks." Cybil's response was emphatic.

"Not even if I found someone fabulous?" I forked another

mouthful of pancakes, rationalizing that since I didn't add syrup, they were actually not all that fattening.

"Well, if he's fabulous . . ." Cybil shrugged, her expression telegraphing just how impossible she considered that to be.

"Nothing like climbing back up on the horse," Richard said, eliciting a glare from Anderson.

"I think Cybil needs a little time to adjust to what's happened." Anderson waved his coffee cup at the waitress, then waited as she refilled it. "It's not always better to jump right back into things."

"No. I think Richard is right." I was wracking my brains trying to come up with Mr. Perfect Antidote to a Bad Breakup. "The best thing Cybil can do is to get back into the game, preferably with someone amazing."

"*Cybil* can speak for herself," Cybil said with a grimace.

"Sorry," I said with a grin. "Occupational hazard."

"I know you mean well." Her smile encompassed us all. "And I certainly wouldn't want to miss Prince Charming, but I think right now all I need is a little time and my friends."

Richard and Anderson reached simultaneously for her hands, and I marveled at how lucky I was to have friends like these. We sat for a moment in self-satisfied carbo-enhanced happiness, and then Anderson brought things full circle stop back to me and my not-so-successful evening.

"So what did Althea have to say?"

What didn't she say would be a better question. I'd felt like a kid caught with a water balloon on the apartment building stairwell. (Okay, so I think biographically. But I only hit Mr. Demateo. And nobody liked him. He was a cantankerous old fart with a tendency to pinch in inappropriate places.)

But we were talking about Althea. And her certainty that everything that had happened was entirely my fault.

"Vanessa?" Richard prompted.

"Sorry." I tried for upbeat, but failed miserably. "Just reliving the humiliation."

"With Grayson?"

"Actually with Althea. After Grayson dressed us down, you'd think I'd have been immune, but . . ."

"That bad?" Richard asked.

"Worse," I sighed. "She insinuated that if I'd let her go first, things would have gone more smoothly."

"Yeah, for her." Cybil added sugar to a fresh cup of coffee.

"Well, she does have a point. I did sort of cut her off at the pass."

"All's fair in love and war," Richard chimed cheerfully.

"Well this was neither, really. And in all honesty, Althea does have more experience in dealing with difficult clients."

"Vanessa, there's no need to be modest." Anderson frowned. "You know as well as I do that you passed Althea a long time ago. That's why you went out on your own."

"I used to believe that. But now I'm not so certain. I mean, how lame is it to risk one's entire reputation?"

"Well," Cybil said, "it's not like you were alone in this. I certainly played my part in the whole affair, and Althea was right there with you."

"Okay, so we're all stupid. Now what?"

"We regroup and figure out what the next move should be." Richard leaned forward, his lawyer's brain already working on the problem.

"*Retreat*," I said. "I think the next move should be retreat. I mean, the man made it pretty damn clear what he thought of matchmaking."

"Matchmaking per se?" Anderson asked. "I'm thinking he

was a lot more upset about the publicity. And that's something that will fade."

"Not after tonight."

"Well, we all have contacts." He was looking directly at Cybil, who nodded her agreement. "Between us we ought to be able to squelch the comments. Or at least water them down. And certainly Althea will be doing what she can for damage control."

"But no matter how you spin it, it's still a big fat public fiasco." I propped my elbows on the table, resting my head on my hands. Have I mentioned that I don't do failure well?

"You said that before Althea came up, you thought he was interested, right?" Richard asked, his wheels still turning.

"Yes. Maybe. Oh, I don't know. He was listening. And arguing. And I thought maybe there was a spark of interest there."

"Then you need to play off of that."

"How? By storming the castle? Because I'm fairly certain he's not going to be throwing open the doors for me, you know?"

"Actually, you don't know anything except that he wasn't ready for you and Althea in one dose. And honestly, Van, I don't think that's all that surprising. The two of you together can be a bit—"

"Overwhelming?" I laughed. "Maybe you're right, but believe me, Mark Grayson is perfectly capable of holding his own even with the two of us."

"Still, considering the situation, I can see that he might have reacted out of self-preservation more than any real animosity toward the two of you. My point being that it ain't over till it's over."

"And what exactly do you propose I do to get back in the

game?" Honestly, at that moment, if I never saw Mark Grayson again it would be just fine with me. I'm not into self-flagellation, believe me.

"I don't know. You'll think of something. If for no other reason than because I'm quite certain that Althea is somewhere scheming right now."

If Anderson was trying to hit my buttons, he was doing a damn good job. I wasn't about to let Althea one-up me. "Okay, so I'm not out of it. But I do seem to be sort of down for the count. As I said, Grayson didn't exactly leave the door open."

"Well, there's got to be a crack. You just have to figure out what it is."

I reached for the bill, but Anderson was faster. "Our treat." Richard nodded.

"But I'm the one who called you out in the middle of the night."

"Please," Richard said. "By Manhattan standards it's still early." He was right, at least for most of Manhattan. But the staff at the Madison seemed ready for us to leave. And to be honest, the carb rush from the pancakes was starting to wear off. I stifled a yawn, and Richard laughed.

"So much for the late-night party girl."

"Too many nights in a row," Cybil said.

"Two if I'm counting right," Anderson teased, joining Richard's laughter. "It's hell getting old."

"Hey, watch who you're calling old," I warned, smothering another yawn. "It's just been a long night." Coming out of a very long day.

Richard headed for the cashier to pay the bill as we all stood up and gathered our things. "You staying with Cybil?" Anderson asked.

I opened my mouth to agree, but Cybil beat me to the punch. "It's not necessary. I'm fine. Or at least closer to it than I was eight hours ago. What you need right now is a good night's sleep, in your own bed."

"I'm not sure that's—" I started, but Cybil interrupted.

"I'm okay. Really. If I have trouble sleeping, there's always the rest of the cupcakes to keep me company."

"Chocolate isn't going to help you sleep."

"No, but I'll be very happily wide-awake. Seriously, I'll be fine."

We've already established that accepting defeat gracefully isn't one of my strong points, but sometimes a person just has to give in. And to be honest I was so tired I was almost dragging on the sidewalk.

Anderson stepped off the curb to hail a cab as I gave Cybil a hug. "I'll call you in the morning?"

"Not too early," she returned with a smile. "But I'll count on it."

Tears pressed against the back of my eyes. For Cybil, for me. Hell, for all mankind. (Okay, that was the remnants of Chivas talking. Did I mention that before I left Bungalow 8, Cybil and I had drowned our sorrows?)

I sniffled and waved at Cybil, then slid into the taxi between Richard and Anderson. We were quiet for most of the drive back, each lost in our thoughts. It was a comfortable silence. The kind that only comes when you've known someone forever.

Or when there's nothing left to say.

The truth was that I hadn't the slightest idea how to wiggle my way back into Mark Grayson's good graces. In point of fact, I wasn't entirely sure I'd ever been there to begin with. But I was certain that I'd seen a spark of interest. Grayson might not have thought he wanted a wife, but he was wrong.

And I was just the person to prove it to him.

All that was left was to figure out how.

Chapter 9

One of my favorite things about a bedroom is, well, the bed. Or, more important, the linens on the bed, which explains why my sheets and duvet cost slightly more than a Birkin bag. Okay, I'm exaggerating. But only a little. My bedding (from Fine Linens) is the most luxurious thing I own. After all, I do spend half of my life there.

And in all honesty, there's nothing more fabulous after a night of humiliation than sinking into the soft cool comfort of your very own Italian-made, six-hundred thread count, Egyptian cotton sheets. The only thing marginally better is waking up in them. You know the drill—luxurious stretch, long yawn, and then a quick snuggle for another ten minutes' sleep?

Heavenly.

Unless the first thing you see is your mother standing at the end of the bed.

"Vanessa, get up." Her voice had a smoker's rasp, the effect much nicer than the habit that precipitated it. "We're due at Tavern on the Green in an hour and a half."

Why in the world did I ever give her a key?

"Go away," I said, turning my face into the cool sanctuary of my pillow. "I had a bad night."

"I know, darling, it's the talk of the town." There was a note of condemnation. I think I mentioned that my mother has never really approved of my choice of profession. Heck, who am I kidding? My mother wouldn't approve of any profession. In her mind the best thing a girl can do is marry rich, spend the better half of the money, and give the rest away.

And so far, I might add, she's been doing a damn good job of it.

I surfaced from the freshly scented heaven into familial hell. "Did it make the papers?"

"Yes," she said, bending now to push Waldo out of the way. "Vanessa, do something about your cat."

I don't know if it's her perfume or the fact that she despises all things feline, but Waldo thinks my mother is one of his conquests. From my vantage point I could just see the tip of his tail as it wove figure eights around my mother's Ferragamos. "He's not a dog, Mother. You can't call him off."

"Well, try."

We'd played this game a million times already, and if anything it had only increased Waldo's ardor. "Come on, Waldo." I sat up and patted the comforter for effect. Nothing happened.

"Waldo." This time there was a hint of exasperation. I wasn't in the mood. And miracle of miracles, Waldo cocked his head, considered the matter, and with a walk worthy of a king, sauntered over to the bed and leapt up beside me.

"See," my mother said with self-satisfaction.

I sighed again, this time for effect, and ran my hand over Waldo's silky fur. "How bad was it?"

"How bad was what?" Mother asked.

"The papers," I said in exasperation.

"Oh that," she answered, emphasizing the last word as if Waldo had left a little present for her. "Fairly tame actually, considering the nonsense you and Althea have been up to."

I sent a silent prayer of thanks to Cybil, Richard, and Anderson, and sank back into my pillows. Another bullet dodged. "I'm too tired to go to one of your benefits, Mother. I just want to stay here and sleep." Waldo, obviously in an obliging mood, curled up beside me.

"Wallow is more like it." She crossed the room, her heels clicking on the parquet floor. With a whoosh she pulled up the shade, the morning sun blinding against the white of my bedroom walls. "You know better than most that the best way to deal with gossip is to face it head-on."

I knew no such thing, but she obviously wasn't about to back down. My mother might look like an aging movie star, but she has the tenacity of a rottweiler. It was simply easier to give in than it was to try to argue with her. Besides, in the end, the result was the same. I did exactly what she wanted.

"I've forgotten where we're going." I sat up again, pushing my hair out of my face, my awakening senses picking up the scent of coffee. "You made coffee?"

"Hardly." Mother laughed, the sound surprisingly musical. "I brought Starbucks."

All the better. I got up and padded into the kitchen, her footsteps echoing behind me.

"It's a benefit for the Make-a-Wish Foundation. A luncheon."

"Oh, joy," I said, pulling the lid off my mocha latte and simply inhaling. What is it about coffee? It smells so divine, but without serious dairy infusion, it tastes like shit. Definitely an acquired taste. But with a little Starbucks mojo, I was definitely on board.

"Darling, everyone will be there."

"Like that makes it better?" I stared over at her, wondering why it was that my mother always managed to make me feel like an adolescent again. And believe me, that's not a time period I'd like to revisit.

"Of course it does." She turned to pick up her own coffee, her plum-stained lips pursing as she tested the heat. "You'll waltz in and show them that last night was a one-off."

I've never waltzed anywhere in my life. Especially with my mother on my heels. "I don't have to prove anything to anyone."

"Of course you don't, darling," she soothed, meaning nothing of the sort. "It's just that your choices have affected other people as well."

"Like you?"

"Among others."

I glared at her, trying to think of a comeback, but I wasn't exactly firing on all pistons. Chivas will do that to you.

"Your father—" she began, but I waved her silent.

"My father doesn't give a damn what I do and you know it." You're probably cheering for my dad right now, but let me remind you that he's not exactly a warm and fuzzy sort of guy. The only reason he isn't bothered by my actions is that except for the holidays he rarely remembers I exist. Which sounds like a hardship, but honestly it's not. My life is what it is. And, frankly, in order to get my father's attention I'd have to wear a ticker tape or something.

In all truth, I prefer Moschino.

"Your father loves you very much," she was saying, "and so do I."

In their own way, I suppose, they did. There are certainly more dysfunctional families. But I had other things to deal with. Like figuring out how to get Mark Grayson to engage (literally). I'd thought about it as I fell asleep—which took longer than you'd think given the situation—and the only thing I'd come up with so far involved throwing myself at his feet and groveling.

"Thanks for the coffee, Mom, but I think I'm going to have to give the luncheon a pass."

"But I'm getting an award." She was pulling out the big guns. Guilt is a powerful persuader.

"I don't have anything to wear." It was a last-ditch effort and we both knew it.

"I sincerely doubt that," she said, already heading for my closet. Of course she was right, and I realized she wasn't going to let me off the hook. Actually I had promised to go. Pre–Mark Grayson. And I supposed a couple nights of drinking and the bet from hell didn't qualify as a break-plans-with-your-mother emergency.

For a moment I considered using Cybil, but since she was probably going to be there, it didn't seem the best of alibis.

"What about this?" Mother pulled out a black and white Norma Kamali that had been delightful in its day, but many seasons later looked more like something from a costume exhibition. Shoulder pads belong on football players, but for way too many years we'd forgotten that.

"Please," I said, stretching the word out for emphasis, "I'd only add fuel to the fire in that."

She pulled out another hanger. This one a red jumper I'd lusted after only a year ago. But now it looked more schoolgirl than socialite. My mother's image of me, no doubt.

"Let me." I elbowed my way past her and pulled out a simple black dress—Shannon McLean, Cosa Bella. "This should do nicely."

"Then you'll come." She said it as if I'd had a choice. *Mothers.*

"Just give me half an hour."

"Twenty minutes." She turned her wrist to look at her watch. "I'll wait in the living room."

Thirty minutes later we were walking into Tavern on the Green. I know, it's sort of a kitschy place. But at its heart, the Central Park restaurant is sort of quintessential New York. Originally a sheep barn—*seriously*—it sits right at the top of Sheep Meadow, which, believe me, wasn't named for its topiaries.

Anyway, in the 1930s the barn was restyled into a resplendent restaurant, where the elite of the day met to see and be seen. Remodeled in the fifties, it continued to be an "in" spot until the early seventies, when it began to show its age. But fortunately, the restaurant was rescued again with yet another makeover. This one funded by Warner LeRoy. Among other additions, he created the glass-enclosed Crystal Room, a rococo fantasy that's over-the-top fabulous, especially in the spring.

Today, the Crystal Room was resplendent, the doors and window thrown open to the lovely garden beyond, the smells of flowers and trees invading the space so that I almost forgot I was in the city.

Almost.

I stood at the back of the room, trying to look invisible, and not succeeding at all. Most everyone had arrived, thank God, but news travels fast and our fellow latecomers were definitely whispering behind bejeweled hands.

Okay, maybe I'm being oversensitive, but this is Manhattan, where gossip is a full-body contact sport. Returning with name badges, my mother shot me an innocent smile.

Uh-oh.

"Did I tell you I'm sitting at the head table?"

"And me?" I already knew the answer. I was being deserted. She might as well have just fed me to a tank of hungry piranhas.

"Oh, I arranged a fabulous table for you. You won't mind, will you?" She handed me my name tag and left me standing in a cloud of First. So much for mothers protecting their young. Come to think of it, aren't there some species where the mother eats the young?

I sucked in a breath, and looked down at the carefully calligraphied name tag. Why even bother with good clothes? Slap this thing on and even Dior became tacky. I considered putting it on my purse, but I swear I could hear the leather protesting, so instead I gingerly stuck it in the vicinity of my left breast.

The murmuring crowd had quieted slightly and I realized it was now or never. And with mother getting an award, never was not an option. Squaring my shoulders I waded into the throng, exchanging banalities and air kisses with people I had known most of my life, but still didn't know at all.

It's shallow, I know. But it's my world and I'll defend it to the death.

Of course, the table Mother "arranged" was all the way up front, so it took almost a full ten minutes to gain access, and by that time the hostess was already standing at the podium welcoming everyone to the fete.

I slid into my seat with a sigh, and smiled in the general direction of my tablemates. The key to dealing with an uncomfortable social situation is to give the illusion that you don't care. And the best way to do that is to avoid making direct eye contact with anyone. I know that sounds difficult, but it isn't as hard as you might think. The key is to look directly into their hairline. They think you're looking at them, you're spared the humiliation of seeing what they're really thinking, and occasionally your spirits are lifted by the fact that their colorist isn't as good as yours.

Believe it or not, I've never been very comfortable in a room full of people. In college, if I had to go to a party by myself, I used to walk in and head straight for the phone. (Yes, I admit it, I predate cell phones.) Anyway, I'd call time and temperature and have a very earnest conversation with the recording, all the while checking out the room. In the process, I had a chance to kill the butterflies and I usually found someone I knew.

Tricks of the trade.

Now you know why newcomers at parties always seem to be on their cell phones. Is there still such a thing as time and temperature?

I'd scanned most of the guests at the table, recognizing almost all of them. The woman on my left, Esther Remaldi, was an old friend of my mother. They'd even shared the same nanny. Well, not at the same time, but you get the point. She was rarely in the city these days, preferring her Bar Harbor estate. (Can you blame her?)

We had a house in the Hamptons when I was growing up, but my father's late life interest in skiing had meant good-bye, Sag Harbor, hello Aspen or Saalbach. Not that I'm complaining.

Directly across from me was the director of a prep school. A dour man who had spent his life on the edges of a society he couldn't possibly afford. It was no doubt an awkward position, but he'd managed it with decorum. His wife sat next to him, and a woman I vaguely recognized from similar functions sat next to her. To the director's left was another couple, the

Gaudier-Smiths. I knew them from my parents' Christmas parties. My presence at the table was definitely bringing down the median age.

Finally, I turned to my right, my social smile freezing in its politely upturned place.

Mark Grayson.

The fact that I hadn't noticed him before was either a blessing or my mind on protective overdrive. Either way the jig was up; he was here and in the flesh. I didn't know if I should kiss my mother or kill her. Although kill was looking like the odds-on winner.

"We meet again." His voice was polite, but glacial. I stole a glance at the rest of the table to see if they were leaning forward, ears extended, but these people had manners flowing through their veins and everyone seemed to be involved in their own conversations.

"Mr. Grayson." I fumbled around for something pithy to say, but my intelligence along with my stomach seemed to have deserted the ship.

"Please, call me Mark," he said, clearly not meaning a word of it.

"And I'm Vanessa."

"I know." His eyes narrowed with the expression. "I can hardly turn around without stumbling over your name."

"I don't control the newspapers, Mr. Grayson," I said, the emphasis on his last name. Something about his attitude pissed me off. And since anger is the great equalizer, my head cleared, my stomach lurched back into place, and my answering smile made his seem almost tropical.

"I wasn't speaking of the tabloids. I was referencing the fact that your constant proximity is bordering on stalking."

"I beg your pardon." I didn't have to pretend to be offended.

I was. "I'm here because my mother is receiving an award." I tipped my head toward my mother, who was deep in conversation with the hostess.

"Anna Carlson is your mother?" He sounded as if I'd just announced I was a Kennedy.

"Sometimes to my chagrin." Mother chose this moment to look up, and with a waggling of eyebrows offered a beatific smile. I know I've said this before, but mothers can be a pain in the ass.

"I've always found her to be quite charming."

"You know my mother?" I don't know why it surprised me. I mean, our social circle is surprisingly small. But somehow I hadn't really considered him a part of it.

"Not well. But I've worked with your father on numerous occasions, and because of that I've had the chance, from time to time, to socialize with your mother."

The fact that my mother had kept this little tidbit a secret was enough to make my head explode, but now was not the time. "How lovely." Okay, it didn't work at all as a comeback, but at least my tone remained frigid.

"I take it you didn't arrange for this?" There was an actual glimmer of sympathy in his eyes, and I wasn't quite sure how to take it.

"No. I hadn't any idea, actually." I frowned over at him, trying to judge his sincerity. "Believe me, after last night, if I had, I would have pulled every string I possessed to be certain that I was seated somewhere else."

"What about the bet?" He was goading me, I was sure of it.

"It's finished. A miserable failure that hopefully will soon be forgotten."

"Somehow I didn't take you for the type who gives up at the first sign of trouble."

I studied his face, trying to figure out what the hell he was playing at. "I'm not. But I'm also not the type to waste my time on lost causes. And you made it pretty damn clear last night that any further effort on my part was going to be rejected summarily. I'm a fighter, Mr. Grayson. But I'm not a fool."

"Clearly you're not." His gaze met mine, and I felt as if I were being scanned by some sci-fi computer. You know, the kind that can record your innermost thoughts. At least I knew why he was so successful in business. He simply locked eyes with his competition and scared the shit out of them.

But I was made of sterner stuff. "Look, I gave it my best shot. You have to understand that I believe in what I do. And I honestly believe that I could have found the right partner for you."

"Not to mention gaining a reputation as Manhattan's best."

"Sure. That was a big part of it. Althea is good at what she does." The minute the words were out of my mouth I regretted them, but better to soldier on. "I started out with her. And even though I'm out on my own now, people still think of me as her protégé. I mean, would you want a hotel designed by a master architect or his apprentice? It's as simple as that."

"You need to make a statement that's all yours."

"Exactly."

"And I fit the bill?"

"Look, you're high-profile, you're single, and in my opinion, you'd be better off if you had a better half."

"Well, I have to give you one thing. You're the first woman who's said that to me and not been angling for the position herself." He smiled and I was surprised again at how it softened his face. But in an instant he regained his usual grim composure. "Unless this is a ruse?"

"You caught me," I said. "My business is all a ruse. I invented the whole thing as a way to meet men. I mean, offering to marry a guy off to someone else is such a great opening line."

"All right. I admit that was a low blow."

"No kidding. I realize my bet with Althea has put the spotlight on you, but I assure you that wasn't the intention. Your involvement was strictly happenstance. You were sitting at a table in the corner—with Tandy Montgomery. Someone said it was high time you were married and the rest is rather overrated history, I'm afraid."

"I don't buy that. I know for a fact that there were at least three other eligible bachelors at Bemelmans. Why me?" There was something in the question that begged more than a flippant response. I looked down at my hands, taking a moment to gather my thoughts.

"Because there was something in your eyes."

"It's impossible to see anything in there."

"Well, I could see your eyes. And there was a look that said, 'I've conquered the mountain. Now what?'"

"And marriage is the 'what'?"

"A partnership is. Look, people weren't meant to operate solo. It just doesn't work. That's why the first humans banded together in groups. It's what makes us come home for Thanksgiving even though we know we'll want to throw things fifteen minutes after we arrive. We all need to belong somewhere."

"I thought you didn't believe in love."

"I don't. At least not as the only basis for a marriage. See, I believe that with the right partner, you not only have someone to come home to, you have someone to share life with. The good stuff and the bad stuff. And even better, since you get to choose, you can avoid the Uncle-Henry-drinks-too-much-and-Aunt-Sophie-never-shuts-up syndrome."

"A manufactured family."

"Sort of. Although I think that's institutionalizing it even more than I would."

"And because I had the 'what next' question in my eyes, you automatically translated that to 'I need a wife'?"

It was a fair question.

"No. Well, not exactly. I mean"—this was getting tricky—"in that moment, yes. That's exactly what I thought. But after—"

"You sobered up," he finished for me.

"Right. After I sobered up, I had a chance to really think about it. And the truth is, you have all this success and no one to share it with."

"What if I like being on my own?"

"It's like I said last night, you're just using that as an excuse to avoid intimacy."

Anger sparked in his eyes, and I recognized in an instant that I'd gone too far. "I hardly think—"

The hostess chose that exact moment to start the proceedings. There was no more time for talk. I wasn't sure if I was relieved or regretful. Besting Althea was a hell of a carrot, but sometimes the donkey needed to get a life.

I sat back in my chair and went through the motions of paying attention, but in truth I didn't hear another word the hostess said. I vaguely remember picking at the rubber chicken while some politician spoke about something or other, and I remember my mother standing up to accept her award, but the rest of the event went by in a haze. Until suddenly it was over, and people were standing, exchanging polite good-byes.

I stood up and was turning to go, when Grayson touched my shoulder. Damn it, I'd thought maybe he'd let it go. Squaring my shoulders I turned, bracing for his rebuttal, but instead he handed me his business card. "I'd like to finish the conversation. Call my secretary and she'll set something up."

I stood there for another fifteen minutes at least. And for the first time in my life I completely understood the phrase "knock me over with a feather."

Chapter 10

Chef & Company. *8 West Eighteenth Street (corner of Fifth Avenue), 646.336.1980.*

New York's premiere corporate and fine dining caterer. Tasteful, thoughtful catering with impeccable taste. Chef & Company chefs come from the finest restaurants and catering establishments in New York City. They have a proven ability to put new spins on traditional dishes, world cuisines, and presentations. Their cuisine is exquisitely presented, dependably delivered, and professionally served.

—www.chefandco.com

Television production sets aren't noted for their opulence. Especially location shots. But Stanley Barrow's sets were an exception to the rule. And this one, filming inside Central Park, was more lavish than most. I stood, arms crossed, waiting patiently for Stanley to finish the last of the day's shots.

Beside me a lavish table of "afternoon snacks" was laid out with the elegant precision of a master chef. Nestled amid peach-colored linens were glorious platters of crostini and tapas, flanked by a magnificent cheese board and an assortment of the most mouthwatering pastries I'd ever seen, meant for cast and crew alike. Working on this set was most definitely not a hardship. At least not where the stomach was concerned.

Stanley barked an order, and actors and crew moved back into position. According to the digital device keeping track of takes, this was number twenty-six. Stanley hadn't gained success by slacking off.

Maybe it wasn't such an easy gig after all.

I think I mentioned that Stanley is a director/producer. His Mean Streets series has put a new spin on "must-see" TV. Currently television's highest-ranked crime drama, *Mean Streets: NY* had spawned equally successful spin-offs including MS: Cincinnati, MS: Houston, and MS: Seattle. A twice-divorced workaholic with bad instincts where women were concerned, Stanley had jumped at the opportunity to break the pattern and find someone worthy of his money and success.

That's where Belinda came in and, if I couldn't manage some real damage control, where she'd be exiting stage left. As the bustling set testified, Stanley was a busy man. Fortunately, we'd already arranged to meet. And so now it was just a matter of waiting. And trying not to think about the business card burning a hole in my pocket.

It had taken every ounce of self-control I possessed not to make the call the minute I'd ditched my mother and slid into the relative safety of a taxi. But as I'd told Lindy last night, playing hard to get could be an asset—especially in business. So I didn't want to seem too eager. I'd managed that only too well last night. There was always the possibility that Althea would find a way to worm her way in first, but I trusted my instincts and intended to wait until after my meeting to call.

Heck, maybe I'd even wait until tomorrow—then again maybe not. Self-control is obviously a good thing, but in truth I don't have a whole lot of it.

A man in a pair of jeans and a grungy letter jacket jumped from a rocky outcrop into a clearing, shooting at the two men in hot pursuit behind him. It looked so realistic I actually took a step backward, but almost at the same time Stanley yelled, "Cut." And the action stopped, only to rewind and start again. The process was repeated enough times for me to consume three tapas, four crostini, and a couple of fabulous slices of Stilton.

It wasn't until I was reaching for a simply scrumptious-looking éclair that I heard Stanley utter the word everyone was waiting for: "Print."

Waving good-bye to the tiny choux pastry, I turned to wait for Stanley. But, as you know, chocolate is seductive and before he could say, "It's a wrap," I'd popped the cream puff into my mouth. Of course that's the precise moment when he came over to talk.

"Fabulous food," he said, his voice still tinged with director's authority. "Only the best for my people."

Chef & Company was definitely at the top of the heap, and their presence here only added to the aura of success surrounding Stanley. "It's amazing," I mumbled, struggling to swallow the last of the little éclair.

"Only the best," he repeated, draping an arm over my shoulder as we walked toward the roped-off area marking the perimeter of the set. Grips or best boys or whatever they're called were packing up equipment that looked more complex than something one would find at NASA. And in some ways I suppose it was more marvelous. After all, machines like that made nighttime bright, rain on a sunny day, and New Paltz look like Paris in the spring. The magic of the media.

"I'm glad you made it," Stanley said as he brushed past the crowds gathered outside the ropes. He might be one of the most powerful men in television, but the beauty of his position is that he is still relatively anonymous. The crowd was far more interested in the rock-jawed stars who played the detectives. "Do you mind walking?" he asked, nodding toward a narrow pathway leading off the meadow and into the park.

"Not at all," I answered, as if there'd really been a choice. He was the client, if he'd wanted to go rock climbing I'd have gone through the motions.

"Did you talk to Belinda?" The fact that he led with Belinda was an indication of just how much he cared. I took it as a good sign.

Stanley Barrow is not handsome by any conventional standards. He's a little too tall, a little too lanky, and there's a David Letterman–style gap between his two front teeth. His hair staged a massive coup and lost, the resulting exit leaving only a small island on the crown of his head, but he's got an innate sparkle that sort of overrides all of that.

It's not exactly charm, he's too much the geek for that, but he's also got a way of putting his finger on the pulse of the nation and calling it exactly the way *they* see it. Which explains the phenomenal success of his television shows.

He started as a writer, but abandoned that years ago to become an idea man, passing off the mundane in favor of the high-rolling pressure exerted by the network execs. To say that he's a player is an understatement.

But like Belinda, Stanley has never been able to find his stride in his personal life. His first wife was a bimbo—and I'm being kind—and his second was a gold digger of the first order. Both of them were blond and beautiful, and both were shrewd in the time-honored way of a sex that has had to become devious to survive.

However, the most interesting thing about Stanley is that despite everything he's been through he's still out there looking.

In the wrong places most of the time, granted, but there's something to be said for his optimism.

A friend of a friend introduced us, and although he initially rejected my offer of service, we became friends. And from there developed the trust necessary for him to take the chance on me and my instincts.

"So what did she say?" He stopped, his earnest expression pushing away my reverie.

"To be honest she was worried she'd offended you."

He opened his mouth to protest and then closed it with a shrug. "I don't like being reminded of my divorces."

"It's not like she did it on purpose, Stanley. I mean, you did ask her about what she was working on."

"I know." He at least had the decency to look contrite. "I shouldn't have shut her out like that, but she's not exactly what I was expecting."

"What you think you want and what you actually need are two completely different things." I started to walk again, sticking to the paths less traveled. "That's why you hired me, remember?"

Part of my job is being tough when it is necessary—like a bossy aunt or something. I genuinely care about my clients, and Stanley more than most, so I have to be honest. Without that, the whole thing would fall apart in an instant.

"I know. And she really did seem great. I just panicked when she started talking prenup—my life flashing before my eyes, you know?"

"Well, she wasn't referencing anything personal. In fact, she's only handling this case as a favor to another partner. Her expertise is in corporate law, not divorce law."

"I guess I overreacted." His smile was sheepish and charming all at the same time. "Any chance I haven't blown it completely?".

"Two-date rule—remember?" I smiled back, silently congratulating myself for getting things back on track. "Why don't you send her a little something to let her know things are all right."

"Flowers?"

"Too boring. You need something that'll prove you're interested, despite your digression into the past." I pulled out my BlackBerry and paged through several entries. "I've got just the thing." I scribbled down a name and phone number and handed it to him.

"What's this?"

"Girlshop on Washington. She saw a pair of earrings there yesterday."

"Kipepeo?"

"That's the designer. They look like really intricate snowflakes. Gold on brass. If you tell the clerk, I'll bet she'll remember. They talked for a bit."

"Won't Belinda realize the idea came from you?"

"Possibly, although she only mentioned it in passing. But even if she does, she'll know you cared enough to consult with me. I promise it's the thought that counts most."

"All right." He reached over and grabbed my hand, engulfing it in his. "I don't know what I'd do without you."

I sighed and pulled back, feeling suddenly awkward. "Well, you won't have to find out—we have a contract, remember?"

It was probably rude of me to pull things back to business, but I was more comfortable there, and quite frankly, so was Stanley.

"So," he said using the word as a segue. "I heard about last night."

"I'm surprised it didn't make the eleven o'clock news." I sounded snarky, but really, wasn't there something more interesting to obsess about?

"It was past deadline," Stanley said with a laugh, ignoring my undertones. "Anyway, I just wanted to say that for my money he made a mistake."

I clutched the business card in my pocket, wondering whether I should share the latest episode. It certainly had the potential for a better ending, but I'd learned from experience that it was better to keep things close to the vest until a deal was finalized. And although Mark Grayson had opened a window, I was fairly certain he was more than capable of slamming that sucker down quicker than I could snag a Louis Vuitton bag at a downtown sample sale.

If you want the God's honest truth, I hadn't the slightest idea what would happen next, but as my grandmother always said, perseverance wins the day. And believe me, the woman had a doctorate in persistence. She was married four times, after all—talk about keeping hope afloat.

We stopped in front of the statue of Balto, the wolf looking on with something akin to amusement, I swear. "In retrospect it probably wasn't the best approach. I hadn't planned on the bet making *Page Six*."

"Unless you made your wager in an underground bunker in the middle of the desert, my guess is it was bound to get out. And Bemelmans is a far cry from the Sahara."

"I know. And martinis have a way of bolstering self-confidence."

"That's one of the main reasons I stopped drinking."

"Well, that seems a bit extreme to me. I was thinking more along the lines of limiting my martinis to two and having a firm no-betting-while-drinking rule." We started walking again, heading toward the Dairy. It's one of my favorite places in the park. There and the Ramble, especially in the fall. Actually I love all of Central Park in the fall, but any time of year the park is peace in the middle of chaos.

And just at the moment that appealed to me.

"Well, as far as I'm concerned," he said, "Grayson missed out on a good thing."

"I don't know about that. But it ain't over . . . ," I said, repeating Richard's words from the night before.

"That's my girl," Stanley said, a smile lighting his craggy face. "Poor bastard doesn't have a chance."

I suppose some people would have taken that as an insult. But me, well, it made my day.

Unfortunately it didn't give me courage. Three hours later, I still hadn't made the call. I know you're thinking I'm a total putz. And maybe I am. I mean, the man had given me an opening. But I needed more than that. I needed a plan of action. A proposal—if you'll excuse the pun.

So I called Cybil. I figured two heads were better than one. And because heavy thinking needs fortification, we were drinking cosmopolitans. I know, not very original. I mean, Carrie and the girls had the corner of the market on the things. And I'll be the first to admit I'm a die-hard *Sex and the City* fan. (Mr. Big is my idea of a hot steamy night.) But in reality the drink is surprisingly good. So while I'll admit the idea started with the TV show, we'd long since adopted cosmos as our own.

Cybil reached for the pitcher to pour a second glass. At my house you get paper cups, at Cybil's you get crystal. "What I don't understand," she said, "is why you haven't called already. I mean, for all you know he extended the offer to Althea, too."

The idea had occurred to me. "Well if he has, he'll wait to hear what I have to say before he makes any decisions. And I figure it won't hurt to make him wait."

Cybil shrugged. "Might work. But it might also backfire. I'm not sure it's a good thing to give him time to reconsider."

I hadn't thought about that. Still, better to stick to my guns.

"Well, the decision's been made for me." I glanced down at my watch to confirm the fact. "It's after hours. I can't call until morning."

"I'll bet a brow wax at Fekkai that he's still at work." She sat back with a self-satisfied smile.

It was tempting. Manana was a miracle worker when it came to brows. But I swallowed desire and held fast. "Nope, I'm waiting until tomorrow. Besides, he said I was supposed to talk with his secretary. And even if he's burning the midnight oil, I'm betting she's long gone."

"You're making excuses."

"Probably. But even so I'm not going to call."

"You're scared," she said, with a self-satisfied smirk.

"I am not." I poured more cosmopolitan, trying for disinterest.

She waited, not saying a word, the silence telling in and of itself.

"Okay. Maybe I'm a little afraid." I'm not big on admitting weakness, but Cybil sees right through me so there isn't much point in pretending.

"Of Grayson?"

"Surprisingly, no. I mean, when I'm not goading him he's actually kind of nice. I think I'm more afraid of failing than anything else."

"Vanessa, I've been your friend for a hell of a long time, and I've never known you to worry about failing."

"I just hide it really well. And besides, this time the stakes are really big."

"Well, it's not worth freaking yourself out over," she said, shaking her head.

"I know, but this is about a lot more than just marrying off Grayson. It's about proving to myself that I can do this on my own. That I don't need Althea."

"But you've made successful matches since you left Althea."

"I have. But all of them were based on connections I'd forged when I was still with Althea, or they were easy matches that didn't really say anything about my abilities."

"I think you're selling yourself short. But I understand what you mean. You just can't let it get to you."

"I'm doing all right. I got the man to crack a window."

"Thanks to your mother."

"Which is pretty damn amazing. She's the last one I'd have expected to help me. She hates what I do."

"She doesn't hate it. She just doesn't understand it. But in her own don't-hug-me-I'm-wearing-couture kind of way, she loves you, and she wants you to succeed."

We were getting perilously close to sob sister territory. I drank from my glass, letting the bittersweet taste of cranberry, grapefruit, and vodka bolster my courage. "All right. I'll call."

Cybil smiled, knowing full well that I'd been working myself up to it all along.

I pulled out the business card and my cell phone and dialed.

One ringy dingy . . .

Two ringy dingies . . .

Four more and the answering machine picked up. I listened as a clipped British voice explained that the office was closed for the day. The beep sounded, and my heart slammed into gear beating loud enough to echo in my ears. All cognizant thought fled, and I shot a panicked look at Cybil, silently begging for help.

Unfortunately she was choking on her laughter.

"Thanks a lot," I said, flipping the phone closed, feeling like an adolescent who had just called the cute boy in class. "He's probably got caller ID."

"It's a cell phone. Maybe it'll just show the number."

"He's a big boy. He'll probably work it out. Now he's going to think I'm an idiot."

"Why? He told you to call. If he does check the number, he'll just think you were following through. No big deal." She paused for a moment, her lips still twitching. "Unless, of course, the answering machine caught the heavy breathing."

"Shut up," I snapped, wishing there was a way to rewind the last few minutes.

"This is really important to you, isn't it?" Cybil asked, sobering.

"Yeah. But not just because of the bet. You know?" I blew out a long breath. "I know it sounds stupid, but I really think Mark Grayson needs someone."

"Everyone needs someone."

"I agree. But some people need it more than most. And I want to help."

"Even if he doesn't see the need?"

"Maybe because of that. I don't know. The cosmos are making me philosophical." I smiled, trying to lighten the moment. "Anyway, it's a good thing he wasn't there. Before I can meet with him, I really need to come up with a pitch."

"You know your pitch backward, forward, and sideways." Cybil said, sipping her cosmo. "Does 'like attracts like' ring a bell?" She waved a hand through the air to emphasize the point—or maybe to dismiss it.

"Yeah, but with Grayson I need something concrete. I need a woman." From anyone but me that would have sounded illegal. But in my business it was the key to success.

"Well, you have a pretty extensive roster, surely one of them . . ."

"No," I waved my glass, "none of them. I've been over the list a million times."

"But a girl would be crazy not to be interested in Mark Grayson. He's got everything. Looks. Charm. Money out the wazoo. I mean, God, he's the catch of the century."

"Believe me, I've been fending off calls since the bet hit the paper. Finding a woman is not the problem. Finding the *right* woman, that's the key." I took a long swallow of cosmopolitan, considering the matter. "I need someone with an impeccable background. Someone beautiful and talented. Someone secure and accomplished. Good with social niceties, and well connected."

"You're not asking for much."

"It gets worse. Grayson is savvy and smart, and he's got a sense of humor. Which means our girl has got to have a razor-sharp wit as well as a good mind."

"Don't forget about the heart of gold." Cybil lifted her glass, the gesture mocking. "You're looking for a fairy-tale princess."

I started to argue but before I could open my mouth an amazing idea popped into my head. The more I thought about it, the more I knew I was right. Cybil was the fairy-tale princess. And to make it even sweeter, she'd just been dumped by the dragon.

"No," I said, draining the rest of my drink. "What I need is you."

Chapter 11

Continuing on my carb quest, pasta ranks right behind pancakes as comfort food. And my absolute favorite restaurant in this city is a little restaurant on Seventy-seventh. Perfect for a romantic evening, a boisterous group of friends, or just a quiet evening of the some of the best home-made pasta in Manhattan. I mean, their lobster linguini is to die for. *Really*. And fortunately for Cybil and me, they also have a midtown location—that delivers.

So I ordered sustenance while Cybil picked her jaw up off the floor.

"You're out of your freakin' mind." This was actually about

the sixth time she had uttered the phrase, each time with a little more emphasis than the last, but I'd known her a long time, and underneath the denial I could see a spark of interest in her eyes.

"Don't you see? It's perfect." Honestly, when I'd originally said it, it had been on impulse, but in the intervening fifteen minutes or so I'd grown quite attached to the idea. There were all kinds of commonalities. Both were wealthy. Both had graduated at the top of their college classes. Both had broken away from their families to make their own success in the world.

Okay, not exactly in an Oprah way, but still, they'd both made a name for themselves in their respective industries. And, of course, there was the matter of societal ties. Grayson might pretend to be a loner, but at his level he had to have made alliances along the way. And Cybil's lineage assured that there were very few doors her name couldn't open.

And more important, I just had a feeling that they were perfect for each other. In the beginning, before Althea, before HEA, before any career aspirations at all, I'd trusted my gut. That's what it was all about, really. That's why I love what I do. I mean what could be better than helping two people find each other?

Cybil crossed her arms over her chest in the same way she'd been doing since the first grade. I told you stubborn was her middle name. "What about Stephen?"

Now there was a question that begged an answer, but not the first one that sprang to mind. I took a long sip of my cosmo, working to formulate a more politically correct answer.

The doorbell rang, and I delayed the moment, jumping to answer the door instead. After paying the delivery man, I followed Cybil into the dining room and began unpacking the divine-smelling food. "This looks fabulous," I said, opening a container of pesto-covered penne.

"Don't change the subject," Cybil said, dishing some lobster linguini onto a plate. "What about Stephen?"

"I know he was important to you. But he's gone. And there's no time like the present for moving on."

"By marrying someone else?"

"No." I shook my head emphatically, while helping myself to both dishes. "By dating again. And what better way to make a start than with someone like Mark Grayson?"

"Vanessa, you're asking me to let you set me up as a potential mate for the man. I hardly call that rebound dating."

"Well," I said, following her back into the living room, "if you think about it, all dates are basically preludes to possible commitment. Otherwise, why go out in the first place?"

"For fun. For hot sex. To see and be seen?"

"Yeah, maybe, but you have to admit that somewhere in there every time we go out we're all thinking this could be the one."

"You don't think that. You don't even want to get married."

"I don't date. If I did, I swear to God I'd be sucked into the same quagmire."

"How can you possibly talk about dating as the doorway to marriage and quicksand all at the same time?"

She'd walked right into it. I smiled and set my plate on the table. "Because most people don't have someone like me to help them sort through the possibilities."

"And choose the right one," Cybil said, with something less than enthusiasm.

"Exactly," I said, gracing her with a beaming smile. "I can't promise that a first date will lead to anything other than a second."

"Two-date rule."

I nodded. "But by doing my homework and trusting my instincts I can give people a chance at finding the right kind of relationship."

"It just sounds so cold."

"Okay. Look at it this way. What have you got to lose? I mean, if Grayson agrees to this, then you'll have a couple of dates with what you yourself described as the catch of the century. And so, worst case, you have a good time and cocktail party stories for years. It's win-win."

"And you really think the two of us might hit it off?" Despite her resistance to the notion, she was intrigued. And that was half the battle.

"Absolutely. Look, Cybil, I love you like a sister. There's no way I'd set you up with someone I think is wrong for you. If nothing else, blame it on professional pride."

This brought a muffled laugh as she swallowed a mouthful of pasta.

"And you'll be helping me out. Giving me one up on Althea. Because trust me, there's no way she can produce someone as wonderful as you. And if I'm right, and you and Grayson really do hit it off, then that'll be icing on the cake."

"But to win the bet, I'd have to marry him."

"Okay, there's a limit to how much I expect you to help me. And marriage is one them. All I want you to do is go out with the man. Then let pheromones do the rest."

"I thought you didn't believe in that sort of thing."

"I'm not denying sexual attraction exists. I'm just saying that if certain other factors aren't present you should run for the hills. So you'll do it?"

There was a beat of silence and then another, and I almost thought I'd misjudged her interest, but then she sighed and drained her drink. "I'm in."

I opened my mouth to thank her, but she waved me quiet.

"There are certain limitations. If he's not interested, then it's off before it starts. And if I go out with him and don't like him, then no pushing for a return engagement." I started to object, but again she motioned for me to shut up. "I'll do the two-date thing. But only if he's in agreement. In addition, I'm not making any promises about where it goes from there, even if we do like each other. All right?"

I nodded, knowing damn well that if I could get Grayson to accept my help and set him up with Cybil, it would be a success. Cybil was the kind of woman men adored. She'd have been married a long time ago if she hadn't insisted on choosing boyfriends like Stephen. A small niggle of worry blossomed at the thought, but I squelched it before it could go any farther. I was a professional, after all. And I had a good feeling about this.

From what I'd seen, Mark Grayson was a stand-up guy. Even angry, he had a quality about him that commanded respect. And today, in his own way, he'd sort of been charming. All of that with a woman he clearly couldn't stand. Just think about how much better it would be with someone he actually liked.

"So how does this work?" Cybil asked, anxiety cresting in her eyes.

"Easy. I just have to convince Grayson to give me a chance. Then tell him about you, and from there we'll let nature take its course. He'll ask you out. You'll say yes. And before you know it I'll be dancing at your wedding."

"Let's just take it one step at a time. Okay?"

"All right." I grinned, feeling like I had just brokered a deal with the axis powers. Of course, I was only halfway there. But that beat where I had been this morning. I had an opening with Grayson, a fabulous woman to recommend, and, for the first time since the bet, an actual shot at winning. Or at least getting in the game.

I grabbed the pitcher and headed for the kitchen. "I'm making another round," I called over my shoulder. "I feel like a celebration."

Unfortunately, I have a bad habit of always getting the cart before the horse. Or in this case the woman before the man. By noon the next day, I was beginning to think Grayson's interest in meeting with me had been feigned.

I'd called again at precisely nine thirty only to be told in a not so warm and fuzzy way that Grayson wasn't in. To add insult to injury his assistant also informed me that she was more than aware of who I was and that she very sincerely doubted her boss had anything at all to say to me. I tried to explain, but was cut off without even being allowed to finish.

Maybe the woman had designs of her own. Hard to say, but whatever the problem, the phone wasn't ringing. I picked it up and listened to the dial tone, feeling all of about fourteen. It was about the twenty-seventh time I'd tried the maneuver, the result always the same—the empty hollow buzzing of the dial tone.

Waldo sat in the window observing my antics with the dispassion only a cat can achieve. "It would serve you right if I got you fixed." The threat rolled right off his silky black back as he lifted a paw and gave it a languid lick of his tongue.

Maybe cats had the right idea. Maybe we should all operate as if we didn't give a damn about anything. As if there was nothing more exciting in the world then a sponge bath and a nap in the sun.

But just at the moment the idea wasn't flying. Patience has never been my strongpoint. Although I talk a good game.

I thought about calling Cybil, but decided against it. One, it would tie up the phone and, two, she might have changed her mind. Better to just wait for Grayson to call. I think I hate being held hostage by the phone more than anything in the world.

I know it's my own fault. Call it a personality quirk, but I can't put it out of my mind. Not even with cell phones. I'd given the icy assistant my cell number, too, but I didn't have the courage to count on it exclusively. By staying here at home, I was doubling my options. Landline and cell phone. Stupid, I know. But then I've never claimed to be rational.

I walked into the kitchen, dumped my tepid coffee, and poured a fresh cup. I'd been doing the same for the past couple of hours, never actually drinking any of it. But going through the motions made me feel good.

I sighed and stood looking out the window. One of my favorite things about living in Manhattan is watching the world through nineteenth-floor windows. You're close enough that you can still see details, but far enough above that they can't see you. The ultimate voyeur.

I once watched a movie shoot through binoculars. Spent most of the day actually watching as they turned the clock back to the 1950s. Pretty cool. Even saw Nicole Kidman. I know, I shouldn't be so easily impressed. And in truth, it's the everyday people I enjoy watching more. The mom with her kids. The old man and his wife. The delivery men, the taxi drivers . . . you know the drill.

Today the street was fairly quiet. Off in the distance I could see the green of Central Park, and directly across from me the streaming sheets of water as they coursed down a courtyard wall.

Manhattan is full of secret beauty. Places that can only be seen when you're above them. It's like a world of secret gardens. I never get tired of looking at it.

Behind me the shrill ring of the phone broke through my reverie and I jumped, dashing across the apartment with shaking hands. Counting to three and breathing deeply, I picked up the phone and said hello in what I hoped was a calm and sensible voice.

"Vanessa, you sound sick."

Mother.

"I'm fine," I snapped. "I thought you were someone else."

"Mark Grayson," she said with the self-satisfaction only a parent can achieve. "I knew it was a good idea to seat the two of you together. Did you call him?" I'd filled her in on the conversation yesterday after the lunch. And to be honest, in face of her general disapproval of matchmaking, I was still surprised she'd facilitated things.

"I called," I said, not really wanting to go into the humiliating details.

"And?" Mother prompted.

There was a moment of silence and then I caved. You know as well as I do that no matter what age you are, your mother can take you back to sniveling child with just a word. And my mother was a master.

"I got his assistant and left a message. And he hasn't called back."

"He will. You just have to be patient. He's a busy man." Actually she was probably dead on. It's just that when something is important, patience isn't as easy to come by.

"Anyway," I paused, taking a deep breath, "thank you for yesterday."

I know what you're thinking. My mother helped me. And so I should be more grateful. But you have to understand a couple of things. First, my mother and I have perfected our relationship over the decades—it may not be perfect, but it's ours. And second, my mother never does anything out of the goodness of her heart, there's always a secondary motive. Always.

I just hadn't figured this one out yet.

"I'm just glad I could help." Modesty didn't suit my mother.

And I wished I knew what she was up to. Maybe she was setting me up to fail. Although that seemed a bit extreme even for her.

"I really should get off the phone."

"That wouldn't be a problem if you had call-waiting." It was an old argument. I hate call-waiting. It just facilitates rudeness. And as such, I bullied my phone company until they agreed to drop the feature from my phone.

The fact that it annoys my mother was an added bonus.

"Well, I don't have it. So I really should hang up. All right? I promise I'll call you the minute I hear from him." Fat chance.

"I've got a better idea," my mother said. Of course she did. She was the queen of "I'll top that." "I'm having lunch with your father. He's taking me to Mark's." Mark's is a lovely restaurant in the Mark Hotel on Seventy-seventh near Madison. An elegant staple for the over-sixty set. "Why don't you meet us?"

An invitation from my mother was one of life's impossible situations. She simply wouldn't take no for an answer. But the idea of spending a couple of hours with her and my father grilling me about the bet and Mark Grayson wasn't my idea of fun. I looked around the apartment, searching for an excuse. Nothing presented itself.

"I'd love to . . . ," I began.

"Oh good," Mother said, efficiently cutting in before I got to the "but." "We're meeting at two."

I closed my eyes, counted to three, and then miracle of miracles, the doorbell rang. "Mother, there's someone at the door," I said, my voice sounding a lot like I'd run a marathon and won. "I've got to go. Sorry. And I'm afraid I'll have to take a rain check on lunch." I hung up before she could even say good-bye. It seems rude, I know, but desperate times and all that.

The doorbell buzzed again, and I wondered who it could be.

The concierge announced visitors, so it had to be someone in the building. Anderson usually knocked, and Richard would have left for work ages ago.

I pulled the little knob that opened the peephole, and felt a lot like I'd exchanged one problem for another. This was not turning into a great day.

Mrs. M.

And from the looks of her tapping foot, she wasn't happy.

I shot a look at Waldo stretched out on the windowsill. He opened one eye and then closed it again. No help from that corner. "You should have been a dog," I whispered, and then dared another peek.

She was still there, this time moving closer, her eye on the peephole. I dropped the little shutter in place and stood frozen, praying she hadn't noticed the movement. There was something unsettling about the thought of Edna Melderson trying to look in through the peephole, even though I knew she couldn't see anything.

"Vanessa?" She really did sound like the Wicked Witch, I swear. I held my breath, motioning Waldo to silence. No way was she carting my cat away in a bicycle basket. My heart was pounding and I pondered the fact that I'd let an old lady cow me into hiding in my own apartment.

"Vanessa?" This time she knocked. I stared at the door like it was going to open itself. One minute passed, and then another, and then just when I thought I'd managed escape, a white envelope slid under the door.

I started to reach for it, and then realized part of it was still on the other side. Mrs. M. was good. I hate to admit it but I actually stood there waiting, counting one Mississippi, two Mississippi, three Mississippi—well you get the idea. I was up to eighty-five Mississippi when I figured I was safe. But to be sure I checked the peephole first.

Unless she was ducked down on the floor, the coast was clear. And while I didn't put it past Mrs. M. to think of that, I didn't actually think she could manage the maneuver. She wasn't exactly a spring chicken, you know.

Besides, I still had the advantage of a closed, locked door.

I bent down and slowly pulled the envelope out from under the door, imagining Chanel red talons following behind. What can I say—too many horror movies as a teenager.

Anyway, needless to say, nothing happened.

The envelope looked harmless enough. I slit it open and pulled the piece of paper out with trepidation. Swallowing, as if it was a summons from the devil himself, I opened it and immediately exhaled.

Not a summons to appear before the board.

There was a God.

Unfortunately that's as far as the good news went. It was a bill—for Arabella. Five hundred dollars for a kitty prenatal visit. What a world.

Still, considering the alternative, it was a small price to pay. I walked over to Waldo and, much to his dismay, pulled him into my arms. Waldo might be a lothario, but he preferred initiating contact, thank you very much. But he was my cat, and I had single-handedly—all right, Richard helped a little—saved his gonads. The least he could do was offer a cuddle and a purr.

Of course, all you really had to do was stroke his belly and all bets were off. He was a cat, after all. He curled against me, warm and furry, and just for a moment I forgot all my worries. Okay, so I was glad Waldo wasn't a dog.

We stood for a moment, me bonding with my cat, Waldo

suffering my ridiculous human sentimentality. And then the phone rang. I dumped Waldo faster than a guy on a blind date dumps an ugly woman.

He yowled and I ran.

"Hello?" I sounded like I'd surfaced from a silk-sheet love fest.

"Vanessa? Is that you?"

Not Mark—Maris Vanderbeek.

I cleared my throat and sucked in a calming breath. "It's me. Sorry. I was in the back room." Considering my apartment is only about nine hundred square feet and that each of the four rooms in it has a phone, the excuse was lame, but Maris had never seen the apartment and I wasn't about to explain that I'd been communing with my cat. "What's up?"

No matter how much I wanted Mark Grayson to call, I couldn't in all good conscience hang up on Maris. After all, Grayson was only a prospective client. Maris was marrying Douglas Larson—a bona fide paying client.

"I need your help," she said, and for the first time I noticed the tremor in her voice. "Douglas called off the wedding."

I swear to God, my life flashed before my eyes.

Chapter 12

Gramercy Park. *Irving Place (between Twentieth and Twenty-first streets).*

One hundred and sixty years ago, Samuel Ruggles developed a tranquil residential area surrounding a private park in New York. . . . Today, almost two centuries later, New York's Gramercy Park remains as private, secure, and serene as it was in the days of Samuel Ruggles. Enjoyment of the park is still limited to those with keys to the park's gate: the homeowners and tenants of Gramercy Park.

—www.coopcommunities.com

An apartment with a key to Gramercy Park is as close to a sure investment as it gets. And Maris Vanderbeek had one.

Maris is a card-carrying member of New York's blue blood society. Not that they have meetings or anything, but their pedigree allows them access to certain privileges above and beyond common celebrity and bourgeois billionaires.

According to the DAR, the original Vanderbeek had come to New York with Henry Hudson. And, according to legend, had been present when Hudson famously bought Manhattan. Hey, you got to love a guy with an eye for a bargain. Anyway, apparently unlike a lot of those early adventurous types, Vanderbeek had held on to his share, which in today's market is worth something in the neighborhood of $17 billion.

And Maris, as an only child, had inherited the lot.

You'd think all that money would make finding a husband a snap, but there were a few flies in the Baccarat-encased ointment. Primarily the fact that Horace Vanderbeek suffered a stroke sometime during his fifties, and with the death of his wife (some say he drove her to it), his daughter was left with the onerous job of caring for her father.

By all accounts—not Maris's, bless her—Horace was a difficult man, and despite having enough ailments to fill a season in one of Stanley's television shows, he held on to life with the tenacity of a broke fashionista at a Prada sale. Finally, at ninety-two, he had succumbed to pneumonia, which doesn't give a whit how much you're worth, and Maris, at fifty-three, was left on her own for the first time in her adult life.

I met her at an after-party for the Broadway opening of *Dirty Rotten Scoundrels*. (The show was amazingly funny—but what would you expect with John Lithgow and Norbert Leo Butz?) She was standing all alone in the corner nursing a lemon-drop martini, the dichotomy of drink and social skills intriguing, to say the least.

Everyone at the party was someone, but Maris's clothes screamed old money while her eyes flashed lost and lonely, an irresistible combination for a woman in my particular line of work. And in just a few minutes I, too, was sipping a sweet and sour libation and chatting up what indeed turned out to be a valuable addition to my list.

Maris had managed to snare Douglas Larson.

Yes. *The* Douglas Larson. Reclusive author of *Essence of Henry*. Douglas was something of an urban legend in Manhat-

tan. An English lit professor at NYU, his family can be traced
back to the *Mayflower*. And unfortunately, like the Vander-
beeks', inbreeding hadn't really done them all that much good.
As a result, Douglas was extremely shy and very awkward
around women, the latter due, at least in part, to the fact that
his first and only love had left him standing at the altar.

His scars were deep, and his novels echoed a haunting sad-
ness that had to be experienced before it could be expressed.
While not a commercial hit in the way of John Grisham or
Stephen King, there was a lyrical resonance to his prose that
had resulted in a devoted following.

We'd known each other socially for years, but never really
talked. He was the kind who hid in the corner, while I was more
the tabletop-dancing type. But one night we'd actually struck up
a conversation, and from there a sort of friendship had developed. Despite that fact, however, I'd been shocked when he'd
called me to request a match.

I mean, some people are better off single, you know? Still, I
have never turned down a challenge, and when Maris presented
herself front and center, I knew the game was on. Not only on,
but amazingly successful.

Maris and Douglas were engaged to be married.

Or they had been.

Which brings us right back to Gramercy Park and Maris's
frantic call. We settled on a green metal bench, the traffic noise
washed away by the singing birds and the wind in the trees. A
Disney moment if ever there was one. "So tell me what happened," I urged. Maris hadn't said much of anything since I'd
met her at the park's gate.

"Everything was going fine. We talked to the caterer last
week, and then this week we finalized the registry. We went to
dinner at Bette." Only someone with Maris's kind of connec-

tions could throw that out without name-dropping. It was nearly impossible to get into Bette. Unless you were independently wealthy and engaged to one of Manhattan's literati. Is that a word? Anyway, you get the point.

"All sounds good to me," I said, waiting for the other shoe to drop. To date, the Larson-Vanderbeek merger was my greatest accomplishment. If it fell apart now, the repercussions would be monumental.

"Exactly, it was. I mean, everything was better than good; it was great. And then this morning I get a phone call from Douglas. And he tells me that he can't do it."

"Do what?" I asked, even though I knew the answer. It was like watching a train wreck; you don't want to, but you can't help yourself.

"Get married." She said, her blue eyes welling with tears.

Most people would consider Maris attractive, although her figure is a bit too full for conventional beauty. And the lines around her eyes and forehead are clear indications that she's probably never even considered Botox. Salt was winning over pepper in her hair, and left to its own, her natural curl frizzed in a way that made one think immediately of electric sockets.

Fortunately, Natasha Magleeva at Limpopo was wonderful with frizz. Which meant that thanks to me, Maris's hair was revitalized in a way that only a good blowout can accomplish.

"Did he say why?" I sucked in oxygen, trying to keep my pounding heart in line. It would never do for the matchmaker to show fear.

"No. He just said it was no use talking about it, he wasn't going to change his mind." She reached over for my hand, squeezing it until I thought my bones might break. "You'll do something, won't you? I . . . I love him."

Love. That nasty four-letter word. It has more power than all curse words combined. If only I could wave the magic wand and take Maris back to the pre-Douglas state. But I couldn't, and even though I usually side with the client—they're paying the bills after all—it was in my best interest to knock Douglas into shape. For his own good.

"I'll talk to him." I nodded sagely as if I knew exactly what needed to be done, all the while searching like a crazy woman for the key to Douglas's defection.

"He's not answering any of his phones. And the university won't tell me anything."

"Don't worry," I said, trying for reassurance. Maybe I'd been wrong about the two of them. But I was never wrong. It had to be something else. "I'll find him. Are you sure he didn't say anything else? Something to give you an idea where all this is coming from?"

"No." She shook her head. "I tried to reason with him. But—"

My cell phone's ring sounded discordant in the quiet of the park. "Vanessa Carlson," I barked into the receiver, my mind still on Douglas.

"Vanessa. Sorry it's taken so long to get back to you."

Some part of my brain recognized that it was Grayson on the other end of the line, but the rest was simply too panicked about Maris's problem to react appropriately.

"I'm sorry. I can't talk right now. I'm in the middle of an emergency."

"And here I was hoping you'd have time for a late lunch."

"I'm sorry, I can't," I said, waving good-bye to all hope of winning the bet. But I didn't have any choice, Maris and Douglas had to come first.

"Anything I can help with?"

Talk about coming out of left field. I mean I didn't really even know the guy. And, to be honest, our previous interactions hadn't been all that positive. "Thanks. But no. I can handle it."

"All right. So how about dinner then?"

My brain screamed yes, but my heart held sway. "I don't know how long this is going to take."

"If I didn't know better, I'd say you were trying to blow me off."

Well, there was a full reversal of situations. "I'm not. I'm just knee-deep in alligators here."

His laugh was surprisingly rich. "Why don't you call me when you're finished. I eat late."

Hope blossomed. "You're on. Should I call the office?"

"No, my cell." He gave me the number and I fumbled around in my purse for a pen. Maris, thankfully, produced a piece of paper. I scribbled down the number and rang off.

"Am I keeping you from something important?" Maris asked.

"No, of course not. That was just a potential client."

"Not Mark Grayson?" she asked.

"No. Of course not." I lied. No need airing my laundry. Besides, Maris would only be more upset. "The whole Grayson thing is on hold. He's not all that interested in matchmaking."

Maris nodded. "I can understand that. I mean, it is sort of difficult to admit to someone that you aren't capable of attracting a mate on your own."

"Oh, Maris, is that what you think?"

She nodded, a hint of embarrassment in her eyes.

"Don't be silly. I'm very selective about whom I ask to be on my list. If I didn't think you had what it takes, I wouldn't have asked you."

"Really?"

"Absolutely," I assured her. Of course, it had taken three hairstylists, a trip to Barneys, and a personal trainer to bring the diamond out of the rough. But the basic elements had been there all along. They just needed a little love and care. "You can attract any man you want. In fact, you did. Douglas didn't ask you to marry him because of me. I might have set the stage, Maris, but you're the one he proposed to."

"Yes, but now he's unproposed."

"I don't believe that at all. He's just got cold feet. You were about to tell me something before the phone call interrupted us. What were you going to say?"

"Just that he wouldn't listen to anything I said. I tried to get him to tell me what was wrong. To understand why he'd changed his mind, but he didn't really say anything coherent. He just kept mumbling something about it being too good to last. It didn't make any sense. And I told him so, but he just said something about playing the fool. Honest to God, Vanessa, I haven't got the slightest idea what he was talking about."

But I did.

"This is about Alyssa." Alyssa Mangrove was the woman who'd left him all those years ago. It had been a public spectacle. A stronger man would have buckled. And Douglas, well, he'd been destroyed.

"But that was years ago. And I'm not her." Maris was a lovely woman, and I still say perfect for Douglas, but insight wasn't her strong point.

"I know that. But Douglas doesn't. Let me talk to him. I have an idea where he might be."

"Thank you." Maris gave me a watery smile. "I just didn't know who else to turn to."

"No worries. That's what I'm here for." I'd been this route before, although never with someone as fragile as Douglas. Still, I was pretty sure I could get him to see reason. And then with a little luck I'd take on Mark Grayson.

At least my job wasn't boring.

A couple of hours later I was downtown looking for Douglas. He was fairly predictable, and I figured the White Horse Tavern was my best bet. The tavern is often billed as the second oldest bar in Manhattan, but its main claim to fame is the fact that Dylan Thomas actually drank himself to death there. Apparently, in November 1953, Thomas beat his own personal record by downing eighteen shots of whiskey. According to the story, soon after the last drink he stumbled outside and collapsed on the sidewalk. He was taken to the Chelsea Hotel and there fell into a coma; the next morning he was transferred to St. Vincent's Hospital, where he died.

There's a lesson in there somewhere.

Anyway, thanks to the notoriety, the bar was a gathering place for writers for the next twenty years or so. A tribute to one of their own, I suppose. And even now there is something about the place. It's segmented into smaller rooms with heavy black beams overhead. A very British feel to it.

Actually, I love British pubs. And for that matter British pints. I was never a big beer drinker until I tasted my first bitter. But I digress.

I walked into the shadowy bar and wove my way through tables and framed portraits of Dylan Thomas, looking for Douglas. He was a smallish man, with a thatch of inky hair that insisted on hanging in his eyes no matter how often he pushed it away.

He also had that professorial air. You know, that distracted, where-the-hell-am-I-and-was-I-saying-something-important look? A very bright, if slightly unfocused, mind. It was only with pencil and paper (or, more realistically, with computer keyboard) that he found his true voice, and in it, I for one, got a glimpse of the man behind the curtain.

Just as I expected, he was sitting in a back room against the far wall, staring broodingly into space. Sort of Heathcliffe meets Ichabod Crane, neither of them better off for the union.

There was a half-empty beer glass and an open laptop on the table. I suspected the glass was getting more use than the computer. But it was just a guess.

"So how long have you been here?"

He stared up at me for a moment, then shrugged. "Since about eleven."

Considering that it was close to five now, that meant six solid hours of drinking. Even sipping slowly, I was guessing he had quite a buzz going. Not that you could tell by looking at him. I took a seat across the table. "Maris is worried about you."

"She is?" He tilted his head with a frown. "I find that hard to believe, considering I dumped her."

"You want to tell me why you did that?"

He stared down into his beer for a moment, then looked up at me with sad brown eyes. "Because I didn't want her to dump me."

"Come again?" I was sure there was logic in there somewhere, but for the life of me I wasn't sure what it was.

"You need a beer." This non sequitur was followed by the appearance of a waitress.

Considering I hadn't had anything to eat since breakfast, a beer was probably the last thing I needed, but if I was going to get to the bottom of this I needed to get with the program, so to speak. "I'll have a Boddingtons." I smiled at the woman and then turned my attention back to Douglas. "So what in hell would make you think that Maris was going to dump you?"

"Because that's what women do."

I resisted the urge to pound my head against the wall.

"That's what Alyssa did. But she's not all women. We've covered this ground before, Douglas."

"I know," he said, doing a fabulous imitation of Eeyore. Wonderful, I was dealing with a misanthropic donkey. Stubborn and irrational all at the same time. A killer combination. Just what I needed. "But who's to say that Maris won't do the same? And the truth is, I don't think I can handle it happening again."

"I can understand your fear, but believe me, it's totally unfounded. Maris loves you."

"*Now*. But who's to say that won't change?" The waitress arrived with my beer and set it on the table, along with a refill for Douglas.

"You really think you need more?" I asked, sounding more like my mother than I was comfortable admitting.

"Absolutely," he said, reaching for his glass, and just missing. I pulled mine to safety and watched as he swallowed half the contents in one go, wiping his mouth with the back of his hand. It was almost as if he'd morphed into a complete stranger. The haunted look in his eyes was all Douglas, though. Drunk or sober, he needed my help.

"Douglas, there aren't any guarantees when it comes to relationships."

"Precisely why I don't need one," he mumbled into his glass.

"You don't mean that." I took a sip for fortification and plunged right to the heart of the matter. "Letting Maris go would be the biggest mistake of your life. She's perfect for you."

"So was Alyssa." He glared at me. "And look how that ended."

"Douglas, you begged me to find a match for you. You said you were ready for commitment."

"I was wrong." He looked so pathetic I almost felt sorry for him. But the engagement had already been announced—in all the best papers. Presents had been bought, invitations responded to. And in all honesty, if it fell apart now, so did my reputation.

Besides, Douglas and Maris belonged together. So there was simply no way I was going to let cold feet get in the way. "So now you want to spend the rest of your life alone?"

"When you put it like that, not so much," he said with a frown, tilting his head from side to side, trying to focus. "But when I think about it rationally, then I suppose the answer is yes. I'm just not ready to take the risk."

Considering the amount of Pilsner Urquell he'd consumed, I wasn't at all sure he was capable of being rational, but I wasn't about to mention the fact. Better to keep trying to get through to the part of him that wasn't drowning in alcohol.

"But you've already done the hard part, Douglas. You've found the girl."

"Actually, *you* found her," he said, still channeling Eeyore. This was going nowhere fast.

"Look, Douglas, I can't make you get married. But I can tell you that you're making a huge mistake if you let Maris go. The two of you are a good fit. Your strengths play off of hers."

"They do." He shook his head, clearly not completely with the program. "But that's not enough."

"Of course it is," I snapped, trying to hang on to my patience. There's nothing more annoying than trying to reason with an inebriated friend when you're sober. And in all truth, Douglas barely qualified as a friend.

"Douglas, what you need right now is to go home and sleep it off."

"I'm fine," he said, waving his beer in the air to underscore the fact. Unfortunately, beer sloshed over the sides, showering the table. I pulled the laptop to safety and watched as he used a cocktail napkin to try to blot up the mess.

It was sort of like using a spoon to drain the bathtub. Not particularly successful. I signaled the waitress for a rag and the check.

"I'm not ready to go," Douglas protested.

"I think you are," I said, already plotting how I was going to get him outside and into a taxi. He didn't weigh all that much, but he still had the advantage over me. "Come on, let's go."

"But I still have beer." He waved at his glass.

"Finish it, then." Two more sips wasn't going to make much of a difference. I glanced at the bill and pulled a wad of twenties from my purse.

"You shouldn't pay. They were my beers," Douglas insisted, trying valiantly to find his wallet, but not quite managing to access the pocket.

"No problem," I said. "It's my treat."

He drained his glass, and then pushed back from the table. For a moment he was actually on his feet, then almost as quickly, his arms windmilled frantically, and he fell backward against the wall.

The bar was still fairly empty, but a burly guy at an adjacent table stood up to help. I shook my head and shot him a smile, moving at the same time to wrap an arm around a jelly-legged Douglas. "We're fine."

I didn't want to make any more of a spectacle than necessary. The White Horse was not part of the celebrity circuit, but you never know when some yahoo with a camera is going to see his chance at making *Page Six.*

"Okay, Douglas, we can do this." He shot me a confused look, and I tightened my grip. Douglas wasn't much of a drinker, and based on the tab, I figured he'd had something like eight beers. "Just put one foot in front of the other."

It was slow going, but we were definitely making progress.

"I'm sorry, Vanessa," Douglas said. "Didn't mean to do this."

"No one ever does," I commiserated. He was a bit morose, but beyond that he was a fairly decent guy—when he was sober. "You'll feel better tomorrow."

"I blew it, though." He shot me a baleful look with Eeyore eyes. "With Maris."

"Yes, you did." I nodded, pulling to the left to counterbalance his listing to the right. "But it's not too late to fix things."

"Maybe I should call her." He stopped so suddenly, I almost fell over. "Got my phone here, somewhere." He patted his pockets and then frowned. "Where's my computer?"

"I've got it right here."

"Good." He started forward again, stumbling over the leg of a chair. "Phone's in the pocket."

I grabbed his elbow, just managing to keep him upright. "You don't need to call anyone right now."

"But I should talk to Maris. Try to make things right."

It was exactly what I wanted him to do, but not in this state. "It'll keep until the morning. Right now we need to get you outside and into a taxi. Think you can help me do that?"

He nodded and shot me a crooked smile. "Sorry to be such trouble."

"You're not any trouble," I reassured him. Actually trouble was an understatement, but there was no sense in making the situation worse. "Come on. Just a few more steps."

We walked out into the street, and I propped Douglas against a lamppost while I tried to hail a taxi. It was the tail end of rush hour, and the cabs that passed by were either occupied or off duty.

"We could walk," Douglas said, pushing off the lamppost. He staggered a couple of steps, then frowned. "I think I'm gonna be sick." He swayed to the right and then alarmingly to the left. I closed the distance between us, barely managing to keep him on his feet.

"Just hang in a few more minutes. You can do it."

He nodded, but closed his eyes. I shook him. "Douglas, stay with me." Out of the corner of my eye, I saw a taxi and lifted my free arm to flag him down. The driver pulled over and I walked Douglas to the curb. Leaning against the taxi, I managed to hold on to Douglas while opening the door.

"Thank you . . ." His mouth kept moving, but nothing else came out. And then he closed the distance between us faster than I'd have thought possible. His lips hard against mine. "You're the best."

If someone had told me that Douglas Larson's kiss would make me see stars, I'd have laughed out loud. But that's exactly what happened.

One minute he was kissing me, and the next the world was filled with light—the cold, harsh flash of a camera.

Shit.

Chapter 13

Marie's Crisis. *59 Grove Street (between Bleecker and Seventh Avenue), 212.243.9323.*

Formerly Marie's, this dark, dive-y piano bar is decorated with Christmas lights strung across a low ceiling and with red, cracked leather barstools. It takes its unusual name from the original owner, Marie Dumont, who, after being diagnosed with cancer in the 1960s, felt it appropriate to memorialize the bad news forever.

—www.nydailynews.com

The name says it all. I had a potential crisis on my hands, and I needed help. Fast. Richard was the best person to help me. And thanks to proximity, and Richard's penchant for show tunes, Marie's was the choice du jour.

There are some who claim the bar, originally the home of Thomas Paine, was named for his revolutionary rabble-rousing pamphlet of the same name. I prefer the other version. But either way, the joint has a wonderful, shady past. These days, however, the only rabble-rousing comes from patrons fighting over which Broadway standard to sing next.

It was still early by Manhattan time, and the bar was relatively empty—one table filled with noisy tourists, and an additional two or three occupied by the over-forty set settling in for a cheerful night channeling Julie Andrews.

"I'm doomed," I said, staring down into my bourbon. Hey, desperate times call for desperate measures. Or at least generous ones.

"Well, you're not in a good position, I'll grant you that," Richard said, "but it might not be as bad as you think. Maybe it was just a tourist. Or maybe no one will buy the shot."

I glared at him over the rim of my glass. "It was definitely paparazzi. And while I may not be A-list, I'm turning into B with a bullet, thanks to the damn bet."

"I was just trying to be supportive," Richard said, with a shrug.

"Thanks. But right now I need unvarnished truth."

"All right. You're screwed." He shrugged and took a sip of his Irish whiskey. Bushmills Black Bush. With Richard, even drinking was about the best of the best.

"Okay, maybe I meant slightly varnished truth?" I sighed, drained my drink, and tipped my head at the bartender for another. "So what am I going to do?"

"Damage control. Have you told Maris?"

"I've called her cell and her home number, but she's not answering."

"But you left a message?"

"Can't. She doesn't believe in voice mail." When she'd agreed to work with me, I'd asked her to get a machine, but she'd flatly refused. Little did I know that I'd be the one who desperately needed the damn thing. "I even went by there. But no luck. She's obviously out for the night."

"Maybe she went over to Douglas's?"

"I thought of that. But no go. He's at home sleeping it off. I checked."

"Well, you'll track her down before morning."

"And when I do?"

"You tell her the truth. That Douglas was drunk and appreciative. She'll understand."

"Maybe if it stayed a private matter. But if that picture hits the papers, she's going to land in the middle of a personal PR nightmare."

Okay, I know what you're thinking. But honest to God, this is Manhattan and we move in a very small social circle at the end of the day. This is the kind of thing that provides years of cocktail party fodder. No one appreciates that kind of attention, but people like Maris avoid it like the plague. Black mark on the family name and all that. I couldn't have planned something more damaging.

And Douglas—well, suffice it to say, the university wasn't going to be keen on him having his picture in the tabloids. Not to mention the man himself. I mean, he didn't even have his photograph on the jacket of his books. To call him private is an understatement.

Of course, on the other side of the coin, if he valued his privacy so bloody much he shouldn't have gotten drunk and kissed me in the first place. Never mind the fact that it was on a public street. This wasn't my fault. It wasn't. I couldn't possibly have seen it coming.

But that didn't change the fact that it had happened, and now, thanks to photo jerk, there was a very real possibility that the business I'd worked so hard to build was going to be killed quite literally with a kiss.

"Oh God," I said, sinking my head into my hands. "I'm dead."

"No, you're not," Richard said, loyal to a fault. Bless him.

"What about a lawsuit?" I asked, reaching for something—anything—that might save my ass. "Anything to be gained there? I mean, it wasn't my fault. The man was drunk. If the tabloids claim differently, don't I have a case?"

"Possibly," Richard shrugged. "But it takes time and money to win. And after the dust settles, all you'll warrant is a single paragraph buried in the sports section. By then the damage has already been done. Better to figure out how to spin it."

"I was caught on film kissing a client's fiancé. There is no way to spin it."

"Everything can be spun. The truth is that he was thanking you for helping him out with his concern over getting married."

"Sounds good, but the real truth is that he was so drunk he didn't know what he was doing."

"Vanessa, when a man kisses a woman, he knows what he's doing, I don't care what state he's in."

"How would you know that?"

"Because I'm a man."

"A gay man."

"All right I should have said that when a man kisses anyone, it's because he wants to. It's part of the genes, hetero or homo. Got it?"

"So now you're telling me that Douglas has a thing for me?" The idea was horrifying. He was a client. And he was engaged to marry someone else. Someone I quite liked.

"In some way, yes." He held up a hand to stop my protests. "But it doesn't mean he's ready to chuck Maris. Only that he, in some way, is attracted to you."

"You're supposed to be making it better."

"Look. He was drinking."

"Heavily."

"So everything was exaggerated. I'm sure he truly meant to thank you. It's just that he chose an inopportune moment to show it."

"He's got the hots for our girl, if you ask me." Anderson slid onto the barstool next to Richard, his eyes dancing. "I wouldn't have thought Douglas capable of it." I'd left an SOS on Anderson's machine at work. Obviously he'd gotten it. "So when's the wedding?"

"That's not funny. Unless you're talking about *Maris* and Douglas. In which case, thanks to the sleazeball with a Nikon, maybe never."

"Surely she's been around enough to realize that almost nothing in the tabloids is based on reality." Anderson waved down the bartender and ordered a cabernet.

"She hasn't been anywhere, Anderson. That's the problem. And even if it isn't real, a picture is worth a thousand words, true or not."

"So what's the worst that can happen?" Richard asked.

"Maris will dump Douglas before he has the chance to un-dump her. She'll hate me, and my career as a matchmaker will be over before it even has a chance to begin."

"Or people will be lining up to sign on with the notorious Vanessa Carlson," Anderson laughed.

"By people, I'm assuming you mean crazies. This isn't funny."

"I know, sweetie, but this too shall pass. The press has the attention span of a two-year-old."

"You're right, but it's the five-second span that has me worried."

"Maybe you should be more worried about Douglas." Anderson was grinning again.

"Stop it."

"Sorry." He actually managed to look contrite.

"Look. This is serious. There's got to be something we can do. You said I should spin it." I looked over at Richard. "How?"

"Well, you could fight fire with fire. Call *Page Six* and just tell them your side of it."

"But then if they haven't got the picture, I've added fuel to a fire that wasn't lit."

"Can you do that?" Anderson asked. I frowned. Usually I found his wit amusing, but at the moment, nothing was funny.

"You know that I mean," I snapped, and was immediately sorry. Anderson hadn't done anything except ride to my rescue. Again. "Sorry. I'm just worried."

"I know. And I understand why. But trust me, even if it's bad, it won't be as awful as you're imagining."

"I just feel so helpless. And I hate that. I need to do something. Take action." Okay, I was all girded up with no place to go. "So what do I do?"

"Well, I think the most important thing is to make sure Maris isn't blindsided. So talking to her tonight is important. Second, if you can pull it off, you need to be sure that the two of them get back together. If the press figures out there's trouble in paradise, it will only add to the innuendo. And third, I meant what I said. You need to talk to *Page Six* and tell your side of the story. But hopefully if you've handled the happy couple, then you can spin it, so that it's all about a grateful client."

"Maybe I could just get Cybil to run something?"

"Where is she anyway?" Anderson asked. "I'd have thought you'd want her in on the powwow."

"She's at a board meeting. The New York Women's Foundation. I'll fill her in later."

"She'll love this," Richard said. "But you can't use her.

You're too close. People know that. And they'll suspect her of slanting things your way. Not good for either of you."

"You're right." I sighed, wishing I could just turn the clock back before Maris's call. "I don't suppose there's any way you all could pull strings and make this go away?"

"I haven't any left to pull," Richard said, with a shake of his head. I shot a hopeful look at Anderson, even though I was pretty sure he'd already used all his allotment of fairy god-mother dust.

"Sorry. I'm afraid I called in all my markers when I helped you with Grayson." Anderson managed somehow to look apologetic and amused all at the same time.

"Grayson." My heart fluttered to my feet. "Oh, my God, I forgot all about him." I glanced at my watch. It was ten to nine. He had said a late dinner. But I couldn't imagine meeting with him now. I had more pressing fires to put out.

"What's to forget?" Anderson asked. "The last I heard you'd hit a dead end. Are you holding out on us?"

"No. Well, sort of. I'm sorry. I've been a bit preoccupied with the Maris-Douglas situation."

"So spill it. Have you talked to him?" Richard asked, sizing me up like a star witness about to be deposed.

I nodded numbly, my stomach dropping down to join my heart. "He called to ask me to lunch, but I said no."

"You turned him down?" Anderson asked. "Have you lost your mind?"

"I had clients in crisis. Paying clients, I might add."

"Well, I admire your work ethic, but maybe if you'd said yes, you wouldn't be in this situation."

"Thanks. That really makes things better." Sometimes Anderson was just too damn honest. Of course, he was also probably right. But it was like telling a hit-and-run victim that if they'd turned left instead of right they probably wouldn't be in the hospital right now.

"I'm just saying—"

I waved him quiet. "He did say something about a late dinner."

"So what are you doing here?" Richard scowled. "This is your chance."

"Right. And then in the morning the photo runs and he, along with the rest of my client list, will never talk to me again."

"Well, if you wait for tomorrow and the picture runs, then it's a sure thing. But right now you still have a shot at working your magic, and then maybe the photograph won't mean that much."

"I was kissing a client." I felt like I was talking in Swahili.

"Yes, but there were extenuating circumstances. And Grayson, of all people, will understand."

"So you think I should tell him?" My heart exited altogether, leaving my stomach alone and threatening revolt.

"Preemptive strike. At least if he's interested. And I can't imagine he'd ask to meet with you if he wasn't. Doesn't make sense."

"But what about Douglas and Maris?" I really did care about them. Besides, meeting with Mark Grayson under any circumstances was nerve-wracking, but in my present state, the idea was positively frightening.

"You've already said that Maris is out," Richard reminded me. "And Douglas is sleeping it off. So there's nothing you can do right now anyway."

"I can head for St. Patrick's and pray."

"Never a bad choice." Anderson smiled, his eyes full of sympathy. "But in this case, I think Richard is right. You need to follow through with Grayson. As to telling him about the photo, I'd wait to see how it goes. If he is ready to take the plunge, then you probably owe it to him to prepare him, otherwise, it's up to you."

"I should probably warn my other clients, too."

"It wouldn't be a bad idea," Richard said, "but really, I think you're overestimating the influence one picture will have."

"You haven't seen the picture."

"Neither have you," Richard said.

Anderson reached over to pat my shoulder. "It'll be okay. Anticipation is the worst, really. Tomorrow, when you know how bad it is, you can start putting out fires. Tonight, I think you should call Grayson. He's not the type to ask more than once."

"Well, technically he's already asked twice." Anderson and Richard glared simultaneously. "I said technically. And you're right, he won't call again." I sighed and pulled out my cell phone, feeling a hell of a lot like a lamb being led to slaughter.

Just to postpone the moment, I called Maris again, but got no answer. Maybe she was with Douglas. One could only hope. Richard was right—if they made up tonight it would certainly make tomorrow's news go down easier. But I'd done everything I could to ward off disaster. And in all honestly it wasn't my fault. I had been trying to help. Surely Maris would understand that. It's not like Douglas wouldn't back me up.

At least I hoped so. Thanks to Richard and Anderson, I couldn't get rid of the ugly notion that somehow Douglas harbored feelings for me. The idea was ludicrous. I'd never given him the slightest encouragement, and in truth I couldn't believe he'd find me attractive. We had nothing in common except the company we kept. And the fact that I liked his novels.

Besides, he loved Maris. He'd asked her to marry him.

And unasked her, the little demon in my head reminded me.

"It's usually better if you dial first," Richard said.

"I'm just trying to think of what to say." I was stalling, trying to find my courage.

"You tell him you're free for dinner," Anderson said. "Honestly, Vanessa, if I didn't know better I'd think you had a thing for Mark Grayson."

"I don't even know him." The idea was as ludicrous as the possibility of Douglas Larson having the hots for me. "And even if I did, he isn't my type."

"Anderson was just kidding." Richard raised a hand, ever the peacemaker. "Weren't you?" He shot Anderson a censorious look.

"Of course I was," Anderson nodded, emphatically. Too much so. I didn't buy it for an instant.

"I'm not in love with anyone. And no one is in love with me." I said it a bit too loud, and it seemed as if everyone in the bar paused to give me a pitying look. "And as far as I'm concerned that's a good thing," I whispered, frowning at the room in general.

"We just want you to be happy," Anderson said.

"I am happy." How in the hell had the conversation turned to me and my love life, or lack thereof? "Although come tomorrow, I may feel differently when that photograph comes out. I called you two here to help me, not to try and fix me up with my own clients."

"Grayson isn't a client."

"Well, he will be." Just saying the words sent my stomach back to its normal position. I could do this. And I could handle the press, too. Maris was right for Douglas, and Douglas was right for Maris. And nothing, not even a drunken kiss, could change that. All I had to do was batten down the hatches and ride out the storm.

"Besides," I said, squaring my shoulders and tossing my head in what I hoped was a fearlessly-facing-the-world kind of way, "I already have someone in mind for him."

"Who?" they said almost in unison.

"Cybil."

That got their attention.

"I guess I can see that," Anderson said, his expression thoughtful. "There are a lot of commonalities."

"Does she know?" Richard asked.

"Yes. I broached the idea last night and she said that if Grayson is interested, she's game."

"What about Stephen?"

"He's out of the picture. Even Cybil agrees with that. So she's a free agent, and I've just got this feeling Cybil and Grayson would be perfect together."

"Not to mention the good it would do you," Richard said.

"Well, of course, that's been the point all along. But I would never ask Cybil to do something like that if I didn't truly believe it was in her best interest. You know as well as I do that Stephen was never right for her."

"But that decision is hers to make. Not ours."

"I know that. And she's made it. So I don't see why she shouldn't explore other options. It's important that she move on."

"Even so, I think you're playing with fire."

"Here we go again with the analogies," Anderson said. "Look, if Vanessa says they're a good match, I believe her. Besides, Cybil's a big girl. She can take care of herself."

When Richard had questioned my motives, I hadn't had any

qualms. But in defending me, Anderson had actually produced a niggle of worry. I loved Cybil like a sister, and meddling in her love life wasn't exactly risk-free.

"There's nothing to worry about," I said, talking as much to myself as to my friends. "I honestly think they'll hit it off. And if I'm wrong, then they'll just go their separate ways and no one will be hurt." Famous last words. "Besides, I've still got to get Grayson on board."

"So call him." Anderson tipped his head toward my phone.

I stared down at the glowing numbers. They were right. Better to talk to him now. Tomorrow, after the papers came out, he might not be so receptive. And I could run down Maris afterward. Surely by then she'd be home.

Maybe, for the moment at least, I could actually have my cake and eat it, too.

But then wasn't that exactly what Marie Antoinette thought right before they led her to the guillotine?

Chapter 14

Flatiron Building. *175 Fifth Avenue (between Twenty-second and Twenty-third streets).*

Not well-known among those not from the area, or not into historic architecture, the Flatiron Building is a favorite of New Yorkers and admirers around the world. Perhaps because it symbolizes so much of how New Yorkers see themselves—defiant, bold, sophisticated, and interesting. The Flatiron's most interesting feature is its shape—a slender hull plowing up the streets of commerce as the bow of a great ocean liner plows through the waves of its domain.

—www.glasssteelandstone.com

I'd never actually been in the Flatiron Building. Actually when you think about it, there are a lot of buildings in Manhattan I've never been in. That may sound like a blinding glimpse of the obvious, but the point is I still know those buildings. They're part of the fabric of the city. The imprint we New Yorkers have made as we trudge through our daily lives.

We might never look up, but that doesn't mean we don't know what's there. And the Flatiron is one of the city's best efforts. And like all buildings in New York, it comes with its own history. Once the tallest building in Manhattan—honestly—it was never supposed to have lasted. Locals actually bet that it would fall down with the next big wind. Even better, that same wind created a wind tunnel that became the subway grate of its day, provocatively lifting women's skirts.

Of course, in 1902, Marilyn Monroe was just a gleam in someone's eye and an ankle was considered quite risqué. But men will be men, no matter the era, and so young men supposedly flocked to Twenty-third in hopes of a glimpse of stocking. So much so that the constables had to chase them away and in doing so coined the term "23 skidoo."

And you thought all I ever thought about was Italian leather.

Anyway, I wasn't exactly sure why I was meeting Grayson here. He had offices on Madison. But I wasn't complaining. The building held that kind of allure. Inside, the man at the desk had me sign in and then directed me to the top floor. I wasn't surprised. Mark Grayson seemed like a top-of-the-building kind of guy.

What was surprising was the fact that the elevator opened onto an empty floor. And when I say empty, I mean e-m-p-t-y. Even the walls had gone AWOL. Obviously the security guy had sent me to the wrong floor. The open space was clearly being renovated. Paint cans littered the tarp-covered floor, and from my immediate vantage point, I could see framing, a couple of saws, and a staple gun.

But even better than that, I was almost completely surrounded by windows. At the apex of the building's triangle, it was sort of like that scene in *Titanic*. Only instead of an endless ocean, I had the sparkle of the city. There were probably better, higher views—but for my money, this one ranked right up there with the best.

I stood for a moment just soaking it in.

"It's amazing, isn't it?"

I whirled around, embarrassed to have been caught gaping. We might love our city, but we don't want to be caught staring at it like starstruck tourists. "It's nice," I offered, wondering why in the world he'd asked me to meet him here.

"It's my favorite view in all of Manhattan."

"So you hold all your meetings here?" I frowned.

"No." He shook his head. "I actually haven't invited anyone here before. You're the first one."

"Well, maybe you should have waited for the walls?"

"I actually like it like this. The truth is that I've loved this building ever since I was a kid. And when I heard the top floor was for sale, I bought it."

"And tore it up." I could see traces of the old molding along the walls. It was dilapidated, but had probably been regal in its day. It seemed a shame to strip the grand dame of her hardware after all this time.

"Actually, I'm restoring it. I found a guy in Brooklyn who can reproduce pretty much everything. We're working from photographs of the day. It may not be exactly like it was, but it'll be as close as you can get a hundred years later."

I liked a man who appreciated history. And so did Cybil.

"So why did you bring me here?"

For the first time since I'd met him he looked a little self-conscious. Or maybe I was transferring from me to him, because I definitely felt awkward. For one thing, I wasn't sure exactly why he'd decided to meet with me. Hopefully it was because I'd intrigued him enough that he was interested in letting me provide a match. But for the first time I considered that it might be for something else altogether. Like throwing me off the top of the Flatiron Building to get me out of his hair.

After all, I'd single-handedly managed to sic the press on him. Normally, he kept a fairly low profile. But thanks to me, the level had gone from blue to orange. People have killed for less.

"I needed to take some measurements, so I figured I'd kill two birds with one stone."

My stomach rumbled, the bourbon swimming around in there all on its own. "I thought we were going to have dinner."

He smiled, the look as usual transforming him from formidable to boy next door. "We are. Right this way, madam, your table is waiting." He bent into a sweeping bow, and despite the butterflies in my stomach, I laughed.

"Lead on."

I followed him around the corner of the elevator bank to the west side of the building. From here I could see Restoration Hardware below. One of my all-time favorite stores. It's like the best of blast from the past. You never know what you'll find there, but it's guaranteed to take you down memory lane.

"I hope this will do."

I pulled my attention from the window and turned to find him standing beside two sawhorses covered by a piece of wallboard and a tarp. The makeshift table held a variety of open containers, all of them emanating mouthwatering aromas.

"*This* is amazing," I said, moving closer. A folding chair sat on either side of the table, artfully arranged so that the occupants would have full access to the view.

"Alberto is the best."

"Alberto?" I considered myself up-to-the-second on great restaurants in the city, a noteworthy feat when one takes into consideration the sheer number of establishments on the East Side alone, not to mention a propensity for closing just after opening. New Yorkers were a tough crowd. But I drew the line at keeping up with chefs. They switched restaurants with more frequency than Paris Hilton switches fiancés.

"My personal chef," he answered, pulling out a chair.

"He delivers?" Okay, Manhattan was the city of order-in, and I was the reigning queen, but this was entirely new territory.

"I eat at odd times, and usually in strange places." He waved a hand at the skeletal walls behind him. "I find it easier to have someone on my payroll than to keep up with who delivers what after hours."

"Makes sense, I suppose. And it certainly keeps it entertaining." I smiled at him and took the seat he was offering.

He pulled the lid off of something scrumptiously Italian in a Styrofoam container. "Veal limone?"

"Please," I said, watching in amazement as he filled my plate with not only the veal, but steaming asparagus, tiny roasted potatoes, and a slab of focaccia covered with garlic and rosemary. I could die happy just from inhaling. There was even a bottle of wine. "This really does look great."

"Alberto's from Tuscany. But he studied in Paris. The perfect blend of grandmother's cooking and haute cuisine."

"He must cost a fortune." It was out before I could stop it. My mother was probably choking somewhere. I'd always had a problem with my mouth, especially when it came to money. I knew the rules. It's just that sometimes I forgot to follow them.

Fortunately Grayson didn't seem to be offended.

"He does. But it's worth it. I travel eight months of the year. So having him along maintains some sense of normalcy. I like it. And he seems to enjoy the variation in location."

"You get continuity and he gets just the opposite—interesting dichotomy."

"It works." He shrugged.

We ate in silence for a moment. Not the uncomfortable kind. More the man-this-is-the-best-food-I've-ever-tasted-and-no-way-am-I-wasting-time-on-casual-banter kind. I'd made it through about half of the veal when I came up for air.

"So I'm assuming you asked me here for something besides an outsider's opinion of Alberto's cooking." I popped the last of the focaccia in my mouth and forced myself not to reach for another piece. "Which is definitely thumbs-up, by the way."

"I told you I wanted to continue our conversation."

"As I recall, it was over. I'd accused you of avoiding intimacy, and you were about to tell me to go to hell." I marveled at the fact that I wasn't the slightest bit afraid of him. Maybe the food had lulled me into some kind of taste-induced nirvana.

"You have a good memory." He smiled again and reached for the bread. Clearly he didn't have to worry about pedestrian things like weight.

"I graduated magna cum laude." I wasn't sure that the tidbit had anything to do with memory, but I wanted him to realize I was more than a piece of fluff.

"I'm sure you did. But that's not what interests me."

"Then why?" I frowned, trying to figure out his angle. There had to be one. Men like Mark Grayson didn't just invite people to dinner for the heck of it.

"Your ideas interest me."

Maybe there was hope. "You're thinking about letting me find someone for you?"

"Well, when you put it that way, I've got to admit it makes me a little uncomfortable. Let's just say I'm more open to the idea of a partnership than I thought I'd be."

"But the idea of someone else finding that person is still unpalatable?"

"Yes. To some degree. Although there is a certain practicality to the idea. Anyway, I decided it was worth considering, and the first step is to get to know you a little better."

"No ulterior motives?"

"Like what?" He actually looked surprised.

"I don't know—a chance to teach me a lesson. No more meddling or something like that?" I'd actually had an experience like that early in my career. I'd been surprised at how much it hurt.

"Believe me, I don't have time for that kind of thing."

"I'm sorry. But it's happened before. And I don't want to go there again."

"Surely you check up on your clients before you accept them?"

"Of course. But I was young and I wanted to impress Althea. It made me less cautious than I should have been."

"But you see, that's what I like in you. You're fearless."

"Hardly," I said, more flattered than I cared to admit. "I'm just good at putting on a brave front."

"Well, that's half the battle, isn't it?"

"It's not a replacement for experience. The episode I was speaking of is a perfect example. Althea would have seen it coming a mile away."

"But she wouldn't have found him a partner."

I frowned, flummoxed. "How in the world did you know I'd made the match? You don't even know who I'm talking about."

"It doesn't matter. I just know that your answer to his duplicity would be to prove him wrong."

"Well, you're right."

"You've got passion, Vanessa. And that's something I'll take over experience any day."

It was the first time he'd used my name, and I kind of liked the way he made it sound. Mark Grayson was a lot deeper than first impressions would have you believe. He and Cybil were going to do just fine. All I had to do was close the deal.

Of course, that was the hardest part.

"I'm not sure what to say. I don't know that anyone has ever called me passionate. In fact, my best friend thinks I'm so dispassionate that I'm in the wrong business."

"Why?" he asked, reaching for the bottle of wine, topping off our glasses.

"Because I don't believe in hormone-driven happily ever after. Which to Cybil's mind means I'm incapable of passion."

"There are all kinds of passion. And they aren't all physical."

I considered the idea, and then nodded. "I think I agree. I'd never really thought about it in those terms. But you're right. And I think you can apply that to relationships as well. If couples share more than a physical passion—if they share other interests, business, or causes, or even hobbies, then they're going to be bound more closely together over the long haul. In fact, even without physical attraction, I'd submit that the union can last, as long as there are other crucial commonalities."

"Don't underrate physical passion."

"I'm not. I'm only saying that on its own it can't support a relationship. At least not indefinitely. And sometimes, it can even undermine one that seems to be on relatively stable ground."

"You're pretty young to be so cynical."

"I'm not as young as I look, believe me. And anyway, Cybil says I'm an old soul. I've always taken that as a compliment, but I'm not sure that's how she meant it."

"That's the second time you've mentioned Cybil."

Perfect opening, now all I had to do was bait the hook. "She was with me the other night. In black lace?" I waited for him to mentally retrieve the image. I knew he'd seen her. Cybil had looked amazing.

He nodded. "Dark hair? Slow smile."

"Exactly." He was a quick study. Well done. "Cybil Baranski. We've been friends since grammar school."

"I didn't think anyone called it that anymore."

"Guess I just dated myself. Anyway, suffice it to say, she's been my best friend as long as I can remember."

"That's nice." It could have been a throwaway, but he sounded like he really meant it. "I've never really cultivated that kind of friend."

"I'm not sure you can. It just sort of happens. You know, you meet someone and bam . . . you just know you'll be friends for life."

"I thought you didn't believe in that kind of relationship?"

The question gave me pause. But I wasn't about to let him know it. "A friendship is a far cry from a long-term coupling. And besides, the kind of connection I'm talking about is exactly what I think makes a good marriage. Two people who have a shared past and mutual respect for one another."

"So your mate, if that's the right word, could be your best friend."

"Well, if I were to marry Cybil, there would be problems. I mean for one we're both into guys. But more seriously, although our relationship is deep, the footing is totally different from the kind of intimacy I'd expect from marriage. Does that make sense at all?"

"So you can't marry your best friend?"

"That's probably putting it too simply, but yeah, I tend to think that there needs to be a different kind of connection in a marriage than simply best friends."

"Okay, I'm not saying I disagree with you, but what you just said seems to be at odds with your stance against physical attraction."

"I said it before. I'm all for physical attraction. I just don't think it should be the primary basis for a union between two people. It's just a setup for failure. Once the passion fades, there's nothing left to sustain the marriage. You see it all the time."

"What if the passion never fades?"

"That'd be a romance novel. And I don't think it's possible.

Relationships go through cycles, Mark." His name just fell off the end of my tongue. And the minute it did, I wanted to take it back. Using it was like crossing a boundary I wasn't sure I wanted to cross. But then I always overanalyze things. "And so when you're in the off cycle you need something else to keep you together."

"And you believe that a third party is better able to find those commonalities?"

"Well, again that's overstating. But I do think that our culture puts too much emphasis on the physical. And because of that, a man, in particular, tends not to see the right woman, even when she's standing right under his nose."

"Enter the matchmaker."

"It's a time-honored profession."

"That died out with the concept of arranged marriages."

"Actually in some countries the idea is still going strong."

"And women's rights activists are having coronaries trying to stop them."

"Yes, but the divorce rate in countries like ours has more than tripled."

"Point taken." He sat back and took a sip of wine. The second one I'd seen him take. Obviously Mark Grayson wasn't a heavy drinker. I wasn't sure if that was a good thing or a bad thing, but overall it meant Cybil would always have a designated driver.

"Look, it can work." I sat forward, pushing aside my plate. "I've got the couples to prove it. We live in busy times. And we're conditioned to want instant gratification." He started to smile, but I waved my hand to stop him. "I didn't mean that kind of gratification and you know it. I'm simply saying most people don't want to take the time to find the right person. Especially when you're talking about our social set. And so one of three things happens. A person acts on pheromones and makes the wrong choice, or he just ignores real intimacy altogether and settles for brief meaningless encounters, or—and of course I think this is the best—a person calls in an expert and lets them do all the legwork."

"Enter Vanessa Carlson."

"Exactly." I smiled at him, feeling as if I'd won the point.

"And I suppose you'd put me in group two."

"Well, if the shoe fits."

"But what about people who make the right choice on their own? I mean, you have to admit that sometimes true love wins the day."

"Sometimes." I thought about Richard and Anderson. "But unfortunately that's the exception and not the rule. You'd be amazed at how many people don't marry their true love, simply because they know it wouldn't have worked."

"So don't you have a lot of miserable people out there?"

"No. Because at the end of the day, most people will choose comfort over kaboom when it comes to the long haul."

"And simply because you're not part of the hormonal equation, you're able to recognize who someone should be with?"

"Not that specifically. No. I just sort of have a feeling when I think two people suit each other. And I surely don't advocate that there's only one person out there. It's just that I can quickly identify from the people I work with who might fit the bill. Sometimes it takes more than one match. But most of the time I get it right the first time."

"And why do you think that is?"

"Mainly because I do my homework. But also because for some reason my natural instincts about people tend to be right. I can't explain it. But I've always been a busybody when it comes to my friends' relationships. And I also think it has to do, in part, with the fact that when someone comes to me, they're truly open to finding the right relationship. That's half the battle really."

"And what if someone is determined to pursue the wrong person?"

I shrugged and drained the last of my wine. "Then I can't help them." Suddenly I realized I'd walked into a trap. All he had to do now was tell me he wasn't interested in finding the "right" type and the trap was sprung.

But instead he only nodded his head and refilled my glass. "I will say you're not like any other woman I've ever met."

I wasn't sure if that was a good thing or a bad thing. Which left me, uncharacteristically, without anything to say. Fortunately, salvation presented itself in the form of my cell phone ringing.

I pulled it out of my bag and checked the screen.

Maris.

"I'm sorry," I said, snapping the little phone open. "I've got to take this."

"Another emergency?" One eyebrow shot up in amusement.

"Same one," I whispered, as the phone connected. "Maris? Is that you?"

"How'd you know?" She asked, astonishment coloring her voice.

"Caller ID."

"Right, I always forget about that." I think I mentioned Maris has a thing about keeping her phone service minimalistic. She's only had a cell phone for about a year. And that was at my insistence. "Anyway, I'm at the St. Regis. The Montgomery gala. I ran into Richard and he mentioned you were looking for me."

"Did he say why?" I asked, and if possible Mark's eyebrow rose even higher.

"No. Just that it was important."

"Well, it is. How long are you going to be there?" Assuming I could grab a cab, it wouldn't take more than fifteen minutes to get to Fifty-fifth.

"Well, actually, I was on my way out. Douglas was supposed to have come with me. And I'm tired of fending off questions."

"Meet me in the bar."

"You want me to sit there alone?"

"Grab Richard. He'll keep you company."

"Never mind, I'll go on my own. What's this all about anyway?"

"Douglas." She started to ask more questions but I cut her off. "Listen, I'm in a meeting. I'll tell you about it when I get there, okay?"

"Fine." She clicked off, and I had the feeling I'd managed to make her angry even before I broke the news. Why was it I always managed to wind up in ridiculous situations?

"I take it there's trouble in matchmaking paradise?"

I could have been offended, but I was simply too worried about Maris. "Got it in one."

"Want to tell me about it? Maybe I can help."

"Not likely, unless you've got a straight line to the gossip rags."

"If I had that . . ."

"I know. You wouldn't have been fodder of the past few days. It seems I'm facilitating a lot of that of late."

"I see." He didn't, of course, but I had the feeling he got the gist of it anyway.

"Look, I'm sorry. I've got to go. I really would love to take you on." He grinned. And I blanched. "I mean, as a client. In fact, I have someone in mind. But I'm afraid this is more important."

"Do you want to me take you? I've got a car outside."

The idea was tempting. It would be faster than hailing a cab.

But he had a way of coaxing more out of a person than they'd planned, and I wasn't in the mood to spill my guts.

"No thanks. I'll just grab a cab." I stood up and started for the elevator, my thoughts already turning to Maris.

"Vanessa?"

I stopped, and turned, realizing I'd just been extremely rude. "I'm sorry. I didn't even say thank you. It was a lovely dinner."

"I'm sorry it had to be cut short. But that seems to be the norm for you."

"Well, usually it's not quite so hectic." Actually now that I thought about it, he was probably right. But then things did seem to be going particularly badly at the moment. "Call me if you want to talk some more."

"Don't worry. I will."

At least I hadn't ruined Cybil's chances. There was still hope. "I'll look forward to it." I shot what I hoped was a confident smile and then turned again for the elevator. I'd almost reached the door when I realized I hadn't told him anything about the photograph. And Belinda had warned me that Mark Grayson was the kind of man who valued honesty above all else.

So after closing my eyes and whispering a prayer, I turned back. "One more thing," I said as he tilted his head, waiting. I licked my lips and sucked in a breath for courage. "There may be a picture of me in tomorrow's papers. A somewhat compromising one." The eyebrow was at work again, and I felt my throat tightening. "I just wanted to say that it isn't what it seems."

Blissfully, the elevator doors slid open behind me. And I whirled around and dashed inside, staring at the back of the wall until the doors closed again, the sound of his laughter still ringing in my ears.

So much for suave and sophisticated.

Chapter 15

King Cole Bar, St. Regis Hotel. *2 East Fifty-fifth Street (corner of Fifth Avenue), 212.753.4500.*

Located in the St. Regis Hotel, the King Cole Bar is popular with guests and non-guests alike. The Red Snapper (better known as the Bloody Mary) was invented here, beneath the Maxfield Parrish mural depicting Old King Cole.

—www.gonyc.about.com

The St. Regis is one of the most elegant places in New York. And the King Cole Bar fits right in. It's one of my favorite places to relax. It's an oblong affair with a huge Maxfield Parrish mural of its namesake, complete with fiddlers three, over the bar. They serve a wicked martini and the original Bloody Mary, and pretty much anything else your little heart desires.

And so at least the setting was a good one, maybe with enough martinis—for Maris, not me—I'd manage to survive the news I had to impart. She was sitting in a corner at a banquette, a martini and the bar's signature almonds and green wasabi peas in front of her. Maybe she was already ahead of the game.

We exchanged air kisses and I slid into the seat across from her. "Sorry to take so long, I couldn't get a cab."

"It's always amazing to me how if you don't want one, they're literally lining the streets, and when you do want one . . . ," she trailed off with a shrug. She was wearing a shimmering silver cocktail dress that I'd seen and coveted in Donna Karan. She looked fabulous. If only Douglas could see her in it, he'd realize in a heartbeat just exactly how lucky he was.

Unfortunately, Douglas was passed out in his apartment. Maybe he was dreaming of Maris. That might move things along more quickly. Of course, if Anderson was right, he was dreaming of me. What a nightmare.

"Did you talk to Douglas?"

I nodded, holding my story until after the waitress had offered libation. I was in definite need of fortification, but held myself to a glass of red wine.

"Where was he?"

"At the White Horse."

Maris gave a delicate little shudder. She wasn't the pub type, no matter how infamous it was. In that respect she and Douglas were on different pages. But then favorite bars weren't exactly on the list of marriageable assets. "Well, I'm glad you found him. Was he very bad off?"

I respected Maris's restraint. Had the situation been reversed, I would have started grilling her for details the moment I walked through the door.

"Let's just say he'd had quite a few." I probably should have drawn a clearer picture, but she loved the man, and I couldn't bring myself to describe the whole knee-walking part. The waitress brought my wine, and I took a sip, giving myself a moment to get my thoughts in order.

"So did he tell you why he did it?" So much for taking it

slow. Although she'd still waited longer than I would have.

"Yes. And I was right. It was Alyssa."

"He still loves her." Leave it to Maris to leap to the wrong conclusion.

"Of course he doesn't. He loves you."

"Right," she said, her cynicism not becoming. "That's why he dumped me."

"No, Maris. He dumped you because he was afraid. He honestly believes that you'll leave him just like Alyssa did. So he was trying to beat you to the punch. He's afraid of being hurt."

"Oh." The word hung there as if it had wings. She took a quick sip of gin and then bit her lower lip. "There's isn't anything for him to be afraid of. At least from me."

"I know that. And I tried to explain it to him, but he was processing things rather slowly, I'm afraid."

"So he's not changed his mind?"

"Actually I think he has, but he's still afraid. So it could be a day or so before he works up the courage to come back."

"Maybe I should speed things up a bit?" There was a spark of hope, followed by resolution. Maris came from sturdy stock. "I could go over there now and talk to him."

"Might be better to wait. I suspect he's either sound asleep or nursing a hell of a hangover."

"That bad, huh?"

"Well, you can take it as a sign of how much he cares. And how upset he was over the breakup."

"But he initiated it."

"To avoid pain. I don't think it's the same as if he'd decided he didn't love you. If you think about it, it was really just the opposite. He cares about you so much that he realizes what a horrible thing it would be to lose you."

"So he causes the pain himself?"

"Well, I guess he believed that if he moved first, he'd save the public humiliation."

"So he's more interested in saving his reputation than taking the risk on a relationship with me."

"Maris, he got dumped on the day of his wedding in front of five hundred guests. That's not the kind of thing you want to go through again."

"But I've given him no reason to believe it could happen again." I could see that she was moving toward being angry with Douglas, and though I couldn't really blame her, it wouldn't help me if she talked herself into believing she was better off without him.

"Of course you didn't," I soothed. "But that's not enough to take away Douglas's fear. And if it helps, he told me that he knew he'd made a mistake."

"Really?" The hope was back.

"Of course. Just before he left, he even said he wanted to make things right. Unfortunately he wasn't in any shape to do it tonight."

"And that's why you wanted to talk with me?" she asked.

"That's part of it." I blew out a long breath. "The best of it, actually."

"What else is there?" She leaned forward, her hand tightening on the stem of her glass.

"Nothing horrible. Just a bit of a faux pas on Douglas's part." That sounded innocuous enough. "After we talked, I walked with him outside—to make sure he was okay."

"Because he'd been drinking."

"Right." Dead drunk was a better description, but I'd leave that for Douglas to tell her. "Anyway, he was grateful that I'd come to talk to him. I think he just needed someone to assure him that things were going to be okay."

"Of course. That's your job really, isn't it?"

I nodded, wishing I could leave it there. "But he chose a rather intimate way of saying thank you."

"What do you mean?" She frowned.

"Well," I started, and then stopped. How in the hell had I gotten myself into this mess? "The thing is, Douglas thanked me with a kiss."

"A kiss?" She was still frowning, but it was with confusion, not anger.

A big fat wet one. But I could hardly say that. "Yes. On the lips."

"Well, lots of people do that. I'm not sure I see why you're worried about it." She sipped the martini again, the wheels turning in her brain. "You surely didn't think he meant anything more by it?" Her face cleared as she laughed, and if I hadn't been so relieved, I'd have probably been insulted.

"No, of course not. It's just that"—I sobered as I prepared to drop the bomb—"the paparazzi was there."

"They photographed it?" This time she was fully with the program.

"Only one. But believe me, that's more than enough."

"Oh, Vanessa, I'm so sorry." She was apologizing to me?

"For what?"

"For the trouble this is going to cause you. Douglas will be beside himself when he finds out what he's done."

This was not the reaction I'd expected. "You're not angry at me?"

"For being caught by a jackal with a camera? No. It wasn't your fault. But the fallout is certainly going to have an effect."

"Not just on me."

She scrunched her nose in thought. "Well, I suppose there'll be talk. But we'll know that it doesn't amount to anything. If anything, it should make Douglas even more contrite. And at the end of the day, I'll take anything that makes him more inclined to forget this silly notion of our breaking up to avoid, well, breaking up. It's ludicrous, really." She tilted her head with a smile. "I suppose, really, the photog did us a favor."

"But what about the university?" I really wasn't at all prepared for her total lack of concern. I'd thought she'd go ballistic. Clearly I'd underestimated Maris Vanderbeek. "Won't they be angry about the publicity?"

"Actually it'll probably increase book sales, which in turn will boost Douglas's reputation as a novelist, which will no doubt raise his value with the university. All in all, with the right spin, it could be considered a blessing."

To say I was impressed was an understatement. In truth I was floored.

"But there's still the negative impact for you." She reached out to cover my hand with hers. "That's a very real problem. And I'm sorry to have been a part of it."

"You weren't, really." It had been 100 percent Douglas.

"Well, you wouldn't have gone to talk to him, if it hadn't been for me. And if you hadn't been there, then he couldn't have kissed you. So at least in part it is my fault."

"It doesn't matter whose fault it is. You're right, it isn't going to play well in the press for me. I can see the caption now—'Matchmaker Makes Own Match.' Or something more insidious."

" 'Playing with Matches a Girl Could Get Burned'?"

"Don't give them ideas." I glanced at the other patrons of the bar, well aware of the dangers of being overheard.

"No one is listening. And I was just kidding. Maybe it won't even make the papers."

"Normally, I'd agree with you. I mean, I'm not really celebrity material. But considering the buzz surrounding the bet . . ."

"Oh, right. I'd forgotten that." Her tone was commiserative. "That does put a different light on things."

"Right. 'Matchmaker Tastes Her Own Success.' I'm screwed."

"Well, I'll talk to Douglas first thing tomorrow."

"Even if you get there at the crack of dawn you can't guarantee that someone won't get to him first."

"Yes, I can." She glanced down at her watch. "Look, I've got a key to Douglas's place. I'll just go over there and let myself in. If you're right about Douglas, he'll be in no shape to complain. And if the phone rings, I'll get it. That should take the wind out of their sails. Especially if I laugh it off, and say that of course he kissed you, you're single-handedly responsible for getting us together. That should play well, shouldn't it?"

It actually sounded like a plan. In fact, I was impressed with Maris's quick thinking. "You'd do that for me?"

"Vanessa, I wasn't spinning when I said you got us together. You did. And on top of that, you made Douglas realize that he was wrong to have killed our relationship simply because he was afraid. The least I can do in return is deny the ridiculous notion that you and Douglas are an item."

Again I had the sense that I should be insulted, but I wasn't. I was grateful. "But you haven't resolved things between you yet."

"I know. But thanks to you the door is open. And I've had a little time to think myself. I really do love Douglas. Every insecure inch of him. And I'd be a fool if I let him dictate our lives based on his fear. It's not that easy to run me off. So if you're right and he still loves me—"

"He does."

"Then it will be fine." She stood up. "And the sooner I'm off, the more likely we are to be able to nip this thing in the bud, so to speak."

I stood up, too, fighting a desire to hug her. Sure as I did, a guy with a zoom lens would jump out from behind the potted palms. "Thank you."

"Not a problem," she said, already heading for the door.

It was a full minute after she'd left that I realized she hadn't paid her tab.

But considering the trade-off, it was a small price to pay.

"I thought that was you."

I turned around, pasting on my best social smile, but relaxed when I recognized Richard standing there. "How was the party?"

"You know the Montgomerys—excess rules. It was entertaining, I suppose, in a gaudy sort of way."

"Where's Anderson?"

"Begged off. He really does hate these things. Especially when Tod Whitman is involved."

Tod was a party planner and an old flame of Anderson's. Tod still hadn't forgiven Anderson for choosing Richard, and once he'd had a couple of glasses of champagne he wasn't shy about speaking his mind—usually at the top of his lungs. If his skills at arranging hadn't been so fabulous, his loose lips would have tanked his career years ago. "I can see his point."

"Me, too." Richard grinned, then sobered. "Did you talk to Maris?"

"Yes. Thanks to your SOS. She was just here."

"And things are okay?"

"Well, there's still the storm to weather, but she was really very pragmatic about the whole thing."

He sat down and motioned for me to sit next to him. "I can't say that I'm surprised. Her father was something of a card. I suspect, in her life, she's had to deal with more than her fair share of bullshit."

"Well, she was very understanding with me. Actually almost insultingly so."

"Didn't think Douglas was making a pass?" He was smiling again.

"Not even a drunken one."

"Says something for their relationship." Richard slid an arm around me to give me a hug.

"Yeah. It does." Said a lot, actually. She trusted Douglas even when he'd been a total shit. People never ceased to amaze me. Still, even though I didn't understand it, I certainly was grateful for it. "She's going over there now."

"I thought you said he was down for the count?"

"He was. But she's got a key. Figures she'll cut things off at the pass if she's answering his phone tomorrow."

"Not a bad idea, actually. But what if Douglas objects?"

"He won't."

"You sound pretty sure of yourself." Richard reached for an almond.

"He knows he's made a mistake."

"Kissing you?" He popped the almond into his mouth.

"No. Although that was clearly a mistake, I doubt he even remembers it. I meant, in dumping Maris."

"So he wants her back."

"That's what he said, and I'm thinking that if she's there when he wakes up, it'll be that much easier for him to make it all right."

"Sounds like you're off the hook."

"Well, not completely. No matter how well Maris and Douglas handle it, there's still going to be fallout if that picture runs. I mean, I do have other clients."

"But they know you."

"Some not as well as others."

"We're not talking about an almost-client, are we?" Richard asked, waving off the hovering waitress. "Say, one named Grayson?"

"Maybe a little."

Richard smirked.

"All right. A lot. But it's not just because of the bet. He's a really great guy."

"This is getting more and more interesting."

"You didn't let me finish. He's a really great guy—for Cybil. Honestly, I think they're perfect."

"So did you warn him about the kiss?"

"More or less."

"Which is it?" he asked.

"Well, if you want to be technical, I'd have to say less. But he's been alerted."

"Then you should be okay."

"Fingers crossed. Are you ready to go, or were you planning to stay a while?" I shot a look around the bustling bar. There were several tables of people we knew. Some of them clearly coming from the gala.

"No, I was on my way out when I saw you. Shall we share a cab?"

"Actually, I think I'd prefer to walk. Clear my head and all that."

"Want company?"

I smiled up at him, thanking God for such a perceptive friend. "Please."

"Listen, Van, if Grayson's got any sense at all, he'll realize that there's no way you'd kiss a client."

"I know. What I don't know is why it matters so damn much." I sighed, grabbing the check before Richard could. "Too much wine, I suppose. What I need is to go home and go to bed."

After all, tomorrow looked like it was going to be a banner day.

Go me.

Chapter 16

Payard Patisserie & Bistro. *1032 Lexington Avenue (between Seventy-third and Seventy-fourth streets), 212.717.5252.*

François Payard's "museum-quality" pastries are so "insanely good" you could eat yourself into a "sugar coma" at his East Side bistro/patisserie, but then you'd miss out on Philippe Bertineau's "marvelous" cooking, which easily "holds its own"; the "elegant" bi-level space has a feel that some find reminiscent of the old Schrafft's chain, but better.

—www.zagat.com

The smell of something wonderful made its way into my bedroom like a cartoon finger, summoning me from sleep with an almost hypnotic pull. I pushed back the duvet and tried to remember when I'd moved into a bakery. With an almost somnambulistic gait, I headed for the kitchen, following my nose.

Since my oven hadn't been used for anything except shoe storage in nearly a year, I felt fairly certain that it hadn't suddenly decided to go back into the baking business. That meant that some well-meaning soul had invaded and brought sustenance. Tantalizingly delicious sustenance.

Since only three people had access to the key to my apartment—Anderson, Richard, and my mother—I figured it had to be one of them. And since my mother had already graced me with her presence this week, I was fairly certain she could be eliminated from the equation.

Besides, the smell was decidedly carb-laden, and she hadn't touched anything containing flour in at least a decade. (Which, of course, explains why she's two sizes smaller than I am. Although I *am* two inches taller.)

In truth, I wasn't sure that I really cared who it was as long as the aroma was attached to something edible. After all, today was most likely going to be trying at best, catastrophic at worst. I needed fortification.

"Morning, sunshine." Anderson turned from the coffee-maker with a smile. "I brought croissants."

Not just any croissants, mind you. These were Payard's croissants. It was like Paris had morphed into pastry and presented itself on a plate. I know that New Yorkers are supposed to consider bagels the bread of life. And I'll grant you that the right bagel and schmear can be a cathartic experience. But putting a bagel up against a croissant is like comparing Fossil to Prada. And face it, given a choice, who's going to choose Fossil?

"Don't you think it's a little early?" The three LED clocks in my four-foot-square kitchen all attested to the fact that it was seven forty-five. Have I mentioned that I'm not a morning person?

"I figured I ought to be here before the phone starts ringing." Anderson moved to open a cabinet, and I saw the stack of papers.

"Is it bad?"

"Food first."

"Oh, God."

"Well, let's just say you look really good in the photo."

Not bothering to wait for a plate, I reached for a croissant and bit in, letting the buttery flakes of pastry seduce my tongue and soothe my soul. "Is it in all of them?" I asked, daring another look at the stack of newspapers.

"Every last one, I'm afraid. And these are just the dailies."

"You think it'll go beyond that?"

"I wouldn't be surprised to see it in the regionals."

"Oh God." I seemed to be saying that a lot.

"Take this," Anderson handed me a mug and a second croissant, "and go have a shower."

"But it's not even morning yet."

"Honey, for most people the day is already waning. Besides, you'll feel better once you've had a shower."

What I wanted was to rip off the bandage and find out just how bad it all was. But Anderson was right, if I went that route I might never get to the shower, and hiding under the bed in my pj's wasn't going to accomplish anything. Still, the newspapers were calling my name.

Literally.

"I want to survey the damage." I put my cup on the counter and moved toward the papers.

Anderson shifted to block my way. (Which wasn't at all hard to do in my kitchen.) "You really should get dressed first." He handed me back the coffee. "And have a little caffeine."

I started to protest, but the doorbell interrupted.

"I'll get it," he said. "You go and put some clothes on."

I glanced down at the Hello Kitty–dotted cotton I insisted on sleeping in. The cartoon image might be hip (I mean, even Judith Leiber is in on the craze), but my jammies really weren't presentable. "All right. I'm going." I grabbed the second croissant and headed for the bathroom.

Twenty minutes later, I walked back into the living room, feeling a whole lot more human and a heck of a lot more awake. Anderson was sitting at the table with Cybil, the two of them enjoying the last of the breakfast he'd provided. The newspapers were stacked neatly in the center of the table.

"Come to share in my humiliation?" I quipped, trying for a flippant smile.

"I didn't have anything more pressing," Cybil returned, pushing her glasses up on her nose. As always, she looked fabulous, the green Ralph Lauren frames on her glasses matching the shade of her silk sueded tank exactly. "Besides, I knew Anderson would have Payard's."

"The big guns," I said, sliding into a chair. "Okay, so I'm clean, caffeinated, and well-fed. It's time. Any particular order?"

"Actually, they're fairly interchangeable," Anderson said, sliding the stack of papers over to me.

I really didn't want to touch them. In fact, part of me wanted to go straight to the ceremonial-burning part of the equation. I know that sounds extreme, but it's easier to accomplish than you think. I live in Manhattan, remember? And my building still has an incinerator. All I had to do was walk down the hall, open the little metal door, shove the suckers in, and fifteen seconds later—whoosh.

But that was the coward's way out.

Better to face the problem head-on. Then I could run screaming from the room.

I have to admit the picture was actually a good one. And if I'd been in love with Douglas it would have been a keeper. But Douglas was engaged to Maris, and I was supposed to be a professional. And believe me, none of that was reflected in the photograph. And, of course, a column wouldn't be a column without pithy captions. Mine ranged from titillating to X-rated.

"It could have been worse," Cybil said, cutting through the silence.

"It's not good." I shook my head as I perused *Newsday* and then a supermarket tabloid I hadn't even heard of. More of the same. "At least I got to Maris before these came out." I pushed the papers away. "She was amazingly practical last night. I'm just hoping that with reality staring her in the face, she doesn't change her mind."

On that thought, the phone rang. At least we'd made it to almost nine o'clock.

"Do you want me to get it?" Anderson asked. I usually try to fight my own battles. Really, I do. But it was still early, and I hadn't even had a second cup of coffee.

"Would you mind?"

"Honey, that's what I'm here for." He headed into the kitchen and grabbed the phone. All the better for me not to hear.

"I take it you've already seen these," I said, as Cybil grabbed the carafe off the table and refilled my cup.

"Yeah. First thing this morning. I wanted to assess the damage before I came over."

"So what do you think?"

"Well, I've got to say that even to me, it looks a lot like Douglas is enjoying himself."

"Oh, please. He was drunk."

"I know. I'm just telling you what it looks like." She smiled and reached over to pat my hand. "You've got to admit it's a bit funny. You and Douglas Larson."

"It most certainly is not," I snapped, surprised at the strength of my anger. "This picture could very well mark the end of my days as a matchmaker. I mean, look at this one." I pulled out a paper at random. "'Matchmaker Lights His Fire.'"

"Well, it is a bit inflammatory." She waited a beat, but I

didn't even smile. "Look, I know this is serious. But you've got to find a way to get through it. The truth is that if anyone stops to consider it for a moment, they'll see that it reeks of a setup. I mean, it's only a snapshot. And most people are capable of recognizing bullshit when they see it. Have you talked to Douglas or Maris yet?"

"I haven't even been awake an hour." I sounded defensive, but hell, it wasn't a good day.

And to emphasize the point, the phone rang again, but only once. Anderson was clearly on the job.

"People were calling me, too," Cybil said.

"Friend or foe?" The latter of course was more likely, gloating being the national pastime for our circle.

"Neither, really," she sighed. "Mainly it was the voyeuristic type."

"Wonderful. The vultures circle. Did Althea call?"

"No," she said, looking down at her hands.

"Cybil. I know that look." The phone rang again in the background, but neither of us reacted. "Spill it."

She sighed. "Fine. She called. But it wasn't to gloat. She just wanted to know what the real story was. And if you were okay."

"So why didn't she call me?"

"She was afraid that it would be rubbing salt in the wound."

"I suppose there's something to that. You swear she didn't sound pleased?"

"Vanessa, you know better than that. Althea is competitive, but she's also your friend."

"I know. I'm sorry. I'm just feeling cornered. I really wanted to win the bet. And now, I'm afraid I haven't a chance in hell."

"Well, at this point I think the bet should be the last of your concerns."

"I disagree. I think it's even more important now. If I could get Mark on board, it would prove to everyone that I'm still in the game."

"It isn't a game, Vanessa. You're talking about people's lives."

"I didn't mean to sound crass. It's just that I feel like I've lost control. And I guess I'm looking for a way to get it back."

"Well, that's understandable." The phone rang again, this time it stopped almost before it could complete the first ring. "So how did things go with Grayson last night?"

"Actually, they went pretty well. He's different from how I pictured him, somehow."

"What do you mean?"

"I don't know if I can put it into words, but he's just more real. Does that make any sense?" The minute it was out of my mouth I realized how stupid it sounded. But Cybil was pretty good at reading between the lines.

"You like him."

"Yeah, I do. And I guess that surprises me."

"Don't you have to like someone to find them a match?"

"No. I mean I don't think I could do it if they were mean, or a bad person, or something, but I don't think my liking them per se has anything at all to do with finding a match. I just have to be able to read their personality. Figure out what it is they really want."

"Sounds impossible."

"It does." I laughed. "But you know as well as I do that I seem to have a knack for it."

There was a long pause, and I almost thought she was going to disagree with me, but instead she asked about Mark. "Did you tell him about me?"

"Not in so many words. I mean I talked about you a lot. And I also told him I had someone in mind for him, but Maris called before I had the chance to connect the dots."

"That's probably just as well," she said, staring down into her coffee cup. "I mean I've been having second thoughts."

"You're just nervous."

"No. I think maybe it's more than that. I mean I just broke up with Stephen; it seems too soon to be jumping into something else."

"It's just a date, Cybil."

"With big expectations."

"No. I swear. None at all. I admit that in the beginning when I thought of you it was because of the bet. But I also meant what I said. I'd never set you up with someone I didn't think was right for you. And the more I get to know Mark, the more certain I am that he's perfect for you."

"Well, I'm not nearly as confident."

"That's understandable. But you do think he's interesting, right?"

"From what I know," she admitted with a shrug.

"And you think he's good-looking."

"You have to be crazy not to think that." She was smiling now.

"So all I'm asking you to do is give it a chance. Go out with the guy. And if I'm right, everything else will follow."

"And if you're wrong?"

"I'm not." I snorted, not even certain I believed it myself. "But if by some miracle I am, then you just chalk it up as a one-off and that's the end of it."

"Really? No pressure?"

"None at all. I swear. Honest to God, Cybil, I wouldn't be suggesting this if I didn't truly believe the two of you suit."

"Now you sound like a matchmaker. Who uses the word 'suit'?"

"Okay," I said. "How about 'I think he'll blow your socks off.' Is that better?"

"Well, it's certainly more appealing," she said with a laugh. "Anyway, it's still a long shot, right? I mean he hasn't agreed to anything."

"No. He hasn't." Reality came crashing in like the ladies who lunch at a Bergdorf's end-of-the-year sale. "And after he sees the photograph, he probably won't. I'm surprised Althea wasn't crowing."

"Well, the truth is that it isn't just a strike against you, it's a strike against the profession, and that includes Althea."

"Are you trying to make me feel worse?"

"No. Just assuring you that at least with regard to the bet, Althea isn't going to benefit from today's journalistic debacle."

"Funny, I think that actually makes me feel better," I sighed. "I'm a rotten person."

"No, you're not, sweetie. You're just human."

"Well, that's six calls," Anderson said, putting the cordless back in its cradle. "Two from so-called friends, one from your mother, and three from reporters requesting the inside scoop."

"What did you tell them?" I asked, feeling slightly sick.

"Well, since I figured 'fuck off' wasn't an option, I told your friends that you were working, your mother that you'd call her later, and the press, 'no comment.'"

"Well done," Cybil said. "I think maybe you missed your calling. You should be in PR."

"Oh, please," Anderson laughed. "Anyone can answer a phone."

"Better you than me," I said. "I'm not sure I could have handled any of them. Especially my mother."

"She was just worried about you," Anderson said, reaching for the *Times*. Thank God there was one paper that wasn't interested in the misadventures of Vanessa Carlson.

"I know," I sighed. "But as much as I hate making a fool of

myself, I hate doing it in front of my mother even more. I want her to be proud of me, not saying 'I told you so.' She's never approved of my business."

"I think it's more your attitude about relationships she disapproves of," Cybil said.

"Well, there's the pot calling the kettle black. She's spent the last ten years trying to fix me up with every single male within her social orbit."

"She's a mom," Anderson said. "It's in the job description."

"Shouldn't you be at work?" I snapped. I mean, after all he was supposed to be taking my side.

"I told them I'd be in late."

"I don't need a babysitter." I sounded petulant, but I couldn't help it. I'd been taking care of myself for a long time. "Besides, Cybil's here."

The two of them exchanged a glance. The poor-dear-she's-not-thinking-straight kind of look. "Well, two friends are better than one," Anderson said, his tone brooking no argument. "And so I'll go in after you get your bearings."

Okay, in case you're thinking I'm a total twit, I know how lucky I am to have friends like Cybil and Anderson. I even know how lucky I am to have my mother on my side—more or less. What I hate is the fact that I need them so damn much. You know? I just want to stand on my own two feet. Take control of my life.

Waldo twined around my ankles, reminding me that I couldn't even control my cat.

"Thanks, guys," I said, pushing back from the table. I grabbed the carafe and headed for the kitchen to make more coffee. It was shaping up to be a two-pot kind of day. Behind me, the phone rang again, and I could hear Anderson telling whoever it was that I wasn't home and then repeating the words "no comment."

Maybe I should have Starbucks pump the stuff directly into the apartment. If David Letterman could do it, so could I. By the time I'd managed to fill the machine with coffee and start it running, the phone had rung another three times. Anderson was more than a friend, he was a godsend.

I was headed back for the living room when I noticed that the front door was ajar.

"How long has this door been open?" I asked, a tenor of panic seeping into my voice.

Cybil shook her head and Anderson frowned as he hung up the phone. "I've no idea. Does it matter?"

"Waldo," I said, in answer to the question, and Cybil whispered the only words that could possibly make my day worse.

"He's gotten out."

"Waldo," we all yelled simultaneously.

"He was just here," I said, wondering if the ankle rub had been his way of saying good-bye. He wasn't generally an affectionate cat. Damn it all to hell.

"Waldo." The name echoed through the apartment as we began to search frantically for my lady-loving cat. I checked in all of his favorite places, even under the bed behind my sweater box, which required a contortion worthy of Cirque du Soleil. No luck.

"He's not here." I surfaced from under the bed just as Anderson emerged from my closet.

"Not here either."

Cybil arrived in the doorway, panting. "I checked the spare room, he's not there either. And I even looked behind the desk."

"He's gone." I sat on the bed and tried to figure out what to do next. Not that I accomplished a lot, my head was too busy presenting a picture of Mrs. M. in a black pointed hat turning Waldo into a flying monkey. "Just because he's out doesn't mean he's with Arabella."

Anderson didn't have time to comment. The doorbell and phone rang simultaneously. Stupidly, I sat frozen on the bed. Neither option appealed. Maybe if I just sat there all day, the ringing would stop. Anderson took his cue from me and sat next to me on the bed.

Cybil stood frozen in the doorway. The cacophony of ringing continued for at least three beats with no one moving.

Anderson came to his senses first. "I'll take the phone," he said, avoiding eye contact. He might be a brave man, but even he wasn't ready to face the possibility that Mrs. M. was at the door.

"Fine," Cybil said. "I'll get the door."

"No," I said, surprising them both. "I'll get the door."

I sucked in a breath and pushed off the bed. Cybil jumped out of the way as I stalked down the hallway, trying to emulate a confidence I did not feel. Rounding the corner, I crossed the living room and, with a small prayer for help, pulled open the door.

"Maris? What are you doing here?" Probably imagining all the ways she'd like to torture me.

"I thought you might need a friendly face." Well, color me surprised. She'd shown a brave face last night, but in truth I'd still fully expected her to do an about-face the minute she saw the photo. "Two of them, actually." She moved aside to show a somewhat recalcitrant Douglas standing beside her.

"Come in." I gestured to the living room where Anderson and Cybil were standing looking just this side of dumbfounded. "We've just been trying to find Waldo."

"Waldo?" Maris asked.

"My cat. I'm afraid he's a cross between Valentino and Houdini."

"Sounds like trouble," she said, giving Douglas a little push. The two of them walked over to the sofa and sat side by side. I followed suit, sitting in the chair across from them.

"I seem to attract it like lint on black pants." I smiled, not entirely sure what to expect next. The tension was palpable. But at least they were together. I'd take victory where I could get it.

"Why don't I get everyone some coffee?" Cybil said, heading to the kitchen without waiting for a response. Chicken.

"I'll help," Anderson said. Make that two chickens.

Maris, Douglas, and I sat awkwardly for a moment. And then I ventured into the potentially shark-infested waters. I mean, someone had to do it.

"So how are you feeling, Douglas?"

His Adam's apple bobbed as he swallowed nervously. Maybe recalcitrant had been the wrong word. Maris reached over to cover his hand with hers, and suddenly I felt hope blossoming like a perfectly aged brandy.

Douglas grimaced but still managed to smile. "I feel like someone drove a Fresh Direct truck through my head. But I guess it's better than I deserve." He paused for a moment and then turning his fingers over, he laced them with Maris's. "Look, Vanessa, I owe you an apology. It's my fault you're getting all the bad publicity. If I hadn't kissed you, none of this would have happened."

It was the absolute truth, and I had every right to be angry. But I wasn't. I understood how difficult it had been for him to apologize. Maybe Douglas and I had more in common than I'd thought. "It's all right. You weren't thinking straight."

"That's a polite understatement." His smile was more genuine. "I was scared shitless, and because of that I got smashed."

"With good reason," I said.

"Well, if it hadn't been for you, I shudder to think of what would have happened."

"You'd have come to your senses on your own. I just pushed things along a little," I assured him.

"See," Maris said. "I told you she'd understand." She beamed at me as if I'd just given her a present.

"So the two of you are okay?"

"What you're asking is whether she forgave me?" Douglas said, the lilt in his voice giving it away before he had the chance to put it in words. But I wanted to hear it anyway.

"So?" I prompted.

"Suffice it to say that the wedding is on again," Maris said, smiling over at Douglas. Score one for the good guys.

"I'm glad," I said. "You two deserve happiness."

"Well, we wouldn't have it if it hadn't been for you," Douglas said.

"Tell her the rest," Maris urged.

"Well," Douglas said, his face more animated than I'd ever seen it. Clearly, making up with Maris had done him a world of good. "My agent called this morning. And apparently there's been all kinds of renewed interest in my books because of the photograph. He even got a call from *Today*. Can you imagine? I might be interviewed by Matt Lauer."

Funny, the networks hadn't been calling me. I guess luck depended upon which side of the kiss you landed. Mine being the should-have-seen-it-coming side.

"So in a backhanded kind of way," Maris was saying, "it's the best thing that could have happened. And it's all because of you."

"Well, I'm just glad it all worked out." And despite the fact that my life was falling apart all around me, I really meant it. Maris and Douglas made a good pair.

"Seriously, Vanessa. We owe you."

I was mumbling something about how it was all part of the job when, thankfully, Anderson and Cybil arrived with the coffee tray.

"What would you like?" Cybil asked. "I've got leaded and unleaded."

Maris shook her head. "We can't stay. We've got loads of things to do." They both stood up. "We just wanted you to know that we're in your corner."

Tears sprang to my eyes as I stood up, too. Maris gave me a hug. And Douglas started to follow suit, stopped, turning bright red, and then with a nod and a nudge from Maris, moved forward again to give me an awkward embrace. I don't know if it was the tension, the hug, or the general ridiculousness of the entire situation, but suddenly everyone was laughing, and for the first time since I'd woken up, I had a feeling that maybe somehow everything would be okay.

I walked them to the door and was turning around with a self-satisfied sigh, when the phone started ringing again. I winced.

"Come on," Cybil said, abandoning her coffee tray and taking my arm. "Let's get out of here. You need a break. And I know just the place to take you."

"What about Waldo?" I shot a look at Anderson, not sure what I should do.

"No worries. I'll find the cat," he said. I started to protest, but he shook his head. "I can handle Mrs. M. if it comes to that. I won't let her haul Waldo away. I promise. Just get out of here."

"But I'm not dressed to go out," I protested, looking down at my jeans. Granted, the jeans were Diesel and my T-shirt was Juicy Couture, but despite the labels, the ensemble was hardly trendsetting.

"You're fine," Cybil said. "Just add a hat and you'll look like every other Manhattan celebrity trying to dodge attention."

She had a point. Cybil wasn't my best friend for nothing. And besides, there was only one thing that could possibly get my mind off the mess I'd made of my life.

"Come on," I said, grabbing my Yankees cap from its hook by the door, ignoring the phone ringing behind me. "Let's go shopping."

Chapter 17

Barneys New York. *660 Madison Avenue (between Sixtieth and Sixty-first streets),*
212.826.8900.

Barneys has been a mecca for discerning fashionistas and clothing connoisseurs
since 1923. As Sarah Jessica Parker once told *Vanity Fair,* "If you're a nice person
and you work hard, you get to go shopping at Barneys. It's the decadent reward."
Barneys stands for taste, luxury, and humor.

—www.barneys.com

Sarah Jessica Parker has it right. Barneys is a
decadent reward. Or, in my case, a decadent escape. Why is it
that you always spend more money when you're on the verge of
losing it, than when you've got an endless supply? It must be
hormones. Or desperation. Either way, in just a couple of hours
I'd dropped a sizable chunk of change on a fabulous Lanvin
Hero bag and an amazing pair of Marc Jacobs Mary Janes. Both
to die for.

And since misery loves company, Cybil had spent money,
too, buying a wonderful Philip Crangi gold cuff bracelet and a
new lipstick from Bobbi Brown. Our shopping urges satiated,

we'd adjourned to Fred's. A ninth-floor restaurant where women go to see and be seen, it wasn't exactly incognito world, but with my cap and jeans I figured I'd be deemed persona non grata and therefore summarily dismissed.

I was wrong.

My mother could recognize me in a gorilla suit.

"Vanessa?" Her voice carried across the entire restaurant. And I swear the temperature in the room dropped thirty degrees. Okay, I know not everyone in the room was looking. But it sure felt like they were. You know that sickly cold prickle that works its way from the base of your spine up to the hairs on your neck? There were definitely snickers. Well-mannered ones, of course, but the intent was the same as if they were pointing their well-manicured fingers.

I met Cybil's gaze, signaling SOS. But there was nothing she could do. It was *my* mother.

"Darling, I thought that was you." She reached out to pluck the Yankees cap from my head. "There now, isn't that better? We can see your eyes."

"That was sort of the whole point, Mother."

"Mind if I join you?" she asked, not waiting for an answer.

I looked frantically at Cybil, searching for a way out, but short of sprinting past the other diners, there didn't appear to be one.

"I wish you'd answered my calls."

"I should have," I assured her. "It's just that I wasn't up to talking to anyone."

"Except Anderson and Cybil." If I hadn't thought it impossible, I'd have sworn she actually sounded hurt.

"They just sort of popped by."

Mother eyed us both for a moment as if considering the idea, and then, with a shrug, reached over to cover my hand with hers. "So how are you?"

"I'm fine." Okay, I wasn't, but it was in the manual somewhere that grown-up daughters are not allowed to run to their mothers for help. Especially when we're talking about my mother. She means well, but the truth is she's practically perfect, and so totally incapable of understanding the varied misadventures of her daughter.

"You're not fine. But at least you're not hiding out in your closet."

It sounded innocuous enough, until you considered the fact that when I was twelve, and Bobby Dormand told everyone at school I'd gotten my period, I refused to come out of my closet for three days. What can I say, I don't deal well with pressure.

"Although, really, when you think about it," she continued, "Barneys isn't all that different from a closet. It's just a little bigger and has more clothes." It takes a certain degree of deeply embedded pedigree to be able to equate Barneys with a closet. Not to mention money. My mother, of course, had both.

"I'm not hiding from anything," I protested.

"Baseball cap not withstanding." She held it up gingerly between two fingers. You'd think it was covered with anthrax or something. "At least you had the sense to bring Cybil along."

As if by mere association, my sin of underdressing could be forgiven.

"Come on, Mother, you didn't follow us to Barneys to lecture me about my outfit."

"Well, actually, I didn't follow you." Her perfectly penciled brows drew together with the denial. "I just happened to be shopping and I saw you in women's shoes."

"Why am I not buying this?" I asked, shooting a look over at

Cybil. She was fighting laughter, and somehow in light of her amusement, my anger faded.

"Because it isn't true." Mother shrugged with the fatalistic air of someone who is perpetually challenged by life. Or more specifically—me. "I talked to Anderson. He said you were coming here."

"Well, the food here is definitely better than in my closet."

"There's no need for sarcasm, Vanessa. I came because I was worried about you."

There was no arguing with that. She *was* worried. I could see it in the tiny lines around her eyes. "I know. And I should have called. It's just that escape seemed the better option."

"From me?"

"No. From everyone else. The phone was ringing nonstop. Even Cybil was getting calls."

"Me, too, I'm afraid. It's seems you're something of a celebrity these days."

"My five minutes of infamy," I said, forcing a smile.

"It's nothing to make light of."

We were spared further conversation for the moment when the waiter approached to take our order. From the looks he kept shooting my way, it was clear he'd either seen the photograph or recognized a mother-daughter powder keg when he saw one.

"I'll have a dry salad," my mother said, "and a Bloody Mary."

Cybil, following my mother's lead, ordered a Bloody Mary and a Caesar salad.

Daring to buck the vegetable-driven solidarity, I ordered crab cakes and, after a moment's hesitation, a martini with two olives. After all, martinis had started this disastrous ball rolling. Maybe a little hair of the dog would make the whole thing go away. Or at the very least, make it more palatable.

In short order the drinks arrived, and after a sip, my mother sat back, ready to begin the inquisition.

"So," she said, with the air of a queen presiding over her court, "where were we?"

"Having a quiet lunch and trying to forget about Vanessa's problems?" Cybil's suggestion was much appreciated but, of course, totally ignored.

"Well, burying one's head in the sand is hardly the way to deal with something this important."

"Actually, Mrs. C., when you put it like that, it sounds a little macabre." Cybil had been calling my mother Mrs. C. since we'd hit puberty and she'd started watching reruns of *Happy Days*. My mother hadn't exactly warmed to the idea, but after a time it sort of caught on among my friends, and she'd grudgingly learned to accept it.

"You know what I mean." She waved her hand, her wedding ring flashing in the light.

"I'm not hiding out or sticking my head in the sand," I said, bringing the conversation back to the subject at hand. "I'm just trying to put a little distance between myself and the tabloids."

"You should have thought about that before you let that man kiss you."

"He didn't actually consult me about it, you know."

She sighed. "I know it's not your fault. But it's still going to be a problem."

"For me. Not for you."

"You're my daughter, Vanessa, if it's happening to you, then it matters to me. And so I want to do what I can to help."

The last thing I needed was for my mother to poke her nose in and make things worse. No matter how well intentioned she was.

"There's nothing you can do."

"I know. And I suppose that's the hardest part. It doesn't matter how old your children get, you want to protect them. Make their pain go away. It's as natural as breathing."

Put like that, it sounded pretty damn wonderful. But I wasn't a kid, and no amount of motherly love was going to make things all right.

"Vanessa?" a familiar voice said. "I thought that was you."

Great, this was turning into a full-blown party.

Belinda Waxman stood beside the table. "I just wanted to come over and see how you're doing."

"Fine," I said, feeling a lot like a fish in a bowl. Or more realistically, a duck in a shooting gallery.

"Really?" she asked, her frown making it perfectly clear that she wasn't buying a word of it.

"Yes. Honestly. I mean I've had better days. But this too shall pass." I smiled brightly, fooling no one at all, but the effort made me feel better nevertheless.

"You and Douglas aren't . . . ," she trailed off, clearly embarrassed.

"God, no." The minute it came out I realized the protestation was a little too strong. I mean, Douglas was a client. "He's marrying Maris."

"So it's still on? I'd heard there were problems."

"Well, if there are, it's nothing to do with Vanessa," my mother asserted.

I shot her a look—chagrin mixed with gratitude—which pretty much sums up our relationship in a nutshell.

"There was a little hitch," I said, returning my attention to Belinda. "That's why I was with Douglas yesterday. But everything's back on track. I talked to them both this morning."

"And the kiss?" Belinda asked, never one to mince words.

"Was simply an overexuberant Douglas saying thank-you."

"You mean an inebriated Douglas," Cybil interjected.

"Well, it all amounts to the same thing. With a little prodding, Douglas was able to overcome his fear of rejection and realize that he didn't want to lose Maris."

"You're a genius."

Both Cybil and my mother worked to cover their laughter. Cybil by starting to cough and my mother, uncharacteristically, by stuffing her mouth with lettuce. I, quite wisely, kept my mouth shut.

"No," Belinda said. "I mean it. First, you fix things between Stanley and me." She reached up to touch the Kipepeo earrings. "And then you make things right for Maris and Douglas. I don't care what the buzz is, I think you're the best."

Okay, I'm not immune to flattery, but there was a big ugly fly in all that sugar. "Buzz?" I asked, holding my breath.

"Oh, you know," she said, suddenly looking uncomfortable, "it's just the usual stuff."

"Come on, Belinda," Cybil said. "Vanessa's a big girl. Just tell us what you've been hearing."

Mother reached for my hand again.

I felt like I was about to be voted off the island.

"It's not anything, really," Belinda said, trying desperately to backpedal.

"Out with it," I said, pulling free of my mother. "Cybil's right. I can handle it."

"All right," she sighed. "Word is that you've not only lost the bet, you've lost credibility. And the scuttle is that Althea is already fielding calls."

"What kind of calls?" Cybil asked, prolonging the moment.

"Clients."

"Mine?" I asked, my voice coming out on a squeak.

"Yes." She nodded. "And then, of course, there's Mark Grayson."

"What are they saying about him?" For some reason my stomach chose that moment to attempt to reject the martini and what was left of the croissants. I laced my fingers tightly and concentrated on the keeping everything down.

"It's just gossip," Mother said. "Most of it with no more credibility than that damn photograph." My mother only curses when she is angry. Maybe she'd really meant what she said about wanting to right my wrongs. At the moment, the idea of a champion wasn't at all distasteful.

"Just that if he's truly interested in the idea of a matchmaker, he'd be better off with Althea."

"Your mother's right," Cybil said. "It's just a bunch of people with nothing else to talk about. There's probably not a kernel of truth in any of it."

"I shouldn't have brought it up," Belinda said. "I'm sorry. But for the record, I agree with Cybil and your mom, and that's what I've been telling anyone who broaches the subject with me."

"No," I said, "I'm glad you told me. Better to know what's being said. It'll give me a leg up on dealing with the fallout." If there was anything left to deal with. Althea might be a friend, but she wasn't a stupid one. And she'd be a fool not to use my misfortune to her advantage. I can't say that I wouldn't have done the same thing if given the chance.

"So far your clients are standing strong," Cybil reminded me, correctly reading my mind.

"Some of them, yes." I shot a grateful smile at Belinda. "But I haven't talked to all of them." I'd actually managed a few calls while Cybil was trying on clothes. And I'll admit, everyone that I talked to had refused to jump ship, even when I'd said I'd understand. So maybe they were right. Maybe it would blow itself out in the wake of something more tantalizing. I mean, that's exactly what I'd be saying if it were someone else in the same predicament.

Only it wasn't someone else. It was me. And currently panic seemed to be winning the day, despite the troops rallying to my side.

My cell phone rang, breaking through my paranoid delusions, and I pulled it from my purse, checking the display before flipping it open.

My heart stutter stepped to a complete stop.

Mother's eyebrows shot up in question, and Cybil tried to peer over my arm at the screen. Belinda, however, had full view of the phone, and she was the one who put them out of their misery.

"It's Mark Grayson."

"Answer it," Cybil said.

"Quickly," my mother added, "before he hangs up."

Something in her tone broke through my inertia and I flipped the phone open. "Vanessa Carlson." I was delighted to hear that my voice actually sounded close to normal.

"When you said compromising, you weren't kidding," he said. Nothing like jumping straight to the point.

"Well, I always try to do my very best." I scrambled for something less flip to say, but nothing came to mind. "Did you call just to give me a hard time?"

His laugh was oddly comforting. "No. Actually I called to see if you're free for dinner."

"Can you hear what he's saying?" Mother asked Cybil, who was closer to the phone. She shook her head, and I shooshed them both.

"Are you sure you're up for it? I seem be a magnet for trouble these days."

"A magnet of your own making, I suspect." I started to argue, but he really did have a point. "But to answer your question, I think I can handle a little innuendo. It's not like I haven't been there before."

"Thanks in part to me."

"So are you free?" he asked again, ignoring my self-deprecation.

I thought about saying no. But then I looked at Cybil. She deserved this. Even if I didn't. "Yes. I'm free."

And just like that, I was back in business again. Althea might have the upper hand for the moment. But my mother was right, tomorrow would yield something juicier than Douglas's drunken kiss.

I just hoped to heaven it didn't involve me.

Chapter 18

Waldorf=Astoria. *301 Park Avenue (between Forty-ninth and Fiftieth streets), 212.355.3000.*

For more than a century, the Waldorf=Astoria has combined luxury with a wealth of amenities and services. This forty-two-story art deco hotel, located in midtown Manhattan, beckons New Yorkers and visitors alike. An official New York City landmark since 1993, the Waldorf=Astoria is synonymous with elegance and grandeur, boasting recent renovations renewing the splendor that has long made it an international icon.

—www.historichotels.org

The Waldorf=Astoria is one of my favorite places. I'm an unabashed fan of everything about the place. From the grand lobbies to the ornately appointed rooms, it embodies my idea of the good life. So when Mark had asked me to meet him there, I'd readily agreed. But when we got on the elevator instead of heading for Oscar's or the Bull and Bear, I had a shiver of concern.

And when the doors opened on the eighteenth floor, my stomach lurched with the elevator. The marbled rotunda was full of people in tuxedos and couture. On the plus side, I'd decided to dress for dinner. Wearing a vintage midnight blue sheath from Oscar de la Renta and rhinestone sandals from Stuart Weitzman, I could hold my own. On the negative side, these were the very people who'd been calling my apartment nonstop. (Anderson had kept a log. It read like a who's who of Manhattan socialites.)

"I thought we were going to dinner," I whispered out of the side of my mouth, simultaneously nodding at Winston and Marjorie Pierce. Just what I needed, an agonizing stroll through the latest incarnation of peacock alley.

"We are," Mark responded, his hand on my elbow as we followed the coiffed and cultured into the exquisitely decorated ballroom.

"Here?" I said, glancing at the milling hoards.

I should stop here to say that the Starlight Roof is a fabulous place. In the thirties, the venue was reputedly one of the most luminous nightclubs in New York. But for more than fifty years its beauty languished behind a modern architectural remuddle. Fortunately, it has been restored to its former art deco glory, complete with two-story damask-covered windows and a fanciful grille that in its heyday retracted to give patrons an unparalleled view of the stars.

Of course, right at that moment, all I could think about were the smirks and whispers that were going to follow me as I walked through the room. "I can't," I said, trying to swallow my panic.

"Of course you can. Just act like you haven't a care in the world."

"Easy for you to say. No one's going to snicker at you."

His hand tightened on my elbow. "And as long as you're with me, no one is going to laugh at you, either."

"How do you figure that?" I snapped, my tone just this side of waspish. "In case you've forgotten, I'm the topic du jour for pretty much everyone in this room." All four hundred fifty of them.

"You certainly seem to have a high opinion of yourself."

"That's not fair. You know how condemning these people can be." Considering a great deal of "these" people were my purported friends, I suppose the comment sounded a bit inane. But that didn't stop me from saying it.

"Yes, I do know," he said, turning so that we were facing each other. "That's why I've brought you here. If people see you with me, then they'll have to assume I've agreed to work with you. And since I'm known for my caution when it comes to business arrangements, it follows that they'll assume that you're on the up-and-up. No flagrant affairs with clients."

It was a brilliant plan. Stunningly simple. To the point. Practically perfect. Except for one tiny little fact. "But you're not working with me." I held my breath—hope springs eternal and all that.

"Yes, but they don't know that."

I nodded, for once totally at a loss for words. On the one hand, his plan had every possibility of saving my reputation. And ergo my business. On the other hand, by agreeing with me, he'd just confirmed the fact that he wasn't interested in a match.

Now, I suppose if I were a better person, I'd have been satisfied with that. But I still wanted to win the bet. And more important, I wanted to prove to Mark that I wasn't all empty talk, that I really could produce exactly what he needed in a wife—Cybil.

"It'll be fine," he said, interpreting my silence as fear. "Just act as if you're having the time of your life. We'll make the circuit, talk to a few key people, and then I'll take you somewhere quiet for dinner."

"Couldn't we just skip to the last bit? I seem to be making a habit of public appearances to fend off innuendo."

"The cancer benefit?" he asked, laughter coloring his voice. "I thought you were there to support your mother."

"I was. Truly. But my mother was the first to point out that it would do me good to let people see that your rather public debasing at Bungalow 8 didn't have me down for the count."

"Hey, I was the one that was cornered."

"I know. And I also know that I should have approached you in a more private setting. And I've said I'm sorry. So hopefully that much at least is water under the bridge?"

"It is." He nodded. "You ready?"

I eyed the glittering crowd, my stomach still churning. "What if they think I'm romancing you *and* Douglas?"

"They won't." This time he didn't try to hide his laughter. "And if they do, then they're too foolish to bother with anyway. Come on."

We stepped into the room and were immediately surrounded with people we both knew. There were polite questions, of course, and the occasional flicker of something in somebody's eyes, but overall everyone was amazingly restrained. Maybe I'd overestimated the impact of the photograph. Or maybe I'd underestimated the power of being associated with Mark Grayson. Either way, it appeared that, for the moment at least, I'd managed to dodge the bullet.

Due in no small part to the man standing beside me. The only thing I still didn't understand was why exactly he was helping me. I mean, it didn't make any sense at all. He didn't strike me as the altruistic type. Noble, maybe. But only for the right cause.

And believe me when I tell you that while I'm the first to

stand up for myself, I don't think a woman hounding a man to sign on for a spouse hunt constitutes a call to nobility. I suppose one could make an argument for the common bond of being stalked by the paparazzi, but when you consider the fact that the commonality is almost entirely my fault, it dies a quick death.

In short, he shouldn't be doing any of this. But I've never been one to slap away good intentions for lack of explanation. I mean, frankly, I needed all the help I could get. And the truth was that when Mark Grayson spoke, people listened. So if he thought swinging from the chandelier would help, I was ready, willing, and able.

Actually, a trapeze act would probably be less stressful.

"Vanessa, will you be all right if I excuse myself for a minute?" The question cut through my tumbling thoughts, and I resisted the urge to shake my head.

"I'll be fine," I lied.

"I just need to tell Bill something." He nodded toward an older man holding court in the corner. I'd known Bill Benson most of my life. A top financier in the city, he and my father went way back.

"No problem," I said, with what I hoped was a careless smile, "I'll just go and get a drink."

"Great," he said, already leaving. "I'll meet you at the bar."

Left on my own, my falsely buoyed courage sagged. I was tempted to pull out my cell phone, but considering I knew pretty much everyone in the room, it really wouldn't have helped all that much. The best thing was to keep moving, and so squaring my shoulders, I pushed through the crowd at the bar and ordered a cabernet.

Then, glass in hand, I took a slow sip and reminded myself that I wasn't some social wannabe. I didn't need to lean on anyone. I had been born into this life, which meant that I knew how to manipulate the game. I could stand on my own two feet, thank you very much.

"Vanessa," someone called.

I turned around, my neck prickling. I knew that voice. Althea.

She emerged from the throng of people, her expression just this side of gloating. My heart fluttered into my throat, and I looked around desperately for moral support. So much for standing on my own.

"I thought it was you." We exchanged air kisses and a sort of limp noodle hug. "You look great." She sounded surprised. Which shouldn't have bothered me, but it did. I glanced over to the corner, where Mark was still deep in conversation, waving his hands to punctuate something he was saying. No reinforcements from that corner. I was on my own.

"Thanks. I'm trying. But this hasn't been the best of days."

"I know," she nodded earnestly. "I've been worried about you."

"Well, I'm fine," I said with more bravado than I'd thought possible. Nothing like a rival to bring on survival mode. "Cybil said you called."

"I didn't want to bother you. I figured you'd be overwhelmed." Buried somewhere in those comforting words was a dig. I was certain of it. Now don't get me wrong, Althea is a lovely person, but she's also tough as nails, and predatory when it comes to her business. So her sudden concern about my well-being was just a tad suspect.

"I was, a little. I mean, you know as well as I do that the papers can be brutal. But I'm better now."

"Well, I'm glad to hear it. And attending a party is the perfect way to elevate one's mood. I haven't seen Douglas and Maris, though, have you?"

Okay, this one wasn't even couched in pretty words. "They're probably at home, engaged in a little makeup sex. Douglas has been forgiven."

"For kissing you?"

I'd walked right into that one. "No. For breaking it off. That's why I was with him yesterday. Maris wanted me to talk to him. To try to figure out what was going on. Seems he'd gotten cold feet. And I helped him realize what he really wanted."

"Maris."

"Exactly. So despite all the scuttle, everything is back on track."

"Well, I'm happy for them," she said, and to give her credit, she really meant it. "But what about you? What are you going to do?"

"About what?" I admit the question was a stalling technique. She was talking about my now tarnished reputation. In the course of two short days, I'd been publicly chastised by Mark Grayson and caught in a lip-lock with Douglas Larson.

"The buzz. I haven't heard all that much, but it's got to be considerable. No?" She asked, her expression almost patronizing.

"It's about what I expected."

"Well, you've got to do something to redeem yourself. As much as I hate to say it, what happens to you happens to me. Albeit without the dire consequences."

And there we had it. The cause for her concern. She was worried about how my antics would affect her business. On a professional level I can't say that I blamed her, but on a personal one it stung. A lot.

"I'm not that worried." Okay, I was lying again, but you try being in my place and admitting your fears to your rival. "You know how it goes. Today's gossip will be forgotten tomorrow in the wake of whatever hits the papers next."

"I suppose that's true, at least in part," she said. "But what about the people who are looking for a matchmaker? Surely you don't think they'll forget?"

I sighed, forcing a smile. "I can't control what they think, Althea. I can only answer to myself. And at the end of the day, although I wish I'd had the foresight to see it coming, Douglas was just saying thank you. A bit overexuberantly, I'll grant you. But if his fiancée doesn't have a problem with it, then I don't see how anyone else can."

"Bravo," she said, nodded her head in agreement. "I just hope you're not underestimating the power of the press." Again with the passive-aggressive digs. But Althea was just being Althea, and I couldn't fault her for that.

"I'll just have to take it as it comes. My clients seem to be okay with it. They all seem to be staying put." They were, actually. Which in and of itself was a small miracle. But then I'd never had much faith in human nature.

"Well, that's certainly a vote of confidence." She reached over to pat my arm. "But I'm just not as sure that new clients, especially the cream of the crop, will be as easy to persuade."

I sighed and fought to keep my voice light. "If you're talking about the bet, then I'm afraid—"

"She's trying to be polite, Althea." Mark appeared suddenly at my elbow, his face a charming mask. "But what she's not telling you is that after much consideration, I've decided to sign on and let her work her magic."

"*You're* Vanessa's client?" Althea asked.

If I could have caught my breath, I probably would have enjoyed the moment more. But if Althea was surprised, I was flabbergasted. I knew I'd captured his interest, but I had no idea he'd decided to come on board.

Emotions rioted inside me. Some of them identifiable, others not. But relief and excitement seemed to be the front-runners. And so when I smiled up at him, the gesture was genuine. "I wasn't certain you wanted to share the news."

"Why not?" he asked, his gaze still locked on Althea. "I'm looking forward to seeing what you've got in mind for me. After all, you do seem to have an in with some of the most beautiful women in Manhattan."

"It's about more than beauty, Mr. Grayson," Althea said, her sharp eyes studying him. If she was looking for a sign of weakness, she was in for a big disappointment. Mark Grayson was one tough customer. In fact, if I hadn't already had someone in mind for him, I'd probably have panicked.

As it was, I still felt a little sick to my stomach, but I knew I would rise to the occasion. Or rather, Cybil would. All I had to do was finalize the details.

"I'm well aware of the fact, Ms. Sevalas," Mark responded. "What I should have said is that Vanessa has access to some of the most interesting and well-connected women in the city."

"The single ones, anyway," I chirped, sounding like a Barbie doll on amphetamines. There was something decidedly uncomfortable about the way Mark was looking at Althea. "And Althea knows just as many as I do. Really."

"So what? Now you're trying to tell me to go with the competition?" There was a teasing note in his voice, and an implied intimacy that I wasn't sure what to do with. Most likely part of his effort to put me at ease and one-up Althea. I wasn't sure why he was going to such lengths to protect me, but I damn sure wasn't going to argue about it.

"Absolutely not." I smiled up at him. "I was just pointing out that Althea is very good at what she does."

"Yes, but not as good as you are." This time his voice carried, and I realized that the people around us were listening. "And

now, Althea, if you'll excuse us, we've got a dinner reservation."
He didn't wait for her to answer, just put his hand in the small
of my back and propelled me forward.

"Lots of details to work out," I called behind me, suppressing
a laugh at Althea's open-mouthed astonishment.

"That was rather heavy-handed of you," I said as soon as we
wore alone in the elevator.

"Do you want me to take it back?" he said, lifting an eyebrow.

"No. Of course not. I'm delighted that you've decided to let
me find you a match. But I thought maybe you were just saying
it, you know, to defend me in front of Althea." I can't explain it
exactly, but the idea appealed to me somehow. My latent fairy-
tale princess syndrome rearing its ugly head.

"Let me assure you that I never do anything I don't want to
do." It wasn't a diss or anything, but it had the same effect, the
Cinderella in me sinking mercifully back into my deeply buried
subconscious.

"Well, whatever the reason, you really helped me in there.
And not just with Althea. You were right, facing it head-on was
really great. Especially with you by my side." It came out sounding really sappy, and I looked down at my shoes feeling particularly stupid. "Okay, that didn't come out right. I just meant
that—"

"I'm glad I could help," he said, his formality making me feel
even more awkward. Fortunately the doors opened to an older
couple clearly staying at the hotel. Both were dressed in that
understated way that screamed money. Everyone exchanged polite nods and then we all rode down in silence.

The doors slid open to the lobby and I stepped out with a
strange sense of relief. "Are we still going to have dinner?" I
asked, trying to find center. There was something about the

man that threw me off-kilter. Or maybe it was just his unexpected kindness.

"Yes. Unless you'd prefer to go home. I know it was hard for
you up there."

"No, I'd like to go. I mean, it should only get easier from
here." Famous last words. "Right?"

Before he could answer, my cell phone chimed at me from
the confines of my evening bag. "Do you mind? I really should
get it."

He nodded and discreetly moved a few paces away. Whatever else he was, Mark was a class act.

"Hello?"

"Vanessa." It was Lindy Adams. "Thank God. I was afraid
you'd be out."

"Well, actually, I am," I said, realizing as the words came out
that Lindy sounded like she was on the verge of tears.

"Oh, I—"

"Lindy, it's all right. I'm never too busy to talk to you. Is this
about Devon?"

"Sort of. But it's not what you think. I'm afraid we're in a
little bit of trouble." She was rushing now, as if she was trying to
get the words out before someone cut her off.

"Are you okay?" My tone must have alerted Mark, because
he moved back within listening range, his expression full of
concern.

"Yes, I'm fine—physically. But we're . . . well, we're in a bit of
a jam. I didn't know who to call and they only let you dial once."

"Lindy, where are you?" I asked, alarm bells resounding in
my head.

"I'm—" I heard a whispered male voice in the background,
and then the static of the phone being transferred.

"Vanessa, it's Devon. I'm afraid we've been arrested."

"What?"

"It's hard to explain on the phone, but suffice it to say that Lindy was following your suggestion."

"What?" Apparently I had use of only one word.

"Vanessa, we're counting on you. We need someone to bail us out."

My head was spinning as I tried to make sense of what he was telling me. "You need bail money?"

Mark lifted his finger to his mouth, and I realized that my pronouncement had just echoed through the Waldorf's oh-so-exclusive lobby. The elevator couple shot a glance our way, the woman dismissive, the man condemning.

I blew out a breath and lowered my voice. "Look, I'm sorry to sound like a nit, but you've just thrown me for a loop."

"Believe me, it's nothing compared to how we feel. Anyway, given the circumstances, Lindy felt it best to call you." I could tell he wasn't in complete agreement, but considering I'd apparently led them to a life of crime, I suppose he had a point. "Can you come and get us?"

"Of course. I'll be there as soon as I can." I started to hang up and then realized I had no idea where to go, but fortunately Mark was more clearheaded. He pulled the phone out of my hand.

"Mark Grayson here. We need to know where you are."

I assumed Devon managed to impart the information, because he said something about not worrying and hung up the phone.

"Where are they?"

"The 19th Precinct," Mark said, his hand against my back again as we moved toward the revolving door. "Do you want to tell me who I was talking to?"

"Devon Sinclair and Lindy Adams. They're clients."

"In jail?"

"Yes. Although I can't imagine why. Devon works on Wall Street and Lindy is a fabulous girl."

"Well, that explains everything." His tone was dry but not condemning.

"Listen, I'm sorry to pull you into this." He must have thought I was a magnet for trouble. "I'll just get a taxi and be on my way."

"Absolutely not. I'm going with you."

"But—"

"No arguments," he said. "I've got a driver, so it'll be faster."

He had a point. Besides, if I was really honest, I didn't want to face the station house on my own. I had no idea what kind of trouble Lindy and Devon were in, but clearly if they needed bail money, it wasn't just a parking ticket.

Mark's driver opened the door, and I slid into the car. Mark followed suit, and after leaning forward to give the man instructions, he sat back, his smile wry. "I'll say one thing, Vanessa, life certainly isn't dull when you're around."

I wanted to respond. Something pithy, with the proper edge. But I couldn't find the words. The truth was that two people I cared about had been arrested for something I somehow had managed to set in motion.

It wasn't a pretty picture. I mean, what kind of matchmaker sends her clients to the big house?

Chapter 19

19th Precinct. *NYPD, 153 East Sixty-seventh Street (between Third and Lexington avenues), 212.452.0600.*

The 19th precinct is a busy place, with more robberies than any other precinct in the city. It's home to haute couture on Madison, coveted residences on Park and Fifth, the bric-a-brac of billionaires at Sotheby's, Gracie Mansion . . . and also Pale Male and Lola, the two peregrine hawks who made their own love nest at 927 Fifth Avenue.

—www.kathleenoreilly.com

So with a payload guaranteed to make the most discerning burglar's day, you'd think that the men in blue would have other more pressing things to do than arrest Lindy and Devon. Of course, I wasn't sure what exactly they'd been arrested for, so I guess I shouldn't have been jumping to conclusions, but honestly, I couldn't imagine Lindy ever doing anything illegal. She's just not the type.

Mark's driver pulled up outside the redbrick building, its blue trimmed windows and doors making it seem almost cheerful, even in the half-light of the street lamps on Sixty-seventh. The building itself, dating back to 1887, is a lovely testament to turn-of-the-century Manhattan.

The inside of the building wasn't as charming as the outside, but there were hints of the past, in the high ceilings and lou-vered doors. But I wasn't here to admire the architecture. With Mark on point, we were quickly escorted upstairs to the room where Lindy and Devon were being held. At least they weren't in lockup.

"Vanessa," Lindy said, flying across the room to throw herself in my arms, "thank God you're here."

I glanced at Devon over Lindy's shoulder, but he just shrugged, refusing to meet my eyes. "So what happened?" I pushed away from Lindy, searching her face. "How in the world did you wind up here?"

"Well, it's my fault really . . . ," Lindy began.

"What about him?" Devon, interrupted, frowning at Mark.

"This is Mark Grayson. You talked to him on the phone."

"I know who he is," Devon said, "but why is he here?"

"He gave me a lift. And he managed to get us up here to see you with a minimum of fuss. So I wouldn't complain if I were you."

"I'm not complaining, I'm just not sure I want Lindy airing our dirty laundry in front of a stranger."

"He's not a stranger," I snapped. "He's my . . . ," I trailed off, realizing I wasn't exactly certain what Mark was to me. As of an hour ago he was a client and quite possibly I could call him a friend, but somehow neither word seemed exactly right.

"I'm here to help," Mark said, coming to my rescue. "It's as simple as that."

Devon nodded, but didn't look all that enthused. In fact, if I had to describe it, I'd say he had the look of a teenager caught

egging the headmaster's house. (Not that I have personal experience, mind you. It was an apartment balcony, not a house, and
I didn't throw anything; I was just along for the ride.)

"Look, we're wasting time talking about this," I said, picking
up the thread of the conversation. "I can't do anything until I
understand what happened."

"Lindy took your advice," Devon said, his tone a mixture of
contrition and defiance.

"What advice?" I asked, addressing them both.

"I watched *Grease*," Lindy said, crossing the room to take a
seat across from Devon, her composure restored.

"The movie?" I scrambled madly to make sense of the statement, but for the life of me I couldn't see anything illegal about
watching a movie.

"You said I should be like Sandy."

I stared at her blankly, trying to remember.

"At Bungalow 8, remember?"

It came to me in a rush. Devon. Wandering eye. New and
improved Lindy. "I remember. But I'm not seeing the connection between the musical and the NYPD."

"Well, I thought that if I changed my appearance, like she
did in the movie . . ." She shot a look at Devon, who first glared
at Mark and then nodded reluctantly.

Lindy opened her coat, and it was all I could do not to gasp. It
was Victoria's Secret revealed in full-on Technicolor. I shot a look
at Mark, but bless him, he was staring intently at the ceiling. The
outfit, if you could call it that, covered only the most strategic
places. Put it this way, if Danny Zuko had seen Sandy in that
getup, the movie would have had an entirely different rating.

Which begged the question. "Okay, I'll admit it's a risqué
outfit, but how exactly did it land you both in jail?"

Lindy closed her coat, wrapping it tightly around her. "Well, I was planning to surprise him at work. You know, arrive at his office and give him a hint of what he had to look forward to. I was just trying to show him that I could be as sexy as the other girls." Fresh tears filled her eyes, and Devon reached for her hand, remorse coloring his expression.

"But I wasn't there," Devon said, with a wince. "I was uptown at my chiropractor's office."

"And I thought . . . ," she sniffled, "well, I thought that I could just surprise him there."

"You wore that to his chiropractor's?" I asked, trying to get a handle on exactly what she was saying.

"Well, I had on the coat." In any other city it would have been insane, but for Manhattan so far it was actually pretty tame. "So when I got there, Devon was still in with the doctor, so I took a seat to wait. And when he came out . . ."

"You flashed the office?" I asked, knowing full well that the answer was going to be far worse than that.

"No. Of course not." For someone wearing less than a foot of silk and lace, she managed to sound pretty damn indignant. "I waited until we were in the elevator."

"The elevator?" It was the first time Mark had said anything, and he sounded alarmingly like my father after one of my bone-headed moves.

"It was empty," Devon said, as if that made everything all right. But we weren't sitting in the 19th Precinct for nothing.

"I just meant to give him a peek," Lindy said. "You know, to give him something to think about."

She was giving me something to think about, and I didn't appreciate the pinup pictures popping into my head.

"It was quite a peek." He swallowed uncomfortably, his fingers tightening on hers. "I thought it was a commercial building.

And it was late, I figured everyone had gone home." He was practically squirming in his seat.

"Go on, just tell us," I urged, although I already had a pretty good idea where we were headed.

He sighed. "I just kept seeing her in . . . well, that . . ." He waved at the raincoat, intimating the garb, or lack thereof, underneath. "And one thing led to another, and we, um . . . well, we sort of . . . got into the moment, if you follow my drift."

It didn't take much imagination, actually, and well, put it this way, it was something I'd just as soon have kept out of my mind, thank you very much, and from the look on Mark's face he was feeling very much the same. However, I knew I had to soldier on, so I bit my bottom lip, striving for something akin to dispassion, and asked the key question. "What I don't understand is how *that* led to *this*?" I waved at the room in general as if the gesture itself would yield answers.

"We didn't think to stop the elevator," Lindy said.

The picture dancing around my head took on new proportions as I anticipated the rest of what she was going to say. Mark coughed into his hand, I think to hide laughter, but I didn't dare look at him, as I was in danger of losing it myself.

"And when it opened, there were, um," Lindy paused, still staring down at her hands, "witnesses."

"Underage ones." Devon had lost all signs of indignation, instead looking very much like he'd like the floor to open and swallow him whole.

"How underage?" Mark asked, his countenance under control again.

"Nine and eleven. Apparently there are apartments in the building." He released his breath on a sigh. "And a rather refined woman and her grandchildren were on their way to dinner."

"How bad was it?" I asked, not certain I wanted to hear the answer.

"Put it this way," Devon said, "they got a whole new meaning for the name Pale Male."

There were certainly parallels. Pale Male was the famous hawk who lived, and loved, on a building on Fifth.

Mark was coughing again.

"So I'm assuming the grandmother is the one who called the police?"

"Yes," Lindy said. "Apparently we didn't notice the doors opening as quickly as we could have. It was nothing short of a high-rise peep show, I'm afraid."

"She actually threatened a civil suit," Devon said, still not quite meeting my eyes.

"Let's tackle one thing at a time," Mark cautioned, his tone all business now. "What are the charges here?"

"Indecent exposure and something about soliciting a minor?"

"I don't think I even want to know how the latter occurred," I said, my mind already presenting various options, none of them good.

"It was a misunderstanding," Lindy said. "I swear it. I only wanted to comfort the child, I don't know how the woman could possibly have thought that I was . . . well, you know, interested in him." She shivered at the memory and Devon pulled her into his embrace.

"It all happened really fast. One minute we were scrambling for clothing and the next the grandmother had called the police."

"It's all so horrible," Lindy said. "I'd never do anything to hurt a child."

"I'm sure they know that," Mark assured her. He really was a nice man. "It's just that it was traumatic for everyone and the woman had no choice but to call the police."

"And they had no choice but to book us," Devon said, shaking his head. "And of course, now there's a question of bail."

"I don't think that'll be a problem. I suspect they're just trying to teach you a lesson. I can't imagine for a minute that they're really going to go through with this. It's clear that you're both remorseful. And I suspect once the grandmother has had a chance to cool off, she'll see that pressing charges isn't really going to accomplish anything."

"And if she doesn't?" Lindy asked.

"Then we'll find a good lawyer. It's not the best situation in the world, but it's not overtly criminal, either. Let's just wait to cross that bridge until we get to it. Right now, I'll go and see about posting bail."

"I should do that," I said, my mind still reeling. "I mean, after all, I seem to have set this whole thing in motion. If only I'd never mentioned *Grease*."

"As I recall," Mark said, shooting another reproving look at Lindy and Devon, "there were no naked people in *Grease*. And certainly nothing to inspire that particular kind of elevator gymnastics. You stay here. I'll be right back."

"I'm really sorry," Lindy said. "I saw the papers this morning, I know this is the last thing you needed today."

"It's fine," I said, shaking my head, either to disagree with my own statement or perhaps in dismissal of the entire fiasco-laden day. "I'm just glad I could help. Although Mark is really the one you should be thanking." That was an understatement, of course. He'd been absolutely amazing. Not only taking appropriate action, but refraining from comment as the story unfolded.

"We didn't mean to hurt anyone," Devon said. "We just got sort of carried away."

"Well, hopefully, your witnesses will see it that way. Especially the one old enough to fully comprehend what was happening."

"You don't think this will make the papers, do you?" Lindy asked, her voice trembling. "My family would be so horrified."

"That's not going to be a problem," Mark said, striding back into the room. "I talked with the arresting officer, and I was right, the woman doesn't want to press charges. It'll only make it worse on the kids."

"So we're free to go?" Devon asked. "What about the bail?"

"There wasn't any. Only a fine. And I paid it. That way you won't have to make a court appearance."

"We'll pay you back," Devon said.

"You sure as hell will," Mark was back to channeling my father, "and I assume you've learned that it's best to keep that kind of seduction confined to the privacy of the bedroom?"

"Maybe not even that," Lindy said, wrapping her coat more tightly around her.

"We'll keep it private from now on. I can promise you that." Devon slid an arm around Lindy, the "we" sounding positively possessive. While I didn't condone the methodology, I applauded the results. Lindy may have set out to seduce Devon, but it was the backfire that had cemented their relationship. It was going to be all right.

And I was never going to work with twentysomethings again.

We hustled them out of the building, relieved to see that the sidewalks were blessedly free of the press. Mark hailed a taxi, and the two of them slid inside, safe and sound, and relatively unharmed.

"Did the grandmother really refuse to press charges?" I asked as we watched the cab pull away.

"Well, it took a phone call and a little persuasion," he admitted, signaling to his driver that we were ready.

"You really are amazing," I said as the black Lincoln pulled up to the curb. "I don't know what I'd have done if I'd had to deal with it on my own."

"You'd have figured out how to handle it," he answered, his smile warm. The driver opened the door, and I hesitated.

"I really should let you go. You've done enough already. I mean, first you rescue me and now you've done the same for two of my clients. It's really above and beyond. I can see myself home."

"Don't be ridiculous. Besides, we haven't eaten yet, and I promised you dinner."

Some part of me wanted to say no. I'm not sure exactly why, considering I'd been all but stalking the man for the past week, but suddenly I felt shy. Still, I hadn't had the chance to tell him about Cybil, and instinct said I should close the deal before he had a chance to think about it all and have second thoughts.

On the other hand, I might be better off just calling it a day. I hadn't exactly been working at the top of my game of late, and I really didn't need another incident. So instead of making a decision, I stood on the sidewalk like an idiot.

I think, quite honestly, that I might have stood there all night, but fortunately for us both, Mark was not so indecisive. "Get in. You need to eat."

Suddenly I realized he was right. I was absolutely starving. "Okay," I said more to myself than to Mark. "Let's go. I'm famished."

I got into the car, settling into the warm leather with a sigh.

It had been quite a day. Mark was quiet for the ride, and I was grateful, I needed a moment to gather my wits.

The lights of Manhattan whizzed by as we drove down Sixty-seventh and turned onto Park, the elegant facades of the buildings almost regal. We passed the Regency, and the Waldorf, and St. Bartholomew's, the church's spires awe-inspiring as they reached into the night sky. Then we drove around Grand Central and down into the Murray Hill Tunnel, coming out at Thirty-third.

This part of the avenue was busier than its uptown counterpart. People were out, enjoying a night in New York. The car pulled up to the curb at Twenty-seventh, and Mark helped me out. "It's just a short walk," he said, breaking the silence, and I nodded, content just to follow along.

The restaurant, i Trulli, was warm and welcoming, the smell of garlic and wine and cheese comforting in the way only good food can be. We wound our way past late-night diners, out to a tree-canopied garden, and I felt all the tensions of the day melting away.

"This is fabulous," I said, accepting the glass of wine the waiter offered. "Just what I needed. How did you know?"

"It's one of my favorite places, and I figured that after the Waldorf, you'd want someplace quiet to unwind. I hadn't counted on our excursion to the 19th Precinct, but I called while we were there to let them know we were only delayed."

"Well, it's perfect," I sighed, taking a sip of the wine.

"Try the bread. The butter is whipped with ricotta cheese. It probably isn't diet-friendly, but it's damn good." He took a slice and slathered it with butter, my mouth watering with every pass of the knife.

He handed it to me and I bit in, closing my eyes with pleasure. "You're right," I said, swallowing. "It's fabulous. Is the rest of the food this good?"

"Better," he answered, opening his menu.

The waiter arrived, and while Mark ordered, I tried to narrow down my choices. It wasn't easy because everything looked wonderful, but I finally decided on the cavatelli, little dumplings with broccoli rabe and almonds. The waiter hurried away, and I sat back with a sigh.

"Long day." It was a statement not a question, and I nodded my agreement.

"You really are full of surprises," I said, realizing that for the first time since making the bet, I was actually feeling contented. As if everything was right with the world. Of course, it was probably just the calm before the storm.

"How so?" Mark asked, pouring himself some more wine.

"Well, this, for starters. But it's more than that. I mean, two days ago you were telling me to get lost, and then you call me out of the blue for a fabulous dinner in a building every New Yorker would kill to see the inside of. And then today you go out of your way to help me and then my clients. Why?" Okay, never look a gift horse in the mouth. I know the saying, but I was really curious.

"I guess the real answer is that you're full of surprises, too. You're not what I thought you'd be at all."

"What does that mean?" I asked, realizing how neatly he'd managed to flip the conversation from him to me.

"Just that you're an interesting dichotomy. On the one hand, you believe fervently in arranged marriages. Or, as you put it, a controlled form of intimacy. But on the other hand, you care so passionately about your clients and friends that you'd do almost anything for them."

"How can you possibly know that?" I asked, intrigued and sort of freaked out all at the same time. I work really hard to keep my emotions in check. I mean, in my business they're a detriment. I can't afford to care.

"I've seen you in action." He smiled and reached for another piece of bread.

So maybe I was more transparent than I thought. Or maybe he was just particularly insightful. Either way, I didn't really relish the idea of being under the microscope, better to move the topic to something less personal.

"I'm just doing my job. And on that note, I think I have someone you might be interested in."

His frown was so fierce, I thought maybe I'd misunderstood. "You haven't had second thoughts?"

"Not as long as you haven't." His expression was still intense, but not as angry.

"Why would I change my mind?" I asked, not certain that I was following his train of thought. "I've been pursuing you for almost a week."

"Yes, you have," he said. "And you've got me. I guess I just didn't expect you to produce someone so quickly."

"Well, I don't always move this quickly."

"So what's different about me?"

"I just want the best for you. And I think Cybil fits the bill."

"Your friend? She's on your list?"

"No, actually, she's not. It's just that the two of you have a lot in common, and she's just broken up with her on-again-off-again boyfriend, and so the timing is perfect."

"But she's rebounding. Surely that's not the best criterion for a prospective match?"

"Usually I'd agree with you. But this is different. I told you last night, Cybil's really special, and she deserves someone who can appreciate the fact. And I think that person is you." Funny, in saying it out loud, I suddenly wasn't as certain as I'd been before, but it really didn't matter. It was up to the two of them now.

"Well, I appreciate your vote of confidence, but shouldn't I be signing a contract or paying you first? After all, you're not running a charity service."

I laughed and reached for my glass. "Absolutely not. In fact, you'll find that I'm quite expensive."

"So maybe we should hold off on the date thing until we get everything squared away."

"I'm not worried. I know you're good for it. And besides, after everything you've done for me, I owe you one."

He nodded, but I could see that he was still troubled.

"Look, Mark," I said, "it's perfectly normal to be nervous about this kind of thing. I mean, everyone wants to believe that they'll fall in love and live happily ever after. And if, by chance, they've avoided that fantasy, then our culture will inundate them with the idea until they capitulate. But the truth is that most people need a little help. And that's where I come in."

"I'm not nervous," he said, shaking his head, but I could still see the concern in his eyes.

"You'll love Cybil. I promise. She's amazing."

"I'm sure she is." Again I was surprised at his lack of enthusiasm. But then most of my clients were a bit hesitant in the beginning.

"I told you that we were best friends, but she's a lot more than that. The Baranskis come from old money. They've been in New York for practically ever. So it would be easy for Cybil to coast, but she hasn't. She's managed to make her life a success without falling back on her family's reputation."

"So what does she do?" he asked, nodding at the waiter as he set our food in front of us.

"She's a columnist. Works for Rupert Murdoch. I think she's syndicated in something like three hundred dailies, and a dozen or so weeklies. She's had articles in *People* and *Glamour.* And she even made the cover of *Time Out New York*."

"How did she handle all the things that have been happening to you?" His frown now seemed less aggravated.

"She helped a lot, actually. She ran interference for me after the debacle in Bungalow 8. The press could have been a lot more vicious, but she called in a lot of markers to help contain the damage."

"But not with the photograph?"

"She's used pretty much everything she had. The best she could do there was tell the real story in her column. But in all honesty, I'm not sure how much that helped. I mean, anything she says is suspect since she's my friend. But it's the thought that counts, right?"

"Sounds like you're lucky to have her."

"I am. And you'll see what I mean when you meet her."

He cut a piece of the veal he'd ordered. "So how does this work?"

"The old-fashioned way," I said, forking a mouthful of pasta. "You call her and ask her out."

"I see," he said. "I guess I thought you'd be there to run interference."

"I hardly think that's necessary. And besides, nothing kills a mood more than a third wheel."

"Well, it isn't as if I'm going to romance her, right? I mean, this is just a business arrangement."

He was twisting my words and throwing them back at me. "I don't think a little romance would hurt. I mean, after all, you want to make a good impression."

"So give me her number."

I was surprised he'd surrendered so easily. For some reason I'd expected more of a fight. And, equally alarming, I was actually disappointed. I fumbled in my purse for a pen, trying to analyze my scattered emotions. Cybil and Mark *were* perfect for each other. I was never wrong about this sort of thing.

So why was I suddenly feeling hesitant? Fallout from a very trying day, no doubt. I shrugged it off and wrote Cybil's contact information on the back of one of my business cards. "Here you go."

"Shall I call her now?" he asked, pulling out his cell phone.

"No. We're in the middle of dinner." The protest seemed ridiculous. It wasn't as if he couldn't eat and talk on the phone all at the same time. "Besides, I want to give Cybil a heads-up."

"You haven't told her about this?"

"Of course I have. And she's delighted at the prospect of getting to know you." Okay, I was exaggerating slightly, but she had agreed. And once they'd gone out, they'd both see that I was right. "But she doesn't know that you've signed on."

"Well, if I were a betting man," he smiled, "I'd put big money on Althea telling anyone who'd listen that you've managed to snag me as a client."

"I think you'd lose that one. Making it public would only make Althea look bad."

"Well, someone else then. There were a lot of people at the Waldorf tonight, and news travels fast."

"Well, either way I want to talk to Cybil first. So why don't you wait until tomorrow to call?"

"Fine," he said, putting the phone away. "We'll do it your way."

My way was actually totally suspect. I didn't need to talk to

Cybil first. When Mark called, she would be more than capable of connecting the dots. So the real question here was why in the world I wanted the delay?

This was exactly what I wanted. A professional coup and a deliciously happy friend all rolled together into a single white wedding. And yet, I'd just told Mark to wait. Clearly, I was losing my mind.

Chapter 20

Park Avenue Floratique. *368 Park Avenue South (corner of Twenty-sixth Street), 800.472.7528.*

Skilled in the latest forms of contemporary floral design, our award-winning team of floral designers can create a dramatic floral creation that will delight the mind and touch your soul. . . . For those who are not content with the ordinary.
—www.parkavenuefloratique.com

I adore flowers. Just walking by the window of a florist or the corner bodega's flower display lifts my spirit. And I'm an equal-opportunity flower lover. For me a daisy or a carnation is every bit as delightful as an orchid or a rosebud. I've been known to buy three bouquets at a time from a stand on Lex just to fill my apartment with the glorious riot of color.

And even though I'm not hesitant to buy my own flora, I like it even better when I arrive in my lobby to find a beautiful arrangement waiting to surprise me. Bearing that in mind, you can imagine how delighted I was when Harry, our concierge,

told me that the exquisite crystal vase of lilies, roses, and irises
was for me.

The creamy envelope indicated that the flowers had come
from Park Avenue Floratique, a fabulous shop on Park Avenue
South. I'd used them myself on occasion. But oddly, what excited me more was the fact that they weren't that far from i
Trulli. Okay, I know that it shouldn't matter at all, but the idea
that Mark Grayson had sent me flowers was pleasing in ways I
couldn't even put a name to.

I shot Harry a smile and slid a finger under the envelope flap.
The card was short and to the point.

*Congratulations, you've hooked the fish. Now let's see if you can land
him. —Althea*

It was a backhanded compliment at best, at worst another
passive-aggressive jab. Fish and flowers did not a pretty picture
make. And to imply that Mark Grayson was a fish. Well, the
idea was ludicrous. Of course, she was right about one thing. In
order to win the bet, I did have to marry the man off.

But I had a secret weapon—Cybil. And things were already
well under way. The hard part had been getting him on board in
the first place. And I'd managed it. Although to be honest, I
wasn't completely sure how. Still, the point was the game was
on. And I was up to the task. I was a matchmaker after all. I had
instincts about these things. Mark and Cybil were a match made
in heaven. Or more realistically a match made on Madison.
And frankly in Manhattan they were sort of one and the same.

"Thanks, Harry," I said, picking up the vase with renewed
vigor.

"Someone special?" he asked with a knowing smile.

"In a roundabout way. Let's just say they're a sign that things are looking up."

Famous last words.

The door to my apartment was open. Most people would immediately fear a burglary. I thought immediately of my cat. Now, before you start thinking that I'm a moron for not running for the elevator while dialing 911, you have to understand the kind of building I live in. Fort Knox isn't as well fortified. There's a doorman, a concierge, a security guard, and enough security cameras to put together a montage of the entire building. Add to that a live-in super, a gaggle of porters, and an army of maintenance men, and you'll begin to have a picture of how safe I really am.

Not only that, Richard and Anderson are right next door.

Or not.

I stopped in the doorway, clutching my flowers, staring into my living room with something akin to complete and absolute terror. No, it wasn't an ax-wielding, fake fireman rapist. It was Mrs. M., and she didn't look happy. And sitting right next to her was Leo Walderstein, president of the co-op board.

Reinforcements in the form of Anderson and Richard were the only thing that kept me from turning tail and fleeing. Dorothy needed her friends, too. In fact, if it hadn't been for the Cowardly Lion's courage, she'd probably have been toast, or gingerbread, or whatever it is that witches turn you into.

I blew out a breath and stepped inside. "So what's happening here? A last-minute board meeting? If I'd have known, I'd have ordered refreshments." Anderson shook his head, Richard smiled, and Mr. Walderstein's face twitched. But Ms. M. was not amused.

"What have you done with my baby?"

"Excuse me?" I said, still holding my flowers, trying to work out exactly what was going on.

"Arabella has gone missing," she said, as if that explained everything.

"And you think she's here?" I shot a questioning look in Richard's direction. I was a lot of things, including the owner of the feline equivalent of Don Juan, but I wasn't in the habit of stealing other people's pets. The one I had was clearly more than enough.

"Actually, we've searched the apartment," Anderson said, his tone apologetic. "Waldo's gone, too, I'm afraid."

"Again? Did you check the garbage room?" Anderson had snagged him from the recycling bin just that morning. Waldo has a decided penchant for slightly used food, particularly when it contains milk products. Yogurt, sour cream, you name it, Waldo craves it.

"He wasn't there."

"So you think they've eloped?" I couldn't help myself.

"This isn't funny." If Mrs. M.'s gaze were lethal, then I would most certainly have expired on the spot.

"No, of course not." I shook my head and walked over to put the flowers on the table.

"Secret admirer?" Richard asked.

"No. Althea. Congratulating me on securing Mark Grayson as a client." In the face of the assembled company, it suddenly didn't seem such a big deal.

"I realize it's a bit imposing for us to have come in without you," Mr. Walderstein said. He is one of those rail thin, stoop-backed men who walk as if they carry the world upon their shoulders. He'd inherited the presidency when Minerva Baker stepped onto an elevator that was unfortunately sixteen floors below her. Thank you, Otis Elevators. I'd often dreamed of luring Mrs. M. to the same fate. All it would have taken was a bottle of Chanel N° 5.

But of course Mr. Walderstein's first official act had been to get the elevators renovated and rewired. So it was sadly nothing more than a fantasy. Okay, I'm not sadistic, I swear. It's just that wicked witches are supposed to get theirs. And there were no buckets of water in sight.

Anyway, I digress. Mr. Walderstein was standing now, nervously lacing his fingers together. Thanks to the fact that everyone in the building feared Mrs. M., no one wanted to be on the board, and certainly not take on the role of president. So I suspected Mr. Walderstein was in it for life.

Poor little man.

"It's fine. I'm sure you did what you thought best," I said, looking first at Mr. Walderstein and then with a sympathetic glance to Richard and Anderson. I'm sure they had far better things to do than protect my humble abode from Mrs. M.'s hysteria-driven hunt.

"I want you to tell me where they are. Now," Mrs. M. said, her red lips pursing in anger. Years of smoking had given her radiating lines around her mouth, her current expression only magnifying the effect.

"I don't know. And in your current state, I'm not sure I'd tell you if I did." I've always managed to let my temper get the best of me. But really, the woman was intolerable. We were talking about cats, not children, not diamonds, not even a good pair of Manolos.

"Well, I never . . ." Mrs. M. crossed her arms over her bony chest, her frown transferring the wrinkles from her mouth to her forehead.

"Look," I said, trying for a more compassionate tone. "I'm sorry that Arabella is gone, but I didn't have anything to do with it."

"If it wasn't you, it was that . . . that animal of yours."

"Waldo is pretty damn amazing, but I don't think he's mastered the art of picking locks."

She snorted and mumbled something under her breath.

"I searched the entire building. Even got the staff involved," Anderson said.

My heart twisted as I considered for the first time that maybe something awful had happened to him. Waldo was my family. I might bad-mouth his behavior, but I loved him, and the idea that something might have happened to him made my stomach flutter.

"No sign of him at all?" I asked, feeling suddenly bereft.

"Nothing. Richard looked, too." Anderson glanced over at Richard and he nodded, his expression full of remorse.

"We tried," he said, lifting his palms in apology.

"I know you did." Guilt washed through me hot and heavy. I was the one who'd left this morning not knowing where he was. "It was my responsibility. If anyone's at fault, it's me."

"See, I told you she was behind it," Mrs. M. said, looking to Mr. Walderstein for support.

He, of course, had no choice but to nod his head, or she would probably have incinerated the poor guy. Think Uncle Henry—who actually always pissed me off for letting Miss Gulch (no way was she married) take Toto in the first place. I mean, his bluster came way too late for it to have had any real impact.

"I'm not behind anything. I just should have watchd out for my cat."

"Well, at least she's admitting that Walter got out."

"Waldo," Richard and I said simultaneously.

"Whatever." Mrs. M. waved her hand, dismissing me and my cat. "What I'm trying to say is that your cat has kidnapped mine."

"Is that even possible?" I asked, looking to see if anyone else was taking the woman seriously.

Unfortunately, Mr. Walderstein apparently knew which side of the bread his butter was on. "You have to admit, Ms. Carlson, there have been numerous *incidents* involving your cat."

There was truth to that. There was the year he'd single-handedly—or pawedly—managed to knock over the lobby Christmas tree. And then there was the time he snuck out the window and onto Mrs. Smyth's balcony. He'd wound up parading around the building in her unmentionables. "But he's never hurt anyone."

"What about Arabella?" Mrs. M. sniffed. "She'll never be the same again."

"Motherhood certainly has a way of changing everything," Richard offered, only to be greeted by a glacial frown.

"Well, I, for one, think we ought to be out searching for them," Anderson said. "We can sort out what happened after we know that they're all right."

"It's been a long time. Do you think they could have left the building?" Mr. Walderstein asked. "They could be any-where by now."

"They're cats," I said, anger mixing with trepidation. Waldo had never been gone this long before. "They're not likely to have taken a taxi or the F train."

"I heard about a cat who accidentally boarded a plane to France. They sent it home first class," Anderson offered.

"You're not helping," I snapped.

"Sorry," he said sheepishly.

"All right," Richard said, taking charge. "I think we should divide the building into sections and each of us can take one."

Mrs. M. opened her mouth to protest, but closed it again at an almost ballsy glare from Mr. Walderstein. It didn't take long to divide up the floors. I drew the short straw—the basement levels, which included a laundry room, the incinerator (don't even think it), and various other dark and dingy places that house the mechanics of the building.

Oh, joy.

Fortunately, Mrs. M. had joined forces with Mr. Walderstein, and Richard had called the super so that he could access any empty apartments. That left Anderson to team with me, which meant that I had company for my descent into hell.

The basement of our building is old. I mean really, really old. It even predates our building, which has been around since the turn of the century (the one before last). Suffice it to say, it's not someplace where you'd want to spend a great deal of time.

But Waldo was my first priority.

"So if you were Waldo, where would you hide?" Anderson asked.

"Anywhere but here?" I said, turning around the dingy hallway in a circle. Before you start thinking I live in a tenement slum, let me assure you the basement was scrupulously clean. It's just that it was surrounded by dank, dark earth, which meant a certain degree of debris and whatnot accumulated despite the erstwhile efforts of the building staff.

And there was the prospect of rats. No matter where you live in Manhattan, they're always an issue. And the lower you go, the more likely you are to encounter beady eyes and sharp little teeth.

Hey, why do you think I have a cat?

"Waldo?" I called, somewhat timidly. I mean, maybe there

was a rat with the same name, and I really didn't want to be calling him.

"Waldo," Anderson said, with considerably more force. "Come on, kitty."

We waited a moment with the ridiculous notion that he'd answer. But, of course, there was nothing but silence.

"Waldo," we cried again, this time moving into the laundry room. Five dryers and eight washers later, we hadn't had any luck. And judging from the interminable silence of my cell phone, neither had anyone else.

"Mr. Walderstein is right. They could be anywhere."

"So you do think they're together," Anderson said.

"I don't know. I just figure it's too odd for them both to be missing on their own. And Waldo has always managed to be a bit of a troublemaker."

"Maybe he's just trying to take care of his lady love."

"Anderson Wright, you're an unabashed romantic."

"Wouldn't do you a bit of harm to be a bit more that way yourself. One of these days Mr. Right is going to show up at your front door and you're not even going to notice."

"Don't be silly. No one can show up on my doorstep without being announced first."

"And that, my dear, is the whole problem."

Since I had absolutely no idea what Anderson was talking about, I ignored him. "Waldo, come out here this minute," I said, trying to imitate my mother's most authoritative voice. Unfortunately, it didn't work any better on Waldo than it worked on me.

"Shall we tackle the boiler room next?" Anderson asked.

I'd never been in a boiler room in my life, but the word called up images of *The Poseidon Adventure*. You know, spewing oil and fire. Sweaty men without shirts . . . Okay, maybe that's from another movie. "All right," I said, preparing myself for the worst.

Instead of finding brimstone and glowing embers, Anderson opened the door to a hobbit-like living room or study. Made up of castoffs from the building, nothing matched, but the decor took second place to the warm comfy feeling of the place. In the corner, the boiler, which wasn't much larger than a Dumpster, hummed merrily in the background.

There was a battered old rocker and a plaid lounger straight from the fifties. There were tables and books, a couple of hideous lamps, and a gilded mirror that was probably worth money. One man's junk is another man's treasure. Isn't that the way the saying goes? The room was evidence of recycling at its very best.

"Does someone actually live here?" I asked, picturing a street person with secret digs on the Upper East Side.

"No. I think the staff comes here. The mechanics, at least," Anderson said, hands on hips as he looked around the room. "It's actually kind of cozy."

"Puts new meaning to the idea of shabby chic."

"Maybe the trend originated here," he said with a smile.

"Well, if Mrs. M. was chasing after me, I'd certainly consider hiding in here." I moved farther into the room. "Waldo?"

Nothing.

"Waldo?" Anderson said, searching among the accumulated bits and bobs.

"He's not here, either," I said, my heart sinking. It wasn't as if he couldn't take care of himself, it was more that I depended on him. His silent understanding. His warmth. Even the two o'clock in the morning kitty breath as he settled on my pillow to sleep.

"Waldo?" I called, praying for an answer.

Nothing.

Anderson's gaze met mine, and with a sigh I followed him toward the door. Maybe he was in one of the storage rooms.

Behind me the boiler's humming stopped, the ensuing silence heavy.

And then there was a squeak. A tiny, tiny squeak. Followed by Waldo's less melodic meow.

"Did you hear that?" I spun around, eyes searching the room. "Waldo?"

This time his answer was crystal clear.

"He's here," I said, smiling at Anderson. "We've found him."

Anderson called him again, and this time his head poked out from a big calico-lined basket that I actually remembered from the trash room. Someone's abandoned Christmas gift.

"What are you doing in there?" I asked Waldo, half expecting an answer. "We've been worried about you."

Not looking the slightest bit repentant, he ducked down again inside of the basket. Anderson, who was closer, knelt down by the basket. It was tucked into a corner, next to the boiler and a pile of old newspapers. "Well, would you look at that," Anderson said, his tone so full of amazement, I ignored the grimy floor and knelt beside him.

Waldo wasn't actually inside the basket. It had been an illusion. He was sitting just beside it, half-hidden behind the newspapers. Inside the basket lay Arabella, a self-satisfied half smile on her furry white face. And next to her were six mewling balls of fluff.

Waldo and Arabella's kittens.

As if reading my mind, my cat lifted his head, preening in the light from the cast-off lamps. "Waldo's a father," I said, reaching out to touch one of the little kittens. It squeaked and wriggled closer to its mother's warmth.

Anderson flipped open the phone and spread the news, and

soon the boiler room was teeming with humanity. Mr. Walderstein was doing everything but passing out cigars, and Anderson was answering questions from a television reporter who lived in the building. Even my cat, it seemed, was newsworthy.

Mrs. M., predictably, had reacted with scorn and downright revulsion. But then an amazing thing happened. Richard had taken one of the tiny fur balls and laid it in Mrs. M.'s hand. At first, she stared at it as if it were a roach or a slug. But then the tiny creature sucked on her finger, snuggling deeper into the palm of her hand.

If you'll excuse my using yet another cinematic example, it was as if her small heart grew three sizes that day. Make no mistake, I'm sure it'll shrink back as soon as the kittens are old enough to claw up her furniture—I don't keep an upholsterer on speed dial for nothing—but at least for now, she was transformed.

After settling the kittens and the exhausted mother, still in her basket, in Mrs. M.'s apartment, Waldo and I went home.

And it wasn't until the wee hours of the morning, when aforementioned kitty breath roused me from sleep, that I realized I'd forgotten to call Cybil. In fact, for the first time in days, I'd forgotten about the bet. And even more important, I'd forgotten about Mark Grayson.

I reached out to stroke Waldo and slid back into sleep, dreams of marriage and merger mixing with kittens and, oddly enough, the sweet floral smell of Chanel N° 5.

Chapter 21

Just Cats. *244 East Sixtieth Street (between Second and Third avenues), 212.888.2287.*

It's always about the dogs. Dog couture, dog parlors, dog runs, dog, dog . . . dog. Well, sometimes it's all about the cat. With a collection of fabulous feline accoutrements strictly for cats and cat owners, the Upper East Side boasts Just Cats. The perfect place to adopt a new friend, outfit her with only the best, and pick up a few feline-inspired human treasures to boot.

—www.nykatz.net

Okay, call me an overenthusiastic grand-mother, but I wanted to find something special for the kittens. And what better place to do it than Just Cats? The matchmaker of the feline world, they were responsible for pairing hundreds of Manhattanites with their beloved pets.

Not me, of course, since I'm more the abandoned-cat-from-the-shelter kind of girl. But that doesn't mean I don't appreciate a good thing when I see it. And besides, I needed advice. I'd never bought a baby gift for a cat before.

In an effort to kill two birds with one stone, I'd asked Cybil to meet me there. But so far, she was a no-show. Which was most likely explained by the early hour. Thanks to the proud father, I'd woken to a paw patting my cheek with the insistence of a Nuremberg inquisitor.

Fifteen minutes after that (I had to take a shower), I'd followed my jubilant cat over to Mrs. M.'s where we'd been admitted for a viewing with somewhat less disdain than she normally showed us. Still cooing over the kittens, I had to admit the woman had risen to the occasion. Her vet was just leaving, pronouncing all six bouncing babies perfectly healthy.

Leaving Waldo to watch over his brood, I'd woken Richard and Anderson, dragged them to breakfast, eaten way more of a Belgian waffle than I should have, sent them home again to keep an eye on Mrs. M., aroused Cybil (after three phone calls), and insisted she come out to meet me. Not bad for a couple of hours' work.

The shop was full of wonderfully whimsical items for cats and cat fanciers alike. It was almost impossible to decide what to get. I could go the practical route and buy food or litter, or maybe the designer route with one of the lovely little cat baskets. But then they already had one of those.

There were treats of all kinds, and toys that squeaked, squawked, and jingled. Catnip and cat grass, cat coats and cat bowls. I finally settled on six tiny collars, four pink and two blue, each studded with rhinestones that glimmered in the light. Okay, so I'm a sucker for style—even when we're talking about cats.

The shop attendant was just ringing them up when Cybil walked in, looking resplendent in black jeans and an asymmetrical silk sweater she'd bought at Bergdorf's. "You look great," I said by way of greeting, taking the sack of collars.

We walked out into the morning sunshine and down the

street to a Starbucks on Sixtieth. Then, drinks in hand, we went out again, settling onto a bench in front of Bed Bath and Beyond. There's something really nice about Manhattan in the morning. The light is softer, the city seems fresher, and, most important, the inhabitants are mostly in a good mood.

Not that I get to see any of it very often.

Cybil smothered a yawn and had a sip of her latte. "So what was important enough to drag me out at this hour of the day?"

Cybil was even less a morning person than I was. She'd had a boyfriend once in college who was one of those happy rising sorts. You know, the kind who jump out of bed, smile on their faces, ready to start the day. He lasted about three months, and only that long because she couldn't smuggle him into the dorm, except on weekends.

"It so happens I have good news."

"Something beyond the late-night arrival of Waldo's off-spring?"

"That was pretty exciting, actually. Sort of like a good, sappy movie. I mean, it's the first time in the six years I've lived in the building that Mrs. M. was actually nice."

"Kittens have a way of doing that. I mean, isn't there a song about it?"

"Huh?" I frowned and took a sip of my coffee. "Not following that at all."

"You know, noodles, strudels—kittens."

Suddenly Julie Andrews was twirling through my mind. "It's 'whiskers on kittens and warm woolen mittens.'"

"Yeah, that's the one," she said, singing loudly enough for anyone within a five-mile radius to hear.

"Great," I said. "And now everyone on the street is humming it."

She laughed. "Well, there are worse songs. So spill it. What's so important?"

I smiled, a smug self-congratulatory expression on my face. "I got Mark Grayson."

"He's agreed to a match?" Cybil almost choked on her latte, which somehow made the moment even better.

"Yes. And he's calling you today."

"You told him about me? Don't you need to sign contracts or something first?"

"That's almost exactly what he said." I was frowning now. This wasn't the response I was looking for. "But I told him I owed him. And that we'd work out the details later. I figured it was better to get the ball rolling before either of you got cold feet. Is there a problem?"

"No, of course not." Her smile was a little too bright. "It's just that I hadn't expected it to happen so soon."

A lightbulb went off. "You mean you didn't think it would happen at all."

"Well, to be perfectly honest, I didn't think it was likely."

"Thanks for the support."

"It's not you," she said, reaching over to touch my arm. "It's Grayson. And all the adverse publicity the bet has garnered. I just figured he wasn't the kind to offer up his private life by doing something so tabloid-worthy."

"He's not. But matchmaking is more than filler for the tabloids. It's serious business. And I think Mark realizes that. I mean, why else would he have agreed to do it?"

"I don't know," she said, shaking her head. "I'm just surprised he said yes, that's all."

"Well, he did. And now I need you to give it a chance."

"So you can win the bet?"

"No. So you can be happy."

"I am happy," she said. "I was singing friggin' *Mary Poppins* not five minutes ago."

"It was *The Sound of Music*. And besides, one song does not a happy person make." We glared at each other for a couple of minutes and then broke out laughing. You know, the kind that won't stop until it's taken your breath away.

If singing had garnered a little attention, you can imagine what giggling uncontrollably did. But somehow that just made it all that much more hysterical. Finally, with a little help from Starbies, we sobered up.

"You haven't changed your mind?" I held my breath, waiting.

"No," she said, scrunching up her nose. "If it's that important to you, I'll go."

"Fabulous," I said, not feeling anything of the sort. It's amazing to me how your mind can rebel at the most ridiculous moments. This is what I'd been working for since the night of the bet. But here I was again, with that telltale pit of the stomach lurch. Maybe it was fear of failure.

After the week I'd had, that totally made sense.

"He'll be calling sometime today. I asked him to give me time for a heads-up."

"And he really seems interested in this?" she asked.

"I can't imagine why he'd agree to it if he wasn't. You should have seen him last night, Cybil. He was wonderful. First he stood up for me in front of practically everyone we know. And then he cut Althea off at the knees, announcing that he'd decided to give my services a go. And *then*, he bailed me out at the 19th Precinct."

"Hang on." She held up a hand. "He bailed you out?"

"Not in the literal sense. He went with me to help out a client. And, quite honestly, I don't think I could have managed without him. Although he said that I could. That's what's really great about him, Cybil. He makes you feel like you can do anything." I stopped to draw a breath, wondering if I'd maybe laid it on a bit too thick.

"Sounds wonderful," she said with a smile, but I could see something else in her eyes.

"What is it?" We'd been friends since the dawn of time. I knew her every mood. "Something's bothering you."

She leaned forward, her glasses making her eyes appear even bigger than they were. "Are you sure this is what you want?"

"Yes, of course I am. I told you—and in fact, I told him—the two of you are perfect for each other. Like attracts like, remember?"

"Yeah," she said, still eyeing me speculatively. "It's just that you talk about him as if you're the one who's interested."

"Interested in what?" I asked, the answer dawning about two seconds later. "In dating Mark Grayson? Me? There's a laugh. We have nothing in common. Nothing at all. It would never work."

"You're right. I don't know what I was thinking," she said, shaking her head. "Where's he taking me?"

The one-eighty almost left me spinning on the sidewalk. "I don't know. I guess you'll have to wait and see. But he does have great taste in restaurants." Dinner at the Flatiron Building had been fantastic, not to mention i Trulli.

"Then I'll look forward to it," she said, finishing her coffee.

"It'll be good for you to go out again."

"I know you're right—" she said, chewing on the side of her lip.

"But?" I prompted.

"But I still think maybe it's too soon. I mean, it hasn't been that long, you know?"

Her blind loyalty to a man who had dumped her not once but

three times was totally misplaced, but telling her that wasn't going to accomplish anything. "It's just one date, Cybil."

"Two, actually. I know the rules."

"All right, then. Two. But the point is, it's not as if I'm asking you to make a commitment."

"But that's the objective, right?"

"Yes." I nodded, my stomach still rebelling. Maybe it was the coffee. "But only if it's right."

"And you truly believe we're a good fit?"

"I do."

"All right, then. I'm in," she said, tossing her empty cup in the trash. "Although he still has to call."

"He will," I said, giving her a hug. "Shall I come along and help you figure out what to wear?"

"I think I can manage to dress myself," she said with a smile.

"Well, then promise to call me the minute you hear from him."

"I promise," she said, making the universal Girl Scout sign (even though neither of us had actually ever been a Girl Scout). We headed for the corner, waiting for the light to change, Cybil still humming "My Favorite Things." Then the light turned green and we split up, Cybil heading for Sutton Place while I headed crosstown toward the park and home.

It didn't take more than a block or so for my ebullient mood to evaporate. I was entirely too moody. I pulled out my Black-Berry and checked the date. Not premenstrual. But then hormones are a totally fickle lot, striking you down when you least expect it.

I glanced down at my watch. It was still early. Maybe a little shopping would make me feel better. I was only a couple of blocks from Bloomingdale's. *And* Dylan's Candy Bar. Except that if I went there in my present mood, I'd probably consume half the Tootsie Rolls in the place (which is a lot, believe me). Tootsie Rolls have always been a weakness of mine.

Although Bloomingdale's could be just as dangerous. But better my wallet than my waistline. See, I can justify just about anything. And even though I prefer Saks or Bergdorf's to Bloomies, a store is a store, and Bloomingdale's handbag department rocks.

Ignoring Dylan's, I crossed Third and paused in front of the revolving door. I've hated revolving doors all of my life, which is kind of a pain when one lives in Manhattan. Give me a good old push-and-pull door any day. Unfortunately, Bloomies wasn't giving me a choice, and purses were calling. I sucked in a breath, stepped into the glass-partitioned space, and pushed.

The door swung into motion and I arrived safely on the other side. Just like always. But despite that fact, I was still totally freaked out. Standing in menswear, I waited until my heart stopped pounding and then began the trek across the store to ladies' handbags. It really is a gauntlet, with overly zealous purveyors of perfume shoving scented cards at you from all angles.

Most of them are out-of-work actors, which means you not only get overwhelmed with scent, but an over-the-top performance as well. The key is never to make eye contact. So staring straight ahead, I managed to get across the store in short order and down the steps that led to the handbags.

At Bloomingdale's purses are arranged in little boutiques with lower-end bags to the right (when you're facing Lex), graduating to progressively more expensive ones as you move to the left. I skipped the more affordable ones. They were lovely, but I needed a pick-me-up and only the very best would fit the bill. I stopped at Fendi, but to be honest I've never really understood why people like these bags.

Across the way was a little Ferragamo medical bag I'd been

eyeing for a month or so. It just had an elegant functionality about it that appealed to me. I put the straps over my shoulder, my mood elevating immediately. But before I had time to reach for my credit card, my cell phone rang.

Saved by the bell.

Literally.

Reluctantly, I returned the bag to its display shelf and flipped open my phone, wondering what new calamity awaited me. "This is Vanessa."

"Hello, Van, this is Stephen." Stephen, not surprisingly, had adopted Cybil's habit of shortening my name. But for some reason, the way he said it grated on my nerves.

"What can I do for you?" I asked, my tone glacial. He'd screwed my best friend—in every possible way. Not to mention the fact that he was interrupting a perfectly wonderful shopping experience.

"I need to talk." There was a pause, and I actually thought about hanging up, but curiosity got the better of me. "About Cybil."

Okay, I didn't want to talk to the guy at all. And I certainly didn't want to talk about Cybil. "It's a little too late for that, don't you think?"

"I don't know. Maybe it's not."

Oh, dear Lord, was he actually thinking about trying to get her back? "I think if you've got anything to say, you ought to say it to her."

"But she won't take my calls."

"Well, what did you expect? You broke up with her."

"I know, but—"

This was going nowhere fast. Best to nip it in the bud. "Stephen, she's dating someone else." All right, she wasn't exactly dating him, but she would be.

"Who?" The word blasted through the telephone so loudly that I actually moved the receiver away from my ear.

"Mark Grayson," I replied. *That* ought to give him food for thought.

Again there was silence on the line. I waited, trying to figure out why in hell Stephen had called me. Surely he wasn't expecting a sympathetic ear.

"I see," he said finally, and I could have sworn I heard a note of desolation. Served him right.

My phone beeped, signaling another caller. Maybe it was Cybil. "Look, Stephen, I've got another call, and I really need to take it. I'm sure you'll find someone wonderful out there. It's just not going to be Cybil." I clicked off before he could protest, switching to the other line.

"Hello?"

"Vanessa, it's Belinda," she said, tears threatening to drown out her voice.

"What's wrong?" It was getting to the point that every time my phone rang, it signaled a crisis.

"It's over," she said, between sobs. "I told him to go to hell." Presumably there was a reason, but it wasn't the kind of thing one discussed on the phone. Especially in the middle of a department store.

"Where are you?"

"I don't know. I've just been walking. Hang on." She fumbled with the phone, the resulting static uncomfortable. "I'm at Seventy-eighth and York."

Belinda lived on the west side, and though walking was a good way to work out one's emotions, it was a stretch to believe she'd walked all that way. Stanley, on the other hand, had an apartment on East Eighty-first—a fabulous condo with panoramic views of the river and the city. My guess was she'd come straight from there. I scrambled to think of a place on York.

"Why don't you meet me at the Barking Dog. It's on Seventy-seventh, I think. I'll grab a cab and be there in five."

I shot a last loving look at the Ferragamo bag and headed out the door, dialing Stanley's number. Six rings and his answering machine kicked in. I disconnected without leaving a message and dialed his cell phone, with the same results. This time, though, I left a brief message.

Then I flagged down a cab and slid inside, telling the driver to take me to York and Seventy-seventh. I could have walked, but time was of the essence. Belinda needed me. I stared out the window at the buildings whizzing by, my thoughts returning to Stephen and his unexpected call. There was just something in his voice. Something I couldn't quite put my finger on.

I opened my phone, thinking that I ought to call Cybil, and noticed I had a text message. Scrolling over to it, I clicked on the message line. Talk about coincidence. It was from Cybil.

Tried to call you, but the line was busy. Mark called, and you were right, he's amazing. He's taking me to Per Se. Still not certain I'm doing the right thing. But as you said, it's only one date. Off to find something fabulous to wear. C.

The churning in my stomach returned with a vengeance. I'd never felt this way about a match. Usually I felt totally removed from the situation. I cared, of course, but not to the degree that I lost sleep over it. I mean, this was a business after all, and I couldn't allow myself to get personally involved. At least not beyond a certain degree. But here I was on the way to help one client, sick at my stomach for another.

Maybe it was just that Cybil meant so much to me. Or maybe it was the call from Stephen. If he was having second thoughts, I ought to tell Cybil. But he was so wrong for her. And Mark was so right. And I was certain that if I did tell her Stephen had called, she'd use it as an excuse to cancel the date.

But I never kept things from her.

My stomach lurched as the taxi took a corner on two wheels, Mario Andretti at the wheel. I clutched the vinyl strap, trying to decide what to do. Oddly, all I could think of was calling Mark and getting his advice. Which was a totally ridiculous notion.

The taxi slowed as it reached the corner. I handed the driver a five and hopped out of the cab, feeling better immediately. I was just borrowing problems. Stephen hadn't actually said that he wanted to get back with Cybil. And if she wasn't taking his calls, then obviously she wasn't interested in the idea anyway.

So I'd just keep my nose out of it. I had my own problems to deal with. Like Belinda's crisis. It was sound logic. I should have felt better. But I didn't. And for the life of me I couldn't figure out why.

Chapter 22

Barking Dog Luncheonette. *1453 York Avenue (corner of Seventy-seventh Street), 212.861.3600; 1678 Third Avenue (corner of Ninety-fourth Street), 212.831.1800.*

This canine-themed luncheonette, with its doggy drinking fountain out front and stuffed animals inside, is a big hit with kids. But adults love it, too, for another reason: The food (all of it made in-house) is the best bargain in the neighborhood.

—cityguide.aol.com

The Barking Dog is the kind of place you go on a lazy Sunday afternoon for brunch. You don't have to dress up and you don't have to spend a fortune, but you can while away the hours talking with friends over an omelet or a burger. It's one step up from the usual diner fare, and, hey, you've got to love a place that gives your dog a drink while you sit at a café table and watch the world go by.

But I don't have a dog and just at the moment I didn't have hours to while away. I could see Belinda inside sitting at a table by the window. I glanced at my cell to make sure I hadn't missed a call from Stanley. Or another message from Cybil. I knew what I wanted the former to say, but I wasn't as sure about the latter. Anyway, no one had called, so I went inside and let the maitre d' lead me to Belinda's table.

"Hi, sweetie," I said, taking the seat next to her. "Are you all right?"

"No," she said, dabbing a Kleenex to her nose. "It was just awful."

"Tell me what happened," I said, trying not to jump to conclusions. "Everything was fine when I talked to you yesterday."

"It was better than fine," she said. "It was wonderful. Last night we went to dinner, and then afterward—well, it was fabulous. But I had to leave early this morning for a deposition."

"On the weekend?"

"It was the only time that worked." She shrugged, still sniveling. "Anyway, the other attorney never showed. So we cancelled it and since it was still early I decided to go back to Stanley's apartment and surprise him. The doorman had seen me leave so it was no problem going up. But I didn't have a key, so I rang the doorbell." With every word she was getting more wound up, tears freefalling now into her coffee. She struggled for composure, but clearly it was a losing battle.

"It's going to be okay. But I need to know what happened."

She nodded and sucked in a deep breath. "I heard voices, and then the door opened. But it wasn't Stanley. It was a w . . . woman," she paused, fighting her tears, "and she was naked."

"Totally naked?" I asked, not sure exactly what I was supposed to do. I'll say one thing for Stanley, when he screws up, he does it really well.

"No. Not completely naked. She had a towel."

"And Stanley just let her answer the door?" Something about this didn't sound quite right.

"I don't know. I didn't stick around to ask. I mean, there was a naked woman in his apartment. I hardly think there's anything he could have said that would have made it all right."

"But you said you told him to go to hell."

"Well, not to his face. I just yelled into the apartment. I heard his voice. I know he was there."

"Maybe there's a reasonable explanation?"

"Like what? She just came over to borrow some soap?" She gave me the smallest of smiles, but the amusement was contradicted by the tears.

"Well, it seems a bit contrived to me. I mean, you said you had a wonderful evening. And believe it or not, Stanley really isn't the type who flits from flower to flower."

A bubble of laughter erupted from behind Belinda's Kleenex, and the waiter, who'd been hovering anxiously, arrived with a salad and a glass of tea. He set them in front of Belinda and looked pointedly at my menu. "You want anything?" The restaurant obviously wasn't interested in table-hogging histrionics.

My stomach was still on protest, so lunch was out of the question. "Just bring me a cup of coffee, please," I said, handing him the menu. The caffeine wouldn't do much for the queasies, but at least it would satisfy the waiter.

With a "humph" and a head twist, he huffed off toward another table. It was my fault, really. It was the weekend, after all, and there were probably people waiting. But this was an emergency. They'd just have to deal. And I'd leave a big tip. What can I say? I'm a pushover.

I turned my attention back to Belinda, who seemed for a moment to have gained control of the waterworks. Not that it was much of an improvement. She was listlessly stirring her salad like it was a bowl of Cream of Wheat. I stand behind my matches. Really, I do. But moments like these make me wonder why the hell anyone makes the effort. Caring about someone seems to cause so much pain.

I know you're thinking that the payoff is worth it. And I suppose I'd have to agree. I mean, in my case the payoff is literal. But still, so much grief just trying to find a partner. And it's not like riding off into the sunset is a guarantee of anything. Why do you think all those books end where they do? Because it's not such a pretty picture once the sun goes down.

Okay, I suppose I'm being a little cynical. But think about what I've been through in the past few days. And all of it for "love." I mean, God, it's so damn complicated. No wonder I get the big bucks.

"It's going to be okay," I said, reaching over to stop the stirring. "I promise you there's a reasonable explanation."

"I agree. He's not the type to flit," she said, looking up at me with mascara-smudged eyes. (I totally swear by waterproof mascara. So what if I won't have any eyelashes left by the time I'm sixty? It beats looking like a raccoon—in public.) "But, Vanessa, I saw what I saw."

"Yes, well, there were Christmas presents left under our tree for almost fifteen years, but that doesn't mean that a fat man in red velvet delivered them, does it?"

She sighed, running a hand through her hair. "We're not talking about Santa Claus. We're talking about Stanley." The tears started in earnest again, and I struggled for the right thing to say. My earlier diatribe aside, I really did believe that Stanley and Belinda belonged together.

"So what did she look like, this woman?"

Belinda's eyes widened, the tears now skiing off the end of her nose.

"I don't mean that part of her. I mean color of hair, height, you know, identifying characteristics."

"She had huge boobs. You can't get more identifying than that."

"Well, I see your point. But honestly, these days a lot of women have big boobs."

"But I don't." Belinda waved a hand at her chest. "And if that's what Stanley likes, then he'll never choose me."

"Belinda, he's already chosen you. I talked to him, remember? And I told you he's not interested in that type of woman anymore. Honestly."

"Well, considering what I saw, it seems to me like old habits aren't that easy to break."

"Wait a minute," I said. Speaking of old habits, my mind immediately pulled forth two photos. Wife number one, and wife number two. "What color was her hair?"

"Redhead—the natural kind. You know, like Julianne Moore. Only a hell of a lot younger." I'd never heard Belinda curse, which meant that despite having only two dates, she'd fallen fast and hard. I should have been ecstatic, but I really quite liked Belinda. And I didn't want her to be hurt.

I trusted Stanley. A lot. But the facts seemed to stand on their own.

At least I'd been wrong about it being one of his exes. Both of them were more the Anna Nicole Smith peroxide-rules-the-day type. It was in the bimbo code somewhere—bleach blondes rule. Anyway, I wasn't sure if this was a good thing or a bad thing. Not that I wanted it to be one of the exes, mind you, I just figured if Stanley was running scared, Belinda was right, he'd head for what was familiar.

But redheads were entirely new territory. Well, maybe not completely. I mean, she did have big breasts. What had I been thinking? A leopard never changes his spots. There'd been a redhead at the shoot in the park. White teeth, copper hair, humongous boobs.

"What is it?" Belinda asked, her voice shaking. "You know something, don't you?"

I fought the urge to curse myself and schooled my expression into what I hoped was calm passivity. "I don't know anything. I tried calling as soon as I talked to you, but he wasn't answering his phone."

"Because he's in bed with . . . with . . . *that woman*."

As descriptions go, that one pretty much fit the bill. I mean, for hundreds of years "that woman" would come along and ruin everything. Or, to be politically correct about it, "that person." There were "those men," after all. In fact, following that train of thought, Stephen could be considered the textbook definition of "that person." He just kept turning up like a bad penny, trying to ruin Cybil's life.

Well, at least I'd done something about that.

Suddenly I felt a bit better. Which, of course, had nothing at all to do with the issue at hand. "I think you need to talk to Stanley." In truth, there was only so much reassurance I could offer. And the picture etched in her brain was going to trump pretty much anything.

"There's nothing to say. Believe me, I've seen it all."

I told you.

But still, I had to try. "You saw something that looked incriminating. But that doesn't mean it was. You have to try giving Stanley the benefit of the doubt. Like I said before, maybe there's a perfectly logical explanation. And even if there isn't, maybe it's still worth talking to him."

"I don't know. I just don't like being made a fool of."

"Well, no one saw you except the woman, right? You said you didn't actually see Stanley."

"No. I just heard him."

"So the only way you can feel like a fool is if you let yourself. It's not like *you* were naked. If anyone should be embarrassed, it's her. And even if what you think happened happened, the only real fool is Stanley."

"Yes, but I don't want him to be a fool, either. I just wish I'd never found out." The tears were back, this time mixing with the salad dressing.

"Well, you have. And now you have to deal with it." It was time to get down to basics. "Which means you can do one of two things. You can confront Stanley and find out the real truth, whatever it is. Or you can run away and pretend none of this ever happened. The choice is yours."

"I've never been a coward."

"No, you haven't. And I don't think you should start now. No matter what you find out, you'll be happier in the long run."

As if on cue, Stanley walked past the window.

"Oh, my God." Belinda had seen him, too. "How did he know I was here?"

"I told you I left a message on his phone."

"You said you'd called. Nothing about a message." Utter panic had replaced all other emotion as she tried, not particularly successfully, to wipe away her tears and the now misplaced mascara.

"I should go," I said.

She grabbed my hand with the grip of a sumo wrestler. "Don't you dare."

There was no time to debate.

"Hello, Stanley," I said, buying a little more time for Belinda, who had retreated behind her Kleenex again. "You got my message." I tried telegraphing my concern, but it was a total waste of time. I could have been sitting there stark naked, and Stanley still wouldn't have seen anyone but Belinda.

Whatever had happened, I hadn't been wrong about the two of them.

"Belinda. I need to explain."

With a last swipe at her left eye, she surfaced from behind the tissue, focusing somewhere in the area of Stanley's chin. "There's no need for explanation. I think I saw more than enough." I could hear the tremble in her voice, but to her credit, she kept her composure. Although I suppose I shouldn't have been surprised. She *is* an attorney, after all.

"But that's just the thing. You didn't see anything," Stanley said.

"There wasn't a naked girl in your apartment?" Belinda lifted her gaze to his, her eyes flashing. I might as well have been watching a movie. The two of them had completely forgotten I was there.

"No. There was. Her name is Christine Menzel. She's got a guest spot on the show."

"Oh well, then, in that case . . . ," she trailed off, ice dripping from every word.

"Belinda," Stanley said, sitting down beside her, "I told her she could use my apartment. She's only here for a couple of days. Helping us promote the show."

"And, of course, all the hotels are full."

"She flew in this morning. The red-eye from L.A."

Okay, so I'd had the wrong redhead. But it didn't much seem to matter. Stanley was still digging himself in deeper by the second.

"Stanley . . . ," I started, only to have him frown at me in warning. Sure, why not—blame it on the matchmaker. "The plane was delayed, and she was due on *The View*. She called and asked if she could use my apartment to make herself presentable."

"But that doesn't—"

Stanley cut her off with a wave of his hand. "I wasn't even there."

"But I heard you." Hurt replaced anger in less than a second. God, now I wanted to cry.

"You couldn't have. I was out looking for you."

"For me?" Her voice now was almost a squeak. The attorney was replaced by a woman who desperately wanted to believe in happily ever after.

"Yes. After you left, I banged around . . ." He lifted his hand again, warding us both off. "Bad choice of words. I puttered around the apartment wishing you hadn't had to go. And then I got a great idea." He smiled timidly at Belinda, the world-renowned director nowhere in evidence. "Bagels."

"Bagels?" Belinda and I said it together, but again I got the glare. From both of them this time. I held up a hand in supplication and clamped my mouth shut.

"H&H." Stanley held up a sad little bag. It looked like it had been run over by a cab, or a garbage truck, or a subway train, or maybe all three.

Belinda nodded, tears welling. "They're my favorite in the whole city."

"I know," he said. "That's why I got them. I thought I'd surprise you at your office. You know, after the deposition. But when I got there, the guard said you'd already gone." His face fell with the words, like the dad in an old Disney movie I'd seen as a kid. He brings ice cream to a Boy Scout meeting, trying to please his son, but when he gets there, it's all melted. You can guess the rest.

"It was cancelled," Belinda was saying. "The other attorney never showed. That's why I was back at your apartment." Hope flared in her eyes, and I dug my nails into my palms. Matchmakers don't cry. "So you really weren't there?" she asked.

"No." He shook his head, reaching out to take her hand. "I was gallivanting around Manhattan like a love-struck teenager."

"Because of me?"

I swallowed the desire to yell "get a room"; after all, this is exactly what I wanted to happen. It's just that sitting there in the face of it all, I felt sort of—well, if you must know—left out. I know, I know . . . occupational hazard. You'd think I'd learn.

As if to emphasize the point, Stanley stood up, pulling Belinda with him. "You don't mind, do you, Vanessa?"

I shook my head and watched the two of them as they walked out the door, hand in hand. Before I had time to examine my emotions, the waiter appeared, a sort of self-satisfied smile on his face. "I assume you'll be paying?"

I nodded, threw a twenty on the table, and shot the twit what I hoped was a glacial glare. You know, the kind you get in the elevator of your building when you decide to go grab the mail in your sweats only to be surrounded by expensively perfumed, fur-clad women of a certain status and age.

Once outside, I started to call Richard and Anderson, but stopped myself. I always seemed to call them when there was a crisis. And this time I'd actually managed to put out the fire all by myself. Although if I were being really honest, I'd have to say that, apart from calling Stanley and getting Belinda to the restaurant, I really hadn't had a whole lot to do with the reconciliation.

I walked aimlessly west, watching people go about the business of living in Manhattan. It was a fabulous city, and no matter what mood I was in, I loved it. But today somehow it seemed a bit dimmer. I noticed the things we pretend don't exist.

The white stain of graffiti on the side of a brick building, piles of garbage on the curb waiting their turn for pickup, an old lady using a walker crossing against the light, angry cabs and delivery trucks honking their displeasure. And there, on the stoop of a forgotten doorway, a transient curled into fetal position, newspapers and trash bags forming a new kind of couture.

I shook my head, my mind clearing, and headed down Lexington to Seventy-second. From there it was a quick walk to Madison.

I love Madison Avenue. There's something so wonderful about it. Park is more regal, but in comparison kind of boring. And Fifth is supposed to be the grand dame of them all, but I've always felt like it was Madison's flashier cousin. It's not the stores themselves, mind you. Although there are some amazing ones. It's more the amalgamation. You know, all of it coming together in an amazingly elegant symbol of Manhattan.

My Manhattan.

I stopped in front of a gift shop. The kind that carries wonderfully useless things that remind an adult what it was like to be a kid. Baccarat vases, Limoges boxes, little glass-blown candies from Murano. There was a plate with the famous Andy Warhol self-portrait, and a ridiculous-looking carved elephant wearing a tuxedo. And all of that just in the window.

I started to go in, then realized my heart wasn't in it. A sure sign that something was wrong. I just couldn't figure out what. I pulled out my phone again and dialed Cybil. But all I got was her voice telling me she wasn't in.

I glanced at my watch. Still too early for her to be out with Mark. I had a moment's hesitation, wondering if maybe she'd changed her mind and was out somewhere with Stephen instead, but I knew she'd have called to tell me if there'd been a change of plans.

Besides, she was finished with Stephen. She'd never have agreed to go out with Mark otherwise. She knew how important this was for me.

I dropped my phone back in my bag, suddenly feeling alone.

Everything was going amazingly well, and yet for some reason I felt just the opposite. The feeling had been hounding me all day, but I simply couldn't put a finger on what was wrong. Everyone was happy. I'd managed to head off all kinds of catastrophes and even get Mark Grayson to agree to go out with Cybil.

I should have been dancing on air.

But I wasn't.

I grabbed my cell again and dialed Althea, but hung up before it could connect. I didn't know what to say. And even if I did, to be honest, I'm not sure she'd understand. Besides, she probably wasn't home anyway. Today was her usual day with Ken, her personal trainer. He's written all kinds of books and is a local celebrity of sorts, but the only reason Althea goes is because, in her words, "he has abs you could bounce a quarter off."

Of course I could call the gym, but sharing my insecurities with her was like admitting I couldn't make it on my own. I needed to solve my own problems. I sighed and stopped at another window. This one filled with fabulous handbags.

Nothing.

Not even a tingle of excitement.

Something was definitely wrong.

I needed a pick-me-up—fast. And I knew just where to go.

Since I was about three, I've loved the Central Park Zoo. I know it doesn't exactly fit my image, and in fact if you ever tell anyone I'll . . . well, suffice it to say that since reaching adulthood, I've usually come by myself.

But none of that changes the fact that I love the place. Especially when I'm not feeling on top of my game. I made short work of the remaining blocks on Madison, ignoring all the glittering merchandise that called my name, crossed over to Fifth, which fortunately on Sixty-fourth is still very residential, and then into the park.

One flight of steps and a game of "dodge that kid," and I was six dollars poorer and standing in front of my favorite bears—Gus and Ida. Eighteen years old and raised entirely in captivity, they're a fixture here. So popular you can Google them and pull up something like a million hits.

Gus is the bigger one. Something like one thousand pounds, and I've been told that's small for a polar bear. Ida's fur is whiter, and at seven hundred pounds she's practically a size two in polar bear world. But it doesn't matter anyway, because Gus only has eyes for her. Of course, there're only the two of them. Which I suppose could be interpreted to mean he doesn't have a choice. But I've seen them together. There's definitely a spark.

Gus is a swimmer. Endless laps back and forth across their pool. He's even perfected a flip turn. Ida is more of a bobber. You know, like a barrel in water. She sways with the current and watches you watching her. She seems to find us entertaining.

Or maybe she's just imagining hors d'oeuvres.

I don't know what it is about them really, but I love to watch them. Gus relentlessly piling on the laps, and Ida placidly going with the flow. They're the perfect couple.

Which, now that I was thinking about it, didn't exactly fit into my theories. I mean, they were the ultimate in arranged marriages, but you really couldn't find two more different bears. Maybe in some cases opposites do attract.

But then we're talking about *polar bears*. And while I might enjoy projecting human emotion on them, in the end, they're still animals. And as such, what applies in my world doesn't necessarily apply in theirs.

My theories were sound.

And I had the couples to prove it. Of course, the ultimate test was still ahead. I needed for Cybil to see that she was better with Mark Grayson than with Stephen.

Which sounded absolutely self-centered when put like that.

What I meant was that I wanted Cybil to be happy—and that wasn't going to happen with Stephen. So my meddling was all for the best. Really.

Unfortunately, I wasn't sure I believed myself. And since Ida and Gus were stubbornly refusing to comment on any of it, I decided I needed someone human. Someone who saw the world through the same Givenchy shaded lens.

And I'm not talking about Cybil.

Or Richard, or Anderson, or even Althea.

I'm talking about my mother. As crazy as it sounds, she's the only one who really knows me. I mean, in that what-the-hell-is-going-on-with-me?-Don't-worry-I-understand-baby kind of way.

Sometimes a girl just needs her mother.

Even when said mother is mine.

Chapter 23

Tiffany & Co. *727 Fifth Avenue (corner of Fifty-seventh Street), 212.755.8000.*

"I don't want to own anything until I find a place where me and things go to-gether. I'm not sure where that is, but I know what it is like. It's like Tiffany's. . . . I'm just crazy about Tiffany's." (Holly Golightly, *Breakfast at Tiffany's*)

—www.imdb.com

My mother is crazy about Tiffany's, too. As far as she's concerned, nothing compares to opening a present carefully placed inside that famous turquoise box tied with the white, satiny ribbon. And I can't say that I disagree. Since I had my very first heartbreak—Matthew Barrington, seventh grade— my mother has made it a practice to take me to Tiffany's. And I've got the blue boxes to prove it.

So it wasn't all that surprising that when she'd heard my voice on the phone, she'd insisted on Tiffany's. I love the store, I really do. But for me it's not quite the religious experience it is for my mother. But then she *was* Holly Golightly. Not now, of course, but once upon a time. Okay, she wasn't a call girl, but to hear my father tell it, she'd been a rather free spirit in her day. So I guess *Breakfast at Tiffany's* had struck a chord.

All I know, really, is that she cries like a crazy woman every time she sees the movie, and owns a first edition signed copy of the book. Who knows? Maybe she had a thing for Truman Capote. Now there's a scary thought.

When I was younger it embarrassed me to think of her that way; now I have to admit I find it amusing. I mean, we're talking about my mother.

It's odd, isn't it? You never really know your parents as people. They're forever relegated in your mind to the roles of mother and father.

But all that aside, coming to Tiffany's with my mother had always been special. The ultimate pick-me-up. A moment out of time that was just about the two of us. All heartaches and troubles checked at the door.

So here we were, Mother and I, walking between glittering cases of jewelry, all that gold and silver the perfect appetizer for the main event—the diamond floor.

"Isn't this divine?" she asked, stopping to look at an Elsa Peretti brooch. It was deceptively simple, gold and silk coming together to form a calla lily or maybe a poppy. It didn't really matter.

"It's gorgeous," I said, picturing it on the lapel of my turquoise coat. "Wish they'd done it in pink."

"No," she murmured, still admiring the pin. "It's perfect in red."

I nodded and moved on to another case. This one was awash with color. Like a rainbow of jewels, a pair of peridot earrings catching the carefully directed light.

"So tell me what's wrong," Mother said, coming to stand beside me.

I waved away the woman behind the counter and blew out a long breath. "I don't know."

"But you called." She linked her arm through mine, pulling me toward the elevator. "There has to be something."

I suppose it's a sad state when your mother honestly believes the only time you call her is when you have troubles. But in our case, I'm afraid it's the truth. I sort of have this thing about maintaining my independence. Maybe it's just a personality quirk, but I don't like admitting I've got problems unless the situation's dire.

Which meant I must be really screwed up, because theoretically I should have been on top of the world, yet here I was, standing in an elevator with my mother. The doors slid open and we stepped out onto the diamond floor. It's an elegant room, with understated lighting designed to highlight the glittering cases filled with the world's most precious commodity. Diamonds.

We stopped in front of a small case containing a flawless yellow diamond on a delicate white gold chain. The diamond was the size of a walnut. Almost gaudy, and yet not.

"You still haven't told me what's going on," Mother prompted with a frown, ignoring the mesmerizing spell of the glittering necklace.

"I guess I'm confused, more than anything."

"That doesn't sound like you." The frown deepened, but only at her eyes, so somewhere out there a plastic surgeon got his wings.

"I know. That's the problem. It isn't like me at all. I mean, everything is going great. You wouldn't believe the week I've had."

"Well, actually, I seem to recall there were a few major bumps in the road." She pointed to a bracelet with three rows of diamonds set in platinum. The clerk didn't even hesitate. He just brought it out on its little velvet bed and stepped back for my mother to have a closer look.

"That's the point," I said. "I somehow managed to dodge every bullet. I mean, I came through it all unscathed. I finally proved to myself I can operate on my own. Without Althea."

"But you've always known that." She shook her head and handed the bracelet back to the clerk, turning her attention to me. "You're the bravest person I know."

What a laugh. I'd actually managed to fool my own mother. "I'm totally afraid of everything. Especially failing."

"Everyone's afraid of that, darling."

"I suppose so." I stared down at a necklace and earring set. The kind that would make even an off-the-rack dress look amazing. Not to mention the girl inside the dress.

"Well, if everything's worked out, you should be elated."

"I know. But I'm not. I don't feel anything, really."

"Well, then we've come to the right place." She signaled another clerk, and in less time than it takes to say "twenty karats," I was wearing the earring and necklace set. A fairy princess in Seven jeans and an Abercrombie and Fitch pullover.

But I wasn't a fairy princess and these weren't my diamonds. I took them off and handed them back.

"Maybe you're just tired of helping other people fall in love."

"I'm not sure what you're getting at." It was my turn to frown, and, believe me, there were wrinkles.

"Just that maybe it's time for you to stop pairing off other people and find someone of your own."

I thought we'd finally gotten past the go-forth-and-have-grandchildren speech, so her comment left me scrambling for words. "I don't think I'm ready for that kind of commitment."

"No one ever is. Not really. It's more about taking a leap of faith. Isn't that what you tell your clients?"

I started to say no. But then stopped. Maybe she was right. Not about the marriage-for-me part. About the leap of faith. No matter how many points of commonality two people shared there was always that element of risk. Maybe part of my job was to make them realize it wasn't as scary as it seemed.

"I suppose you're right," I answered. "Although the key is to make sure the leap isn't too much of a stretch."

"Likes attract likes," she said. "I know."

Actually I had no idea she'd ever really listened.

"Well, it works."

"So what's the problem?"

"I don't know, it's been a crazy week. I guess I just needed some moral support."

"Well, that's what mothers are for." We stopped in front of a case full of dinner rings. Diamonds mixed together with rubies and emeralds and sapphires to stunning effect. "Try one on," Mother urged.

I pointed to a simple circle of emeralds with a round-cut diamond at the center. The clerk held it out for me to put on and I slipped it into place. There was just something magical about well-cut stones. "It's beautiful."

"So what's up next?" Mother asked, segueing nicely away from the schmaltz of the moment.

I tipped my hand in the light, admiring the ring one last time, and then slipped it off and handed it back to the clerk.

"Mark and Cybil."

"He's agreed to be a client?" she said, looking confused. "Just like that?"

"Well, not exactly. At first the fates did seem to be conspiring against me. I mean, you know about the disaster at Bungalow 8, and then the luncheon that ended before I could close the deal. Of course, he said to call. And I did. Twice. But he wasn't there and I wasn't holding my breath, you know, waiting for him to call back. But then he did.

"Only I was with Maris and had to hang up. And that should have been that, but he said to call him if I wrapped things up, and since Douglas finalized things a little too personally, I called. And we had dinner, but I hadn't talked to Maris about the kiss and so when she called, I cut things off again."

"The man either has infinite patience or is a glutton for punishment."

"I know. I was kind of surprised myself when he called again. But the point is he did. You were there—at Barneys." We sat down on a banquette by the window.

"Right." She nodded. "He asked you to dinner."

"Well, instead he took me to the Waldorf. You know, the Philharmonic benefit. But I told him I couldn't go in. I mean, not with that photo on everyone's mind. But he insisted. Said I should face things head-on."

"Smart man."

"I suppose so. But I could never have done it without Mark. He was a rock. He even took on Althea."

"She was there?"

"Yes. And she was throwing passive-aggressive digs at me about the photograph. About my chances for success, actually. And just as it was getting really uncomfortable, Mark told her that he was my client. Right there in front of everyone. Talk about a triumph."

"Sounds to me like he was bailing you out of a bad situation."

"He was, actually. For the second time. But the important part is that he agreed to let me find him a match."

"Definitely a triumph, darling." She reached over to pat my hand.

"So why aren't I more excited about it?" And there it was in a nutshell. I'd accomplished the impossible. I'd convinced Mark Grayson to sign with me. To go out with Cybil. My best friend in the whole world and one of the nicest men I'd ever met. It was perfect.

My stomach apparently didn't agree, and I groaned.

"What, darling? What is it?" Concern flashed in her eyes and her hand tightened on mine.

"Nothing. Really, it's nothing." I smiled. "Just qualms about Mark's date with Cybil tonight."

"I'm sure it will go smashingly. Cybil's wonderful, and from what you're saying, so is your Mr. Grayson."

"He's not my . . . oh well, I suppose in a legal sort of way he is." I was still trying to grapple with the awful thought that had planted itself in my mind. You know, with the tenacity of trumpet vine or kudzu.

A clerk materialized beside my mother and handed her a credit receipt. She signed it and exchanged paper for a little blue bag. I shouldn't have been surprised. She wasn't exactly a window-shopper when it came to Tiffany's.

"So what does Cybil think of all this?" she asked, as the clerk discreetly withdrew.

"She was really enthusiastic about the idea." There it was again—that sickening lurch in the stomach.

"She was or you were?"

"Both of us, really. I mean, who wouldn't be enthusiastic about Mark?"

"I see." She nodded, but I got the distinct feeling that she was off on her own train of thought. Not that unusual, really. "What about Stephen?"

"He's not part of the picture anymore."

"How can you know that for certain?" she asked.

"He's dumped her three times. Besides, Cybil has nothing in common with him. She's successful. Stephen's not."

"Do you have any idea how hard it is to make a go of it in the art world? It takes years to find a foothold. Let alone success. And even then it's often only fleeting. Even here," she waved her hand at the sparkling cases in front of us. "This year it's Elsa Peretti, next year it will be someone else."

"If I didn't know better, I'd say you're defending Stephen."

"I'm not. I don't even know him, really. If I'm defending any-one, it's Cybil."

"What?" Okay, this conversation had taken a really weird turn. "You're not making sense."

"Darling, every time you put down Stephen, you're putting down Cybil. She chose to take Stephen back. Not once, but twice. So unless you think Cybil is an idiot, there has to be something good about Stephen."

"Hot sex."

"Vanessa." Her tone had me sinking into the velvet seat.

"Okay. I see what you're saying. There has to be something redeemable in Stephen, or Cybil couldn't have fallen in love with him." I tried to sound as if I meant it, but I sounded more like Natalie Wood in *Miracle on 34th Street*. You know the line—"I believe, I believe . . ."

"Exactly. You just need to give Cybil more credit."

"But I do. I think she's the most amazing person on the planet."

"With really bad taste in men?" she coaxed.

"No. I mean, well, yes. She does sort of seem to have a knack for picking losers."

"In your opinion."

"Yes. But after all I know what I'm doing." I sat back, feeling sort of smug.

"Do you?" she flung back. "Then why are you sitting here at Tiffany's with me? Shouldn't you be out with your friends celebrating?"

"They all have someone else." The minute it was out I wanted to take it back. It sounded so lame. Or desperate. Or something. I thought about Stephen. His voice on the phone. He'd sounded desperate, too. And I'd blown him off. Maybe I should have at least tried to listen. After all, I was supposed to be the expert. "I didn't mean that the way it sounded. I'm delighted everyone is so happy. Especially Cybil. She deserves someone like Mark. It's just that . . ."

"Now that everything's so neatly arranged you feel empty."

I nodded.

"Have you considered that there might be another reason?"

It was like she was reading my mind. "Stephen called."

"What?" She looked almost as confused as I felt.

"Cybil's not taking his calls. So he called me. He wanted to talk. I think he wants her back. I blew him off."

"And you haven't told Cybil."

"No. If I do, she might not go out with Mark."

"And that would be a bad thing?" There was something in her voice that I didn't quite recognize. Or maybe I just didn't want to.

"Well, yes. I mean, no. I mean, oh God, I don't know. I'm always so certain about these things. I have to be. Maybe it's because it's Cybil." I sighed, my heart feeling sort of like it had lost something important. Only I had no idea what. Maybe if I talked to Stephen. Maybe that's where the answer lay. Or at least maybe I'd feel better for giving him the chance to say whatever it was he had to say.

Only problem was, I hadn't the slightest idea where to find him. I obviously couldn't call Cybil. I glanced at my watch. She'd be getting ready for Mark about now. My stomach flipped again. I was always nervous when a new client had his first date. But this was ridiculous. Maybe I just needed to concentrate on something else, like Stephen.

"Mother, would you mind terribly if I took off?"

"Dare I ask why?" Her eyes glittered with something I couldn't quite put a name to.

"There's just something I need to do."

"Well, take this, then." She held out the blue bag. "For luck." I opened the sack and pulled out the blue box. Inside was the little ring, its diamond and emeralds winking at me in the light. I felt tears sting the back of my eyes. "Thanks, Mom," I said, sliding the ring onto my finger.

Her smile said it all.

And so, armed with my mother's love, I headed out to find Stephen.

Which turned out to be a whole lot easier than I'd imagined. He was waiting for me in the lobby of my building. Harry tried to apologize, but I waved him away with a smile. "It's okay, Stephen is a friend." It probably served me right to see Stephen so surprised, but, in truth, I hadn't ever gone out of my way to get to know him. I made a living on first impressions, and Stephen just wasn't the kind of man a mother would choose for her daughter. You know what I mean?

But with my mother's admonishment ringing in my ears, I thought maybe I ought to try to see him the way Cybil did. We took the elevator in silence and were still fighting awkwardness as we sat across from each other in my apartment. Waldo, on leave from parental duty, watched us both from his perch in the window. Stephen stared at the floor, and I stared at Stephen.

He looked tired, but he'd had his hair cut, and his clothes were free of paint stains. Okay, I know that sounds judgmental, but I don't mean it that way. There's never been any question about Stephen's looks. He's hot. I can admit that. But that's not enough. There has to be more. Right? I mean, a good body doesn't guarantee a good relationship.

Case in point.

"I didn't know where else to go," he said finally, his gaze meeting mine.

I try to maintain a neutral place when I deal with clients. They're the ones on the emotional roller coaster, and they expect me to be the voice of reason. But Stephen wasn't a client. And it was almost impossible not to react to the pain in his eyes. It was so palpable, even Waldo recognized it, jumping from his perch to rub against Stephen's legs, offering his own specialized form of comfort.

Stephen automatically reached down to pick Waldo up, scratching him behind the ears. Clearly, my cat had no reservations about the man. He wasn't usually big on sitting in strangers' laps. But with Stephen, he seemed right at home. Two peas in a pod, maybe.

Or maybe he was seeing something I'd simply refused to acknowledge.

"I'm sorry I cut you off earlier. I shouldn't have done that."

"It's all right. I probably deserved it. I've hurt Cybil more times than I care to count." An understatement surely. But there was no questioning his regret, it showed in every pore. "I didn't want to hurt her."

"But you have," I found myself saying. "Deeply." Now I'm

not altogether sure that this is what Cybil would have wanted me to say. I mean, something snarky seemed a much better way to go, but I just couldn't bring myself to do it.

He ran a hand through his already disheveled hair. It was part of his charm actually, his little-boy-lost appearance. "I shouldn't be here." He started to rise, but I waved him back in his seat.

"You're here. So you might as well say what you came to say."

He nodded, swallowing awkwardly, and I realized something else about Stephen Hobbs. He was shy. Painfully so, if I had to call it. Which explained a lot of his previous social faux pas. What was surprising was that I hadn't noticed it before. I mean I'm good at reading people.

Unless I'd already categorized them.

I felt the hot stain of guilt and jumped to my feet. "Would you like a drink? I've got pretty much everything." Thanks to a rather intoxicating New Year's Eve party last year.

"A beer, maybe?" Okay, so I didn't have everything.

"I'm sorry. That's the one thing I don't have. How about some wine? Or a scotch or something?"

"I'll have scotch, then. On the rocks."

I walked over to the little table that served double duty as a bar and pulled out the bottle of scotch. It was nothing special, a bottle of Cutty Sark, but in my mind's eye I saw the bottle of Chivas Mark had been drinking at Bungalow 8. With that thought, I glanced down at my watch, the time snapping me sharply back to reality. Mark was probably getting ready to pick Cybil up about now.

I poured some of the whiskey into a glass for Stephen and a double for myself. It had been a long day. I deserved it. Turning around I noted my purring cat, contentedly kneading Stephen's leg. It's really hard to dislike a man who loves cats. And I didn't even know he liked them.

On and off, Stephen had been part of Cybil's life for almost three years. So why the hell didn't I know him better?

Because you prejudged him and wrote him off as not good enough for Cybil, the little voice inside my head admonished. *Well*, said another slightly louder voice, *it's not as if you weren't right. After all, he did dump her three times.* I shook my head again, this time to dispel the voices before I turned into Sybil—with an S.

"Here you go." I handed Stephen the glass and returned to my inquisitioner's seat. "So I take it you're having second thoughts."

"And third and forth and fifth ones," he said, taking a long sip of scotch. "I . . . ," he started and then stopped, staring down into his drink. "I made a huge mistake."

"Yes, you did," I agreed, not at all inclined to gloss over the truth. Better that he face it and move on.

"But I had the best of intentions."

"I beg your pardon?" I said, staring at him now as if he had two heads. "You broke Cybil's heart because you thought it would be good for her?" Again I'd said more than I meant to, but the idea that this man had hurt her on purpose absolutely made me cross-eyed. I drank half of my scotch, and then slowly pulled in air until I was calm enough to look at him.

If he'd seemed wounded before, he was positively crestfallen now. "You don't think I'm good enough for her."

It was an odd segue and caught me off guard. "I . . ." It was my turn to stumble. "I don't think the two of you work as a couple. No." There I'd said it. And it was nothing more than the truth. So why did I feel like I'd kicked a puppy?

"Well, that's what I think, too." If his earlier admission had surprised me, this one floored me.

"Say what?"

"That's why I broke it off. I know that she deserves something

better than me." He shrugged, lifting his gaze to meet mine, the
naked longing there making me shiver. "I want her to be happy."

"But what if you're the only one who can do that?" I couldn't
believe I'd said it. Hell, I wasn't even certain that I believed it.

"But you said . . ."

"It's not about me, Stephen. It's about you and Cybil. And
no one else's opinion should matter in the least." Great, now I
was channeling my mother.

"I tried to believe that. I mean, she makes me so incredibly
happy. She completes me in ways that you can't even imagine."
And don't want to, thank you very much. "But I'm not sure I do
the same for her."

And suddenly I saw the complete picture. The two of them
together, laughing and happy. Cybil did need him. And in some
inexplicable way, he completed her, too. I'd just been too judgmental to see the truth of it. Oh God, what had I done?

"Do you want her back?" I asked, my thoughts spinning
with revelations.

"Yes."

"For good this time. No more running away?" I'd moved
from channeling my mother to Dr. Phil.

"Absolutely not." He shook his head solemnly and reached
into his pocket, producing a little velvet box. I got a lump in my
throat, and the damn thing wasn't even meant for me.
"Look . . . well, I've had a lot of time to think. In fact, aside
from trying to get hold of Cybil, I haven't done much else. And
the truth is, what I really want is to spend the rest of my life
with her. If she'll have me."

I nodded, unable to string together three words. Me. And
I'm not even sentimental.

"Of course," he said, looking dejected again. "She won't take
my calls. So I'm not even sure I'll get the chance to ask her. Es-

pecially with Mark Grayson in her life. I mean, how can I compete with that?"

"It's easy, Stephen. She loves you. Not him." And of course *that* was the absolute truth of the matter. Cybil did love him. With all her heart. I had the cupcake crumbs to prove it. "She's only going out with Mark for me. Because of the bet." And I recognized then that that was the truth as well. My best friend had put aside her heartache and was going out with Mark Grayson on my account. So that I could win a stupid bet. And all I'd done for her was diss the man she loved. But not anymore.

I knew exactly what to do.

It would no doubt give the gossip hounds fodder for weeks to come, the resulting press proving to Mark that I was no better than his initial impression of me. But if I had to lose whatever it was I had with Mark in order for Cybil to be truly happy, so be it.

I loved her, too. It was as simple as that.

"Stephen," I said, reaching over to take his drink, sure for once that I was doing exactly the right thing. "She and Mark should be on their way to Per Se. Go and get her."

Chapter 24

New York Palace. *455 Madison Avenue (between Fiftieth and Fifty-first streets), 212.888.7000.*

Guests enter this hotel through tall iron gates via a courtyard lit by Florentine lanterns. The heart of it is the Italian Renaissance–style palace designed in 1882. Public spaces are rich with architectural details including coffered ceilings, bronze doré moldings, mosaics, murals, and stained glass by Tiffany. Fireplaces include a beauty in the upper lobby crafted by Augustus St. Gaudens.

—www.gayot.com

Three months later ...

There's something absolutely magical about the New York Palace. The moment you step through the iron gates into the soft lighting of the Grand Courtyard, it's as if you've stepped back in time. Elegance and opulence at its very best. And it isn't just the courtyard. It's the hotel itself. From the magnificent three-storied staircase in the lobby to the luscious Villard Ballroom, the Palace evokes the graceful style of the Gilded Age.

And today the ballroom was even more beautiful, white peonies everywhere—on the tables, in the alcoves set into the oval walls, even in the center of the fabulous six-tiered wedding cake. Their heady smell filled the room, and when added to the seemingly endless supply of Perrier Jouet, it was enough to leave a girl positively giddy

"Isn't it gorgeous?" Anderson said, snagging a smoked salmon canapé from a passing waiter.

"Almost as lovely as the wedding," Richard agreed, exchanging his empty crystal goblet for a full one.

The wedding had indeed been fabulous. Held in the Reid Salon, it had almost been too sublime for adjectives. Limited to only the closest of friends, it had an intimacy that only magnified the beauty of the ceremony.

And now, here in the ballroom, the joy had expanded to include the glitterati of Manhattan. Friends and enemies coming together despite their differences to celebrate the happiness of one of their own.

"Well, I thought everything went magnificently," my mother said, her pale blue Versace sheath making her look almost incandescent. But then my mother was always at her best at parties. "Have you seen the bride?"

"No. Not since the ceremony. I don't think they've come in yet."

"If they're smart," Richard said, "they'll skip the whole thing."

"Richard," Anderson scolded, "just because you don't like parties . . ."

"It's not the parties. It's the crush. Look at this place—you can't move a muscle without bumping into someone."

"Ignore him," Anderson said, sotto whisper. "He's just mad because he ran into an old flame who didn't even recognize him."

"Well, I haven't changed that much," Richard snapped.

"Oh, stop sulking," I said. "You don't really care anyway. It's just your pride hurting."

"I suppose you're right," he said, still sounding grumpy.

"Of course she is," Anderson said. "The man was obviously an idiot. Trust me, you're not the sort of man one forgets."

The two of them moved away, Richard laughing at something else Anderson had to say.

"They look so happy," I sighed, caught up in the prevailing mood of the moment.

"Well, they love each other, and at the end of the day, that's what it's all about." Mother shrugged, the ice in her vodka tonic tinkling with the gesture.

If nothing else, that much I'd come to accept. Despite all my theories to the contrary, it seemed that in more cases than not, love did win the day. I just had to look at Belinda and Stanley or Maris and Douglas to know that. Even Lindy and Devon seemed to be building their relationship based on the power of the emotion. I might have been the catalyst that brought them all together, but it was love that kept them that way.

Thank goodness for my successes, because quite frankly to hear the papers tell it I was more a catalyst for disaster than anything else. Even after three months the buzz hadn't died. Apparently Stephen had made quite a spectacle at Per Se. The maitre d' had refused him entrance without a reservation. Not to be outdone, Stephen called the man on his cell phone and requested one.

But the maitre d' was made of sterner stuff. This was Per Se, after all, and apparently he informed Stephen there were no tables available until August. Nonplussed, Stephen made the reservation, hung up the phone, and reapproached the maitre d'.

When the man insisted that Stephen couldn't come in without a reservation, Stephen informed him he had one. The man was flummoxed just long enough for Stephen to slip by him and begin searching among the restaurant's tables.

His first circuit did not yield success, and by the time he'd started the second, the maitre d' had collected his wits and called security. By now most of the restaurant's patrons were glued to the floor show, following a now determined Stephen as he moved from table to table. The arrival of the security guard didn't faze him at all, he merely gave the man a shove and continued searching.

A second security guard had more luck, impeding Stephen's progress by grabbing him from behind. However, again they'd underestimated Stephen's tenacity, and in a move worthy of the World Wrestling League he managed to shake the guard, sending the man sprawling into a neighboring table.

With a quick apology to the couple sitting at said table, Stephen started his search again in earnest. This time calling Cybil's name at the top of his lungs. By now, the police had been called, and things were getting rather heated. But fortunately, or unfortunately, depending on which side of the story you fall on, Stephen found Cybil—and Mark.

Not realizing who Stephen was, and understandably believing him to be a madman, Mark leveled a punch that sent Stephen crashing into a second table. All hell seems to have broken loose at that point, with patrons taking sides, to the point of fisticuffs.

The police arrived, and not able to sort out exactly what had happened they arrested Cybil, Stephen, and Mark. It wasn't until they reached the station house that Stephen got a chance to explain why he'd barged into Per Se in the first place. Suffice it to say, Cybil was overwhelmed, and Mark was furious. But he handled it all with decorum, explaining things to the judge (yes, they were arraigned) and managing to square things with Per Se.

The story made the front page of the newspapers of something like seventeen cities in five countries. Along with the three major networks. Mark's face—along with Cybil's and Stephen's—was splashed everywhere. And, of course, my part in the sordid little tale was gleefully bandied about in every tabloid from New York to L.A.

As a result, I lost Mark as a client, my reputation was in tatters, and I still hadn't fully recovered from all the bad press. However, none of that mattered in comparison to what was accomplished.

Cybil and Stephen.

As if on cue, the happy couple burst into the ballroom, Cybil looking resplendent in Vera Wang. She'd changed from her wedding gown to a fabulous cream beaded halter dress. She'd never looked more beautiful. Stephen had eyes only for his bride, but he, too, looked fabulous, his Paul Smith suit fitting him like a glove. But quite honestly, it wasn't their clothes that made them beautiful. It was their happiness. It was almost a tangible thing. Like the cake, or the flowers, or the ballroom itself.

Mother reached for my hand, giving it a squeeze. "You did the right thing, you know."

"I know." I smiled at my mother, and then reached out to hug Cybil, who'd managed to make her way over to where we were standing. "You look amazing," I whispered.

"I feel amazing." Cybil pulled back, her face glowing. "I just never imagined I could feel like this. And we owe it all to you."

Of course they didn't owe me a thing. If it hadn't been for my meddling, they'd probably have gotten back together sooner. I must have frowned instinctively, because Stephen pulled me into a hug. "She's right, Van. It was because of you. If you hadn't set her up with Mark, I might not have come to my senses. So in a backward kind of way you did us a favor."

He'd said it all before, of course. Several times in fact, but I appreciated the repetition. I figured it'd take about fifty more protestations before I finally forgave myself.

"A toast to the happy couple," Richard said, he and Anderson moving back into our circle. "Congratulations."

We all lifted our glasses, clanging noisily. And then we stood for a moment just content to be together on this happy occasion.

"Well, if this isn't the event of the year, I don't know what is," Althea's raspy voice carried over the crowd as she pushed her way toward us, martini glass in hand. "Everything is just perfect."

"You look fabulous," Anderson said with a smile. Leave it to Althea to come to a wedding in a red Valentino.

"This old thing?" She laughed, her glass bobbing as a result. Cybil twisted out of range with a smile, but Stephen wasn't quite as fast. Clearly it wasn't Althea's first martini. "Sorry, Stephen," she said, sopping at the spot with a napkin.

"It's fine." Stephen laughed, waving her ministration away. "What's a little splash of gin among friends?"

Three months ago I wouldn't have even called Stephen an acquaintance. He was simply the man who dumped Cybil. But now . . . well, now I really knew him. Saw him through Cybil's eyes. And I was proud to call him "friend."

"So when's the show?" Mother asked, exchanging her vodka for a passing glass of champagne.

"Two months," Stephen said. "It still seems a long way off."

"It'll be here before you know it," Richard said. "And about time, too."

Richard had pulled strings with a gallery in Soho. Friend of a friend of a client type thing. And despite the negative publicity, or maybe because of it, Stephen was having his first show. Complete with an opening night party to rival the reception.

My mother was in charge of the guest list. Which meant there'd be booze and money flowing—a fabulous combination when it comes to art.

"Well, right now we're concentrating on this party," Cybil said, lifting their joined hands, her solitaire sparkling in the light. *"Capisce?"*

We all nodded solemnly, and then burst into laughter.

Mrs. M. emerged from the crowd, a dapper-looking man in pinstripes at her side. "I wanted to congratulate you," Mrs. M. said, her red lips moving into a smile. She'd been doing that a lot more frequently of late.

"Thank you," Cybil said, linking her arm with Stephen's. "We're very happy."

"It shows," Mrs. M. said and then introduced us to her companion. Morgan Baxter. A New York Supreme Court judge of some notability. No wonder she'd been smiling so much.

"So what happened with the last kitten?" my mother asked.

The kittens had gone like Gucci bags on a half-price table. All except the littlest one. N°. 5, coincidentally. She was too scrawny for anyone to fall in love with. More Waldo than Arabella, bless her heart.

"Oh, she's fine," Mrs. M. said, her smile broadening. "I've decided to keep her. I've kind of gotten attached to the little thing. And so has Arabella."

Waldo, too, if truth be told. But I wasn't going to press my luck by mentioning the fact.

"Oh, that's wonderful," Althea said. "The perfect little family."

"We'll see how long it lasts," Richard whispered in my direction.

But somehow I had the feeling that Mrs. M. was changed for

good. Blame it on the judge, or the kittens, or maybe even Waldo, but any way you looked at it, Mrs. M. seemed to have shed the curmudgeon once and for all.

Across the room I spied Belinda and Stanley. Belinda blew me a kiss and winked, and I smiled. Maris and Douglas were here somewhere as well. I'd seen them at the wedding. Maris's family and Cybil's went way back. Devon and Lindy moved in a different circle, but I'd talked to Lindy just yesterday and Devon was still playing the role of reformed rake. Time would tell, but I thought they had a good chance.

"Oh, there's the band," Richard said. "Aren't you supposed to have the first dance?"

Stephen swallowed nervously. "I've been practicing."

"Stop it," Cybil said, her eyes on her husband. "You're a wonderful dancer."

"She just doesn't know any better," Stephen said with a laugh. "Fred and Ginger we're not." He held out his hand. "You ready?"

"As I'll ever be." They walked to the center of the now cleared floor, and the band struck up a waltz. I don't even re-member the tune, but it was lovely. Stephen and Cybil starting their new life together by dancing.

"It's perfect," I whispered, to no one in particular. But An-derson heard me.

"You done good, kid."

Suddenly I felt like crying, but popular myths withstanding, weddings were not the place to cry. At least not your best friend's wedding. The song finished and another started, more people moving onto the dance floor. I saw Douglas and Maris, their dancing amazingly graceful. Then Richard and Anderson, and even my mother and father.

Everyone was paired off. Leaving me alone with Althea. The two matchmakers, without a match.

"At least we were invited to the wedding," Althea said, with a chuckle, clearly following the direction of my thoughts. "That's a step forward."

"I suppose so," I said, still watching the dancers.

"And your business is going to be just fine," she said. "The talk is already dying down. Someone else will provide the story du jour before you know it. And you can go back to what you do best—matchmaking."

Which, of course, is exactly what I wanted to do. Although I have to admit, the idea appealed less than it might have a couple of months ago. Not my career per se, mind you, that I still loved, but I'd realized somewhere along the way that it was important to have something more in my life than just my job.

My friends and Waldo topping that list.

"Your business seems to be booming," I said to Althea, still watching the dancers, now gyrating to an old Buddy Holly song. "I saw that you'd made a match for Brendon Walker."

Brendon Walker was a infamous bad boy with more money than sense. Unfortunately, he was an aging one as well, and he'd decided it was time to settle down and produce offspring. Talk about marriage as a merger. Definitely not an easy man to find a match for.

Althea had pulled it off, though, finding just the right woman to capture Brendon's attention—permanently.

"I was getting a little nervous about it all. But I took a page from your book and kept after them. It worked, too." She smiled over at me, and for the first time I felt like maybe she saw me as an equal. It was a sobering moment, except that I was on my third champagne and enjoying the buzz—thank you very much.

"Well, I'm glad it all worked out," I said, watching as Stephen twirled Cybil underneath his arm, and then out and back again. Fred Astaire would be proud.

"Which brings me to something I've been meaning to talk to you about," Althea said. There was something in her voice that made me abandon the dancers and turn to look at her.

"Something bad?"

"Good heavens, no. At least I don't think so. It's just a bit awkward." She swallowed the last of her martini and I'll be damned if a waiter didn't appear with another one almost before she'd finished. "Thanks," she called in his direction, and then turned back to me. "So, here's the thing. I have a client, who has . . . well, who has expressed an interest in you."

"One of your clients wants me to represent him? I'd never do that." I frowned up at her, trying to figure out where all of this was going.

"No. No. It's not that. He wants me to fix him up with you."

"Are you serious? You want to make a match for *me*? Is that even legal? I mean, shouldn't a matchmaker make her own match?"

"Look, I told him I'd broach the subject with you. See if you had any interest. No pressure at all."

"Well, thank God for that," I said, waving my champagne at her. "Glad to know there's no pressure."

"Look, Vanessa, I'd never do this if I didn't think maybe my client was right. I mean, you would be perfect for each other. Honestly. Besides, a married matchmaker is a lot more credible than an unmarried one."

"Oh please," I spat, beginning to feel a little cornered. "You're not married and you're the best I've ever seen." Not that I'd really seen that many matchmakers in action, but there'd been a couple, and I'd read about a few more, and none of them had Althea's class and integrity.

"Just give it one chance. For me."

"Do I know this man?"

"You've met him," she said, pointing. "He's right over there."

I turned to follow the direction of her finger and froze.

Mark Grayson was standing on the edge of the dance floor, looking absolutely fabulous in a gray suit the exact color of his eyes. Not that I'd ever really thought about the color of his eyes or anything. Really. My stomach lurched and I reached for Althea, but she'd disappeared into the crowd.

Mark came closer, and I swallowed nervously before tipping my head up to meet his gaze.

"Would you like to dance?" he asked.

"I didn't even know you were invited to the wedding," I said, playing the part of brilliant conversationalist.

"Well, Cybil thought I ought to come. I mean, I did play a rather major role in the engagement."

"Oh, God," I said, going from bad to worse. He took my hand and led me out onto the dance floor. Of course, the band immediately launched into a Frank Sinatra standard. "I'm not a good dancer," I squeaked, as his hand found my waist.

"No problem. I'm leading this time. All right?"

The question wasn't about dancing at all. And all I could do was nod, numbly, my voice finally deserting me altogether.

My memories of that dance are limited to the way Mark moved, and looked, and smelled. The million different sensations that connect between a man and a woman. Oh yeah, and one other thing. I remember seeing Althea watching us as we danced. She was standing with my mother, who was grinning like she'd won the freakin' lottery.

I smiled at them both, and then nestled my head against Mark's shoulder.

Un-fucking-believable.

It looked like Althea just might win the bet after all.